THE PLANET
STRAPPERS

THE PLANET STRAPPERS

RAYMOND Z. GALLUN

WILDSIDE PRESS

THE PLANET STRAPPERS

Published in 2008 by Wildside Press.
www.wildsidepress.com

I

The Archer Five came in a big packing box, bound with steel ribbons and marked, *This end up — handle with care*. It was delivered at a subsidized government surplus price of fifty dollars to Hendricks' Sports and Hobbies Center, a store in Jarviston, Minnesota, that used to deal mostly in skin diving equipment, model plane kits, parts for souping up old cars, and the like. The Archer Five was a bit obsolete for the elegant U.S. Space Force boys — hence the fantastic drop in price from two thousand dollars since only last June. It was still a plenty-good piece of equipment, however; and the cost change was a real break for the Bunch.

By 4:30 that bright October afternoon, those members who were attending regular astronautics classes at Jarviston Technical College had gathered at Hendricks' store. Ramos and Tiflin, two wild characters with seldom-cut hair and pipe stem pants, who didn't look as if they could be trusted with a delicate unpacking operation, broke the Archer out with a care born of love, there in Paul Hendricks' big backroom shop, while the more stolid members — and old Paul, silent in his swivel chair — watched like hawks.

"So who tries it on first?" Ramos challenged. "Dumb question. You, Eileen — naturally."

Most Bunches have a small, hard, ponytailed member, dungareed like the rest.

Still kidding around, Ramos dropped an arm across Eileen Sands' shoulders, and got her sharp elbow jabbed with vigor into his stomach.

She glanced back in a feminine way at Frank Nelsen, a tall, lean guy of nineteen, butch-haircutted and snub featured. But he was the purposeful, studious kind, more an observer and a personal doer than a leader; he hadn't much time for the encouraging smiles of girls, and donning even an Archer Five now instead of within a few hours, didn't exactly represent his kind of hurry.

"I'll wait, Eileen," he said. Then he nodded toward Gimp Hines. That the others would also pick Gimp was evident at once. There were bravos and clapping, half for a joke.

"Think I won't?" Gimp growled, tossing his crutches on a workbench littered with scraps of color-coded wire, and hopping forward on the one leg that had grown to normal size. He sort of swaggered, Frank Nelsen noticed. Maybe the whole Bunch swaggered with him in a way, because, right now, he represented all of them in their difficult aim. Gimp Hines, with the nylon patch in his congenitally imperfect heart, and with that useless right underpinning, had less chance of taking part in space-development than any of them — even with all his talent for mechanics and electronics.

Two-and-Two (George) Baines, a large, mild person who was an expert bricklayer in his spare time, while he struggled to absorb the intricate math that spacemen are supposed to know — he used to protest that he could at least add two and two — bounced forward, saying, "I'll give yuh a hand, Gimp."

Mitch Storey, the lean colored kid with the passion for all plant life, and the specific urge to get somehow out to Mars, was also moving to help Gimp into the Archer. Gimp waved them off angrily, but they valeted for him, anyhow.

"Shucks, Gimp," Storey soothed. "Anybody needs assistance — the first time . . ."

They got his good leg, and what there was of the other, into the boots. They laced carefully, following all they had learned from books. They rolled the wire-braced silicone rubber body-section up over his torso, guided his arms into the sleeves, closed the zippersealers and centered the chest plate. While the others checked with their eyes, they inspected the nipples of the moisture-reclaimer and chlorophane air-restorer capsules. They lifted the helmet of clear, darkened plastic over his head, and dogged it to the gasket with the automatic turnbuckles. By then, Gimp Hines' own quick fingers, in the gloves, were busy snapping this and adjusting that. There was a sleepy hum of aerating machinery.

"It even *smells* right, in here," Gimp growled muffledly, trying to be nonchalant.

There was loud laughter and clapping. Ramos whistled piercingly, with two fingers. The huge Kuzak twins, Art and Joe — both had football scholarships at Tech — gave Indian yells. Eileen Sands clasped her hands over her head and went up on her toes like the ballet dancer she had once meant to be. Old Paul, in his chair, chortled, and slapped his arm. Even little David Lester said "Bravo!" after he had gulped. The applause wasn't entirely facetious.

Gimp's whole self had borrowed hard lines and an air of competence from the Archer Five. For a second he looked like somebody who could really cross millions of miles. There was a tiny, solar-powered ionic-propulsion unit mounted on the shoulders of the armor, between the water-tank and the beam-type radio transmitter and receiver. A miniaturized radar sprouted on the left elbow joint. On the inside of the Archer's chest plate, reachable merely by drawing an arm out of a sleeve, emergency ration containers were racked. In the same place was a small airlock for jettisoning purposes and for taking in more supplies.

"What do yuh know — toilet facilities, yet!" Ramos chirped with spurious naivete, and there were guffaws which soon died out. After all, this *was* a serious occasion, and who wanted to be a jerk? Now that the price had been shoved down into the ground, they could probably get their Archer Fives — their all-important vacuum armor. They were one more hurdle nearer to the stars.

Two regular members of the Bunch hadn't yet shown up. Ten were present, including Gimp in the Archie. All were different. Each had a name.

But Frank Nelsen figured that numbers, names, and individual variations didn't count for much, just then. They were a crowd with an overall personality — often noisy, sometimes quiet like now, always a bit grim to sustain their nerve before all they had to learn in order to reduce their inexperienced greenness, and before the thought of all the expensive equipment they had to somehow acquire, if they were to take part in the rapid adaptation of the solar system to human uses. Most of all, their courage was needed against fear of a region that could be deadly dangerous, but that to them seemed wonderful like nothing else.

The shop smelled of paint, solvent and plastic, like most any other. Gimp, sitting in the Archer, beside the oil-burning stove, didn't say any more. He forgot to play tough, and seemed to lose himself in a mind-trip Out There — probably as far as he would ever get. His face, inside the helmet, now looked pinched. His freckles were very plain in his paled cheeks. Gimp was awed.

So was everybody else, including Paul Hendricks, owner of the Hobby Center, who was approaching eighty and was out of the running, though his watery blue eyes were still showing the shine of boyhood, right now.

Way back, Paul Hendricks used to barnstorm county fairs in a wood-and-fabric biplane, giving thrill rides to sports and their girls at five dollars a couple, because he had been born sixty years too soon.

Much later in his spotty career, he had started the store. He had also meant to do general repair work in the backroom shop. But in recent years it had degenerated into an impromptu club hall, funk hole, griping-arguing-and-planning pit, extracurricular study lab and project site for an indefinite horde of interplanetary enthusiasts who were thought of in Jarviston as either young adults of the most resourceful kind — for whom the country should do much more in order to insure its future in space — or as just another crowd of delinquents, more bent on suicide and trouble-making than any hot rod group had ever been. Paul Hendricks was either a fine, helpful citizen — among so many who were disinterested and pre-occupied — or a corrupting Socrates who deserved to drink hemlock.

Frank Nelsen knew all this as well as most. He had been acquainted with Paul ever since, at the age of seven, he had come into the store and had tried to make a down payment on a model building kit for a Y-71 ground-to-orbit freight rocket — clearly marked $49.95 in the display window — with his fortune of a single dime. Frank had never acquired a Y-71 kit, but he had found a friend in Paul Hendricks, and a place to hang around and learn things he wanted to know. Later on, as now, he had worked in the store whenever he had some free time.

Frank leaned against a lathe, watching the others, the frosty thrill and soul-searching hidden inside himself. Maybe it was hard to guess what Eileen Sands, standing near, was thinking, but she was the firm kind who would have a definite direction. Perhaps unconsciously, she hummed a tune under her breath, while her feet toyed with graceful steps. No doubt, her mind was also on the Big Vacuum beyond the Earth.

But what is there about a dangerous dream? When it is far out of reach, it has a safe, romantic appeal. Bring its fulfillment a little closer, and its harsh aspects begin to show. You get a kick out of that, but you begin to wonder nervously if you have the guts, the stamina, the resistance to loneliness and complete strangeness.

Looking at a real Archie — with a friend inside it, even — did this to Frank Nelsen. But he could see similar reactions in some of the others.

Mitch Storey sat, bent forward, on a box, staring at his big, sepia hands, in which he tossed back and forth a tiny, clear capsule containing a fuzzy fragment of vegetation from Mars. He had bought this sealed curio from Paul a year ago for fifty dollars — souvenirs that came from so far were expensive. And now, in view of what was happening to hopeful colonists of that once inhabited and still most Earth-like other planet, ownership of such a capsule on Earth seemed about to be banned, not only by departments of agriculture, but by bodies directly concerned with public safety.

Did the color photographs of Mars, among all the others that the Bunch had thumbtacked to the shop walls, still appeal as strongly to Mitch? Did he still want to go out to that world of queer, swirled markings, like the fluid flow in the dregs of a paper coffee cup? Mitch would — more so than ever. He had plant life in his soul, maybe from wandering in the swamps near his home in Mississippi. He had been supporting himself here at school by fixing gardens. If it was plant life of a different, dangerous sort, with other billions of years of development behind it, that just made the call stronger. Mitch just sat and thought, now, the mouth organ he seldom played sagging forward in his frayed shirt pocket.

Ramos — Miguel Ramos Alvarez — only stood with his black-visored cap pushed back on his head, and a cocky smirk of good humor on his mouth. Reckless Ramos, who went tearing around the country in an ancient motor scooter, decorated with squirrel tails and gaudy bosses, would hardly be disturbed by any risky thing he wanted to do. The thumbtacked pictures of the systems of far, cold Jupiter and Saturn — Saturn still unapproached, except by small, instrumented rockets — would be the things to appeal to him.

The Kuzak twins stood alertly, as if an extra special home-coming football game was in prospect. But they weren't given to real doubts, either. From their previous remarks it was clear that the asteroids, those fragments of an exploded and once populated world, orbiting out beyond Mars, would be for them. Osmium, iridium, uranium. The rich, metallic guts of a planet exposed for easy mining. Thousands of prospectors, hopeful characters, and men brutalized by the life in space, were already drifting around in the Asteroid Belt.

Two-and-Two Baines wore a worried, perplexed expression. He was a massive, rather lost young man who had to keep up with the times, and with his companions, and was certainly wondering if he was able.

Little David Lester, the pedant, the mother's boy, who looked eighteen but was probably older, pouted, and his heavy lips in his thin face moved. "Cores," Nelsen heard him whisper. He had the habit of talking to himself. Frank knew his interests. Drill cores withdrawn from the strata of another planet, and inspected for fossils and other evidences of its long history, was what he probably meant. Seeing Gimp in the Archie had set off another scientific reverie in his head. He was a whizz in any book subject. Maybe he had the brains to be a great investigator of the past, in the Belt or on Mars, if his mind didn't crack first, which seemed sure to happen if he left Earth at all.

But it was Glen Tiflin's reactions that were the strangest. He had his switch blade out, and was tossing it expertly against a wall two-by-four, in which it stuck quivering each time. This seemed his one skill, his pride, his proof of manhood. And he wanted to get into space like nobody else around, except maybe Gimp Hines. It wasn't hard to sense how his head worked — the whole Bunch knew.

Tiflin's face seemed to writhe, now, with self-doubt and truculence; his eyes were on the photos of the heroes, beginning way back; Goddard. Von Braun. Clifford, who had first landed on the far side of the Moon. LaCrosse, who had reached Mercury, closest to the sun. Vasiliev, who had just come back from the frozen moons of Jupiter, scoring a triumph for the Tovies — somebody had started calling them that, a few years ago — up in high Eurasia, the other side of an ideological rift that still threatened the ever more crowded and competitive Earth, though mutual fear had so far kept the flare ups within limits. Bannon, whose expedition was even now exploring the gloomy cellar of Venus' surface, smothered in steam, carbon dioxide and poisonous formaldehyde.

To Tiflin, as to the others, even such places were glamorous. But he wanted to be a big shot, too. It was like a compulsion. He was touchy and difficult. Three years back, he had been in trouble for breaking and entering. Maybe his worship of space, and his desire to get there and prove himself, were the only things that had kept him straight for so long — grimly attentive at Tech, and at work at his car-washing job, nights.

In his nervousness, now, he stuck a cigarette savagely between his lips, and lighted it with a quick, arrogant gesture, hardly slowing down the continuous toss and recovery of his knife.

This had begun to annoy big Art Kuzak. For one thing, Tiflin was doing his trick too close to the mass of crinkly, cellophane-like stuff draped over a horizontal wooden pole suspended by iron straps from the ceiling. The crinkly mass was one of the Bunch's major projects — their first space bubble, or bubb which they had been cutting and shaping with more care and devotion than skill.

"Cripes — put that damn shiv away, Tif!" Art snapped. "Or lose it someplace!"

Ramos, who was a part-time mechanic at the same garage where Tiflin worked, couldn't help taunting. "Yeah — smoking, too. Oh-oh. Using up precious oxygen. Better quit, pal. Can't do much of that Out There."

This was a wrong moment to rib Tiflin. He was in an instant flare. But he ground out the cigarette at once, bitterly. "What do *you* care what I do, Mex?" he snarled. "And as for you two Hunky Kuzaks — you oversized bulldozers — how about weight limits for blastoff? Damn — I don't care *how* big you are!"

In mounting rage, he was about to lash out with his fists, even at the two watchful football men. But then he looked surprised. With a terrible effort, he bottled up even his furious words.

The Bunch was a sort of family. Members of families may love each other, but it doesn't have to happen. For a second it was as if Ramos had Tiflin spitted on some barb of his taunting smile — aimed at Tiflin's most vulnerable point.

Ramos clicked his tongue. What he was certainly going to remark was that people who couldn't pass the emotional stability tests, just couldn't get a space-fitness card. But Ramos wasn't unkind. He checked himself in time. "No sweat, Tif," he muttered.

"Hey, Gimp — are you going to sit in that Archie all night?" Joe Kuzak, the easy-going twin, boomed genially. "How about the rest of us?"

"Yeah — how about that, Gimp?" Dave Lester put in, trying to sound as brash and bold as the others, instead of just bookish.

Two-and-Two Baines, still looking perplexed, spoke in a hoarse voice that sounded like sorrow. "What I wanna know is just how far this fifty buck price gets us. Guess we have enough dough left in the treasury to buy us each an Archer Five, huh, Paul?"

Paul Hendricks rubbed his bald head and grinned in a way that attempted to prove him a disinterested sideliner. "Ask Frank," he said. "He's your historian-secretary and treasurer."

Frank Nelsen came out of his attitude of observation enough to warn, "That much we've got, if we want as many as twelve Archies. And a little better than a thousand dollars more, left over from the prize money."

They had won twenty-five hundred dollars during the summer for building a working model of a sun-powered ionic drive motor — the kind useful for deep-space propulsion, but far too weak in thrust to be any good, starting from the ground. The contest had been sponsored by — of all outfits — a big food chain, Trans-Columbia. But this wasn't so strange. Everybody was interested in, or affected by, interplanetary travel, now.

On a workbench, standing amid a litter of metal chips and scraps of color-coded wire, was the Bunch's second ionic, full-size this time, and almost finished. On crossed arms it mounted four parabolic mirrors; its ion guide was on a universal joint. Out There, in orbit or beyond, and in full, spatial sunlight, its jetting ions would deliver ten pounds of continuous thrust.

"A thousand bucks — that's nowhere near enough," Two-and-Two mourned further. "Doggone, why can't we get blasted up off the Earth — that costs the most, all by itself — just in our Archies? They've got those little ionic drives on their shoulders, to get around with, after we're in orbit. Lots of asteroid hoppers live and ride only in their space suits. Why do they make us get all that other expensive equipment? Space bubbs, full-size ionics, lots of fancy instruments!"

"'Cause it isn't legal, otherwise," Mitch Storey pointed out. "'Cause new men are green — it isn't safe for them, otherwise — the Extra-Terrestrial Commission thinks. Got to have all the gear to get clearance. Traveling light isn't even legal in the Belt. You know that."

"Maybe we'll win us another prize," Ramos laughed, touching the crinkly substance of their first bubb, hanging like a deflated balloon over the ceiling pole.

Tiflin sneered. "Oh, sure, you dumb Mex. Too many other Bunches, now. Too much competition. Like companies starting up on the Moon not hiring ordinary help on Earth and shipping them out, anymore — saying contract guys don't stick. Nuts — it's because enough slobs save them the expense by showing up on their own . . . Or like most all of us trying to get into the Space Force. The *Real Elite* — sure. Only 25,000 in the Force, when there are over 200,000,000 people in the country to draw from. Just one guy from Jarviston — Harv Diamond — ever made it. Choosy? We can get old waiting for them to review our submitted personal data, only to have a chance to take their lousy tests!"

Joe Kuzak grinned. "So down with 'em — down with the worthy old U.S.S.F.! We're on our own — to Serenitatis Base on the Moon, to the Belt, Pallastown, and farther!"

Ramos still hovered near Eileen Sands. "What do you say, Sweetie?" he asked. "You haven't hardly made a comment."

Eileen remained tough and withdrawn. "I'm just listening while you smart male characters figure out everything," she snapped. "Why don't you become a listener, too, for a change, and go help Gimp out of that Archer?"

Ramos bowed elegantly, and obeyed the latter half of her suggestion.

"I have a premonition — a hunch," little Lester offered, trying to sound firm. "Our request for a grant from the Extra-Terrestrial Development Board will succeed. Because we will be as valuable as anybody, Out There. Then we will have money enough to buy the materials to make most of our equipment."

Joe Kuzak, the gentler twin, answered him. "You're right about one thing, Les. We'll wind up building most of our own stuff — with our own mitts . . . !"

Some noisy conversation about who should try the Archer next, was interrupted when the antique customer's bell over the street door of the store, jangled. There was a scrape of shoe soles, as the two previously absent members of the Bunch, Jig Hollins and Charlie Reynolds, arriving together by chance, came into the shop.

Jig (Hilton) Hollins was a mechanic out at the airport. He was lean, cocky, twenty-four, with a stiff bristle of blond hair. Like Charlie Reynolds, he added up what had just been happening, here, at a glance. Both were older than the others. They had regular jobs. Their educations were completed, except for evening supplementary courses.

"Well, the *men* have arrived," Jig announced.

Maybe Charlie Reynolds' faint frown took exception to this remark. He was the only one in a suit, grey and tasteful, with a subdued flash to match the kind of car he drove. Few held this against him, nor the fact that he usually spent himself broke, nor the further fact that J. John Reynolds, tight-fisted president of the Jarviston First National Bank, was his grandfather. Charlie was an engineer at the new nuclear powerhouse, just out of town. Charlie was what is generally known as a Good Guy. He was brash and sure — maybe too sure. He had a slight swagger, balanced by a certain benignancy. He was automatically the leader of the Bunch, held most likely to succeed in their aims.

"Hi, gang," he breezed. "Otto is bringing beer, Pepsi and sandwiches from his joint across the street. Special day — so it's on me. Time to relax — maybe unsnarl. Any new problems?"

"Still plenty of old ones," Frank Nelsen commented laconically.

"Has anybody suddenly decided to back out?" Charlie chuckled. "It's tiresome for me always to be asking that." He looked around, meeting carefully easy grins and grim expressions. "Nope — I guess we're all shaggy folk, bent on high and wild living, so far. So you know the only answer we *can* have."

"Umhmm, Charlie," Art Kuzak, the tough, business-like twin, gruffed. "We can get the Archers, now. I think Frank has our various sizes noted down. Let everybody sign up that wants an Archie. Better hurry, though — there'll be a run on them now that they're being almost given away ... List all the other stuff we need — with approximate purchase price, or cost of construction materials, attached. Sure — we'll be way short of funds. But we can start with the items we can make, ourselves, now. The point is not to lose time. New restrictions may turn up, and give us trouble, if we do. We'll have to ride our luck for a break."

"Hell — you know the lists are ready, Art," Frank Nelsen pointed out. "A bubb for everybody — or the stuff to make it. Full-scale ionic drives, air-restorers and moisture-reclaimers, likewise. Some of the navigation instruments we'll almost have to buy. Dehydrated food, flasks of oxygen and water, and blastoff drums to contain our gear, are all relatively simple. Worst, of course, is the blastoff price, from one of the spaceports. Who could be rich enough to have a ground-to-orbit nuclear rocket of his own? Fifteen hundred bucks — a subsidized rate at that — just to lift a man and a thousand pounds of equipment into orbit. Five thousand dollars, minimum per person, is what we're going to need, altogether."

Gimp Hines, who always acted as if he expected to get off the Earth, too, had yielded his position inside the Archer to Tiflin, and had hobbled close.

"The cost scares a guy who has to go to school, too, so he can pass the tests," he said. "Well, don't worry, Frank. A thousand dollars buys a lot of stellene for bubbs. And we can scratch up a few bucks of our own. I can find a hundred, myself, saved from my TV repair work, and my novelties business. Charlie, here, ought to be able to contribute a thousand. Same for you, Hollins. That'll buy parts and materials for some ionic motors, too."

"Oh, certainly, Gimp," Hollins growled.

But Charlie Reynolds grinned. "I can kick in that much, if I hold down a while," he said. "Maybe more, later. What we've got to have, however, is a loan. We can't expect a grant from the Board. Sure they want more people helping to develop resources in space, but they're swamped with requests. Let's not sweat, though. With a little time, I'll swing something . . . Hey, everybody! Proposition! I move that whoever wants an Archer put his name down for Frank. I further move that we have him order us a supply of stellene, and basic materials for at least three more ionic motors. I also suggest that everybody donate as much cash as he can, no matter how little, and as much time as possible for making equipment. With luck, and if we get our applications for space-fitness tests mailed to Minneapolis within a week, at least some of us should get off Earth by next June. Now, shall we sign for the whole deal?"

Art Kuzak hunched his shoulders and displayed white teeth happily. "I'm a pushover," he said. "Here I come. I like to see things roll."

"Likewise," said his brother, Joe. Their signatures were both small, in contrast to their size.

Ramos, fully clad in the Archer, clowned his way forward to write his name with great flourishes, his ball point clutched in a space glove.

Tiflin made a fierce, nervous scrawl.

Mitch Storey wrote patiently, in big, square letters.

Gimp chewed his lip, and signed, "Walter Hines," in a beautiful, austere script, with a touch as fine as a master scientist's. "I'll go along as far as they let me," he muttered.

"I think it will be the same — in my case," David Lester stammered. He shook so much that his signature was only a quavering line.

"For laughs," Eileen Sands said, and wrote daintily.

Two-and-Two Baines gulped, sighed, and made a jagged scribble, like the trail of a rocket gone nuts.

Jig Hollins wrote in swooping, arrogant circles, that came, perhaps, from his extra jobs as an advertising sky writer with an airplane.

Frank Nelsen was next, and Charlie Reynolds was last. Theirs were the most indistinctive signatures in the lot. Just ordinary writing.

"So here we all are, on a piece of paper — pledged to victory or death," Reynolds laughed. "Anyhow, we're out of a rut."

Nelsen figured that that was the thing about Charlie Reynolds. Some might not like him, entirely. But he could get the Bunch unsnarled and in motion.

Old Paul Hendricks had come back from waiting on some casual customers in the store.

"Want to sign, too, Paul?" Reynolds chuckled.

"Nope — that would make thirteen," Paul answered, his eyes twinkling. "I'll watch and listen — and maybe tell you if I think you're off beam."

"Here comes Otto with the beer and sandwiches," Ramos burst out.

They all crowded around heavy Otto Kramer and his basket — all except Frank Nelsen and Paul Hendricks, and Eileen Sands who made the ancient typewriter click in the little office-enclosure, as she typed up the order list that Nelsen would mail out with a bank draft in the morning.

Nelsen had a powerful urge to talk to the old man who was his long-time friend, and who had said little all during the session, though he knew more about space travel than any of them — as much as anybody can know without ever having been off the Earth.

"Hey, Paul," Frank called in a low tone, leaning his elbows across a workbench.

"Yeah?"

"Nothing," Frank Nelsen answered with a lopsided smile.

But he felt that that was the right word, when your thoughts and feelings became too huge and complicated for you to express with any ease.

Grandeur, poetry, music — for instance, the haunting popular song, *Fire Streak*, about the burial of a spaceman — at orbital speed — in the atmosphere of his native planet. And fragments of history, such as covered wagons. All sorts of subjects, ideas and pictures were swirling inside his head. Wanting to sample everything in the solar system . . . Home versus the distance, and the fierce urge to build a wild history of his own . . . Gentleness and lust to be fulfilled, sometime. There would be a girl . . . And there were second thoughts to twist your guts and make you wonder if all your savage drives were foolish. But there was a duty to be equal to your era — helping to give dangerously crowded humanity on Earth more room, dispersal, a chance for race survival, if some unimaginable violence were turned loose . . .

He thought of the names of places Out There. Serenitatis Base — Serene — on the Moon. Lusty, fantastic Pallastown, on the Golden Asteroid, Pallas . . . He remembered his parents, killed in a car wreck just outside of Jarviston, four Christmases ago. Some present! . . . But there was one small benefit — he was left free to go where he wanted, without any family complications, like other guys might have. Poor Dave Lester. How was it that his mother allowed him to be with the Bunch at all? How did he work it? Or was she the one that was right? . . .

Paul Hendricks had leaned his elbows on the workbench, too. "Sure — *nothing* — Frank," he said, and his watery eyes were bland.

The old codger understood. Neither of them said anything for a minute, while the rest of the Bunch, except Eileen who was still typing, guzzled Pepsi and beer, and wolfed hotdogs. There was lots of courage-lifting noise and laughter.

Ramos said something, and Jig Hollins answered him back. "Think there'll be any girls in grass skirts out in the Asteroid Belt, Mex?"

"Oh, they'll arrive," Ramos assured him.

Nelsen didn't listen anymore. His and Paul's attention had wandered to the largest color photo thumbtacked to the wall, above the TV set, and the shelf of dog-eared technical books. It showed a fragile, pearly ring, almost diaphanous, hanging tilted against spatial blackness and pinpoint stars. Its hub was a cylindrical spindle, with radial guys of fine, stainless steel wire. It was like the earliest ideas about a space station, yet it was also different. To many — Frank Nelsen and Paul Hendricks certainly included — such devices had as much beauty as a yacht under full sail had ever had for anybody.

Old Paul smirked with pleasure. "It's a shame, ain't it, Frank —

calling a pretty thing like that a 'bubb' — it's an ugly word. Or even a 'space bubble.' Technical talk gets kind of cheap."

"I don't mind," Frank Nelsen answered. "Our first one, here, could look just as nice — inflated, and riding free against the stars."

He touched the crinkly material, draped across its wooden support.

"It *will*," the old man promised. "Funny — not so long ago people thought that space ships would have to be really rigid — all metal. So how did they turn out? Made of stellene, mostly — an improved form of polyethylene — almost the same stuff as a weather balloon."

"A few millimeters thick, light, perfectly flexible when deflated," Nelsen added. "Cut out and cement your bubb together in any shape you choose. Fold it up firmly, like a parachute — it makes a small package that can be carried up into orbit in a blastoff rocket with the best efficiency. There, attached flasks of breathable atmosphere fill it out in a minute. Eight pounds pressure makes it fairly solid in a vacuum. So, behold — you've got breathing and living room, inside. There's nylon cording for increased strength — as in an automobile tire — though not nearly as much. There's a silicone gum between the thin double layers, to seal possible meteor punctures. A darkening lead-salt impregnation in the otherwise transparent stellene cuts radiation entry below the danger level, and filters the glare and the hard ultra-violet out of the sunshine. So there you are, all set up."

"Rig your hub and guy wires," old Paul carried on, cheerfully. "Attach your sun-powered ionic drive, set up your air-restorer, spin your vehicle for centrifuge-gravity, and you're ready to move — out of orbit."

They laughed, because getting into space wasn't as easy as they made it sound. The bubbs, one of the basic inventions that made interplanetary travel possible, were, for all their almost vagabondish simplicity, still a concession in lightness and compactness for atmospheric transit, to that first and greatest problem — breaking the terrific initial grip of Earth's gravity from the ground upward, and gaining stable orbital speed. Only a tremendously costly rocket, with a thrust greater than its own weight when fully loaded, could do that. Buying a blastoff passage *had* to be expensive.

"Figuring, scrounging, counting our pennies, risking our necks," Nelsen chuckled. "And maybe, even if we make it, we'll be just a third-rate group, lost in the crowd that's following the explorers . . . Just the same, I wish you could plan to go, too, Paul."

"Don't rub it in, kid. But I figure on kicking in a couple of thousand bucks, soon, to help you characters along."

Nelsen felt an embarrassed lift of hope.

"You shouldn't, Paul," he advised. "We've overrun and taken possession of your shop — almost your store, too. You've waived any profit, whenever we've bought anything. That's enough favors."

"My dough, my pleasure . . . Let's each get one of Reynolds' beers and hotdogs, if any are left . . ."

Later, when all the others had gone, except Gimp Hines, they uncovered the Archer, which everyone else had tried. Paul got into it, first. Then Nelsen took his turn, sitting as if within an enclosed vault, hearing the gurgle of bubbles passing through the green, almost living fluid of the air-restorer capsule. Chlorophane, like the chlorophyl of green plants, could break up exhaled carbon dioxide, freeing the oxygen for re-breathing. But it was synthetic, far more efficient, and it could use much stronger sunlight as an energy source. Like chlorophyl, too, it produced edible starches and sugars that could be imbibed, mixed with water, through a tube inside the Archer's helmet.

Even with the Archer enclosing him, Nelsen's mind didn't quite reach. He had learned a lot about space, but it remained curiously inconceivable to him. He felt the frost-fringed thrill.

"Now we know — a little," he chortled, after he stood again, just in his usual garb.

It was almost eight o'clock. Gimp Hines hadn't gone to supper, or to celebrate decision on one of the last evenings of any kind of freedom from work. He couldn't wait for that . . . Under fluorescent lights, he was threading wire through miniature grommets, hurrying to complete the full-size ionic drive. He said, "Hi, Frank," and let his eyes drop, again, into absorption in his labors. Mad little guy. Tragic, sort of. A cripple . . .

"I'll shove off, Paul," Nelsen was saying in a moment.

Out under the significant stars of the crisp October night, Nelsen was approached at once by a shadow. "I was waiting for you, Frank. I got a problem." The voice was hoarse sorrow — almost lugubrious comedy.

"Math again, Two-and-Two? Sure — shoot."

"Well — that kind is always around — with me," Two-and-Two Baines chuckled shakily. "This is something else — personal. We're liable — honest to gosh — to *go*, aren't we?"

"Some of us, maybe," Nelsen replied warily. "Sixty thousand bucks for the whole Bunch looks like a royal heap of cabbage to me."

"Split among a dozen guys, it looks smaller," Two-and-Two persisted. "And you can earn royal dough on the Moon — just for example. Plenty to pay back a loan."

"Still, you don't pick loans off trees," Nelsen gruffed. "Not for a shoestring crowd like us. We look too unsubstantial."

"Okay, Frank — have that part your way. I believe there still is a good chance we *will* go. I *want* to go. But I get to thinking. Out There is like being buried in millions of miles of nothing that you can breathe. Can a guy stand it? You hear stories about going loopy from claustrophobia and stuff. And I got to think about my mother and dad."

"Uh-huh — other people could be having minor second thoughts — including me," Frank Nelsen growled.

"You don't get what I mean, Frank. Sure I'm scared some — but I'm gonna try to go. Well, here's my point. I'm strong, willing, not too clumsy. But I'm no good at figuring what to do. So, Out There, in order to have a reasonable chance, I'll have to be following somebody smart. I thought I'd fix it now — beforehand. You're the best, Frank."

Nelsen felt the scared earnestness of the appeal, and the achy shock of the compliment. But in his own uncertainty, he didn't want to be carrying any dead weight, in the form of a dependent individual.

"Thanks, Two-and-Two," he said. "But I can't see myself as any leader, either. Talk about it to me tomorrow, if you still feel like it. Right now I want to sweat out a few things for myself — alone."

"Of course, Frankie." And Two-and-Two was gone.

Frank Nelsen looked upward, over the lighted street. There was no Moon — site of many enterprises, these days — in the sky, now. Old Jupiter rode in the south. A weather-spotting satellite crept across zenith, winking red and green. A skip glider, an orbit-to-ground freight vehicle, possibly loaded with rich metals from the Belt, probably about to land at the New Mexico spaceport far to the west, moved near it. Frank felt a deliciously lonesome chill as he walked through the business section of Jarviston. From somewhere, dance music lilted.

In front of Lehman's Drug Store he looked skyward again, to see a dazzling white cluster, like many meteors, falling. The gorgeous display lasted more than a second.

"Good heavens, Franklin Nelsen — what was that?"

He looked down at the slight, aging woman, and stiffened slightly. Miss Rosalie Parks had been his Latin teacher in high school. Plenty of times she used to scold him for not having his translations of Caesar worked out. A lot she understood about a fella who had to spend plenty of time working to support himself, while attending school!

"Good evening, Miss Parks," he greeted rather stiffly. "I think it was that manned weather satellite dumping garbage. It hits the atmosphere at orbital velocity, and is incinerated."

She seemed to be immensely pleased and amused. "Garbage becoming beauty! That is rather wonderful, Franklin. I'll remember. Thank you and good night."

She marched off with the small purchase she had made, in the direction opposite his own.

He got almost to the house where he had his room, when there was another encounter. But it was nothing new to run into Nancy Codiss, the spindly fifteen-year-old next door. He had a sudden, unbelievably expansive impulse.

"Hi, Nance," he said. "I didn't get much supper. Let's go down to Lehman's for a hamburger and maybe a soda."

"Why — *good* — Frankie!"

They didn't talk very much, walking down, waiting for their orders, or eating their hamburgers. But she wasn't as spindly as he used to think. And her dark hair, even features and slim hands were nicer than he recalled.

"I hear you fellas got your space-armor sample, Frank."

"Yep — we did. We're ordering more."

Her expression became speculative. Her brown eyes lighted. "I've been wondering if I should look Outward, too. Whether it makes sense — for a girl."

"Could be — I've heard."

Their conversation went something like that, throughout, with long silences. Finally she smiled at him, very brightly.

"The Junior Fall dance is in two weeks," she said. "But I guess you'll be too busy to be interested?"

"'Guess' just isn't the word, Nance. I regret that — truly."

He looked and sounded as though he meant it. In some crazy way, it seemed that he *did* mean it.

He walked her home. Then he went to the next house, and up to his rented room. He showered, and for once climbed very early into bed, feeling that he must have nightmares. About strange sounds in the thin winds, over the mysterious thickets of Mars. Or about some blackened, dried-out body of a sentient being, sixty million years dead, floating free in the Asteroid Belt. A few had been found. Some were in museums.

Instead, he slept the dreamless sleep of the just — if there was any particular reason for him to consider himself just.

II

Gimp Hines put the finishing touches on the first full-scale ionic during that next week. The others of the Bunch, each working when he could, completed cementing the segments of the first bubb together.

On a Sunday morning they carried the bubb out into the yard behind the store and test inflated the thirty-foot ring by means of a line of hose from the compressor in the shop. Soapsuds dabbed along the seams revealed a few leaks by its bubbling. These were fixed up.

By late afternoon the Bunch had folded up the bubb again, and were simulating its practice launching from a ground-to-orbit rocket — as well as can be done on the ground with a device intended only for use in a state of weightlessness, when the operators are supposed to be weightless, too. The impossibility of establishing such conditions produced some ludicrous results:

The two Kuzaks diving with a vigor, as if from a rocket airlock, hitting the dirt with a thud, scrambling up, opening and spreading the great bundle, attaching the air hose. Little Lester hopping in to help fit wire rigging, most of it still imaginary. A friendly dog coming over to sniff, with a look of mild wonder in his eyes.

"Laugh, you leather-heads!" Art Kuzak roared at the others. He grinned, wiping his muddy face. "We've got to learn, don't we? Only, it's like make-believe. Hell, I haven't played make-believe since I was four! But if we keep doing it here, all the kids and townspeople will be peeking over the fence to see how nuts we've gone."

This was soon literally true. In some embarrassment, the Bunch rolled up their bubb and lugged it into the shop.

"I can borrow a construction compressor unit on a truck," Two-and-Two offered. "And there's a farm I know . . ."

A great roll of stellene tubing, to have a six-feet six-inch inside diameter when inflated, was delivered on Monday. Enough for three bubbs. The Archer Fives were expected to be somewhat delayed, due to massive ordering. But small boxes of parts and raw stock for the ionics had begun to arrive, too. Capacitors, resistors, thermocouple units. Magnesium rods for Storey or Ramos or the Kuzaks to shape in a lathe. Sheet aluminum to be spun and curved and polished. With Eileen Sands helping, Gimp Hines would do most of that.

So the real work began. Nobody in the Bunch denied that it was a grind. For most, there were those tough courses at Tech. And a job, for money, for sustenance. And the time that must be spent working for — Destiny. Sleep was least important — a few hours, long after midnight, usually.

Frank Nelsen figured that he had it relatively easy — almost as easy as the Kuzak twins, who, during football season, were under strict orders to get their proper sack time. He worked at Hendricks' — old Paul didn't mind his combining the job with his labors of aspiration. Ramos, the night-mechanic, Tiflin, the carwasher, and Two-and-Two Baines, the part-time bricklayer, didn't have it so easy. Eileen, a first-rate legal typist employed for several hours a day by a partnership of lawyers, could usually work from notes, at the place where she lived.

Two-and-Two would lift a big hand facetiously, when he came into the shop. Blinking and squinting, he would wiggle his fingers. "I can still see 'em — to count!" he would moan. "Thanks, all you good people, for coaching me in my math."

"Think nothing of it," Charlie Reynolds or David Lester, or most any of the others, would tell him. Two-and-Two hadn't come near Frank Nelsen very much, during the last few days, though Frank had tried to be friendly.

Lester was the only one without an activity to support himself. But he was at the shop every weekday, six to ten p.m., cementing stellene with meticulous care, while he muttered and dreamed.

The Bunch griped about courses, jobs, and the stubbornness of materials, but they made progress. They had built their first bubb and ionic. The others would be easier.

Early in November, Nelsen collected all available fresh capital, including a second thousand from Paul Hendricks and five hundred from Charlie Reynolds, and sent it in with new orders.

That about exhausted their own finances for a long time to come. Seven bubbs, minus most of even their simpler fittings, and five ionics, seemed as much as they could pay for, themselves. Charlie Reynolds hadn't yet lined up a backer.

"We should have planned to outfit one guy completely," Jig Hollins grumbled on a Sunday afternoon at the shop. "Then we could have drawn lots about who gets a chance to use the gear. That we goofed there is your fault, Reynolds. Or — your Grandpappy didn't come through, huh?"

Charlie met Hollins' sneering gaze for a moment. "Never mind the 'Grandpappy', Jig," he said softly. "I knew that chances weren't good, there. However, there are other prospects which I'm working on. I remember mentioning that it might take time. As for your other remarks, what good is equipping just one person? I thought that this was a project for all of us."

"I'm with Charlie," Joe Kuzak commented.

"Don't fight, guys — we've got to figure on training, too," Ramos laughed. "I've got the problem of an expensive training centrifuge about beat. Out at my old motor scooter club. Come on, Charlie — you, too, Jig — get your cars and let's go! It's only seven miles, and we all need a break."

Paul Hendricks had gone for a walk. So Nelsen locked the shop, and they all tore off, out to the place, Ramos leading the way in his scooter. At the scooter club they found an ancient carnival device which used to be called a motordrome. It was a vertical wooden cylinder, like a huge, ironbound, straight sided cask, thirty feet high and wide, standing on its bottom.

Ramos let himself and the scooter through a massive, curved door — conforming to the curvature of the walls — at the base of the 'drome.

"Secure the latch bar of this door from the outside, fellas," he said. "Then go to the gallery around the top to watch."

Ramos started riding his scooter in a tight circle around the bottom of the 'drome. Increasing speed, he swung outward to the ramped juncture between floor and smooth, circular walls. Then, moving still faster, he was riding around the vertical walls, themselves, held there by centrifugal force. He climbed his vehicle to the very rim of the great cask, body out sideways, grinning and balancing, hands free, the squirrel tails flapping from his gaudily repainted old scooter.

"Come on, you characters!" he shouted through the noise and smoke. "You should try this, too! It's good practice for the rough stuff to come, when we blast out! . . . Hey, Eileen — you try it first — ride with me — then alone — when you get the hang of it! . . ."

This time she accepted. Soon she was riding by herself, smiling recklessly. Reynolds rode after that, then the Kuzaks. Like most of them, Frank Nelsen took the scooter up alone, from the start. He was a bit scared at first, but if you couldn't do a relatively simple stunt like this, how could you get along in space? He became surer, then gleeful, even when the centrifugal force made his head giddy, pushed his buttocks hard against the scooter's seat, and his insides down against his pelvis.

Storey, Hollins and Tiflin all accomplished it. Even Gimp Hines rode behind Ramos in some very wild gyrations, though he didn't attempt to guide the scooter, himself.

Then it was David Lester's turn. It was a foregone conclusion that he couldn't take the scooter up, alone. Pale faced, he rode double. Ramos was careful this time. But on the downward curve before coming to rest, the change of direction made Lester grab Ramos' arm at a critical instant. The scooter wavered, and they landed hard, even at reduced speed. Agile Ramos skipped clear, landing on his feet. Lester flopped heavily, and skidded across the bottom of the 'drome.

When the guys got to him, he was covered with friction burns, and with blood from a scalp gash. Ramos, Storey and Frank worked on him to get him cleaned up and patched up. Part of the time he was sobbing bitterly, more from failure, it seemed, than from his physical hurt. By luck there didn't seem to be any bones broken.

"Darn!" he choked in some infinite protest, beating the ground with his fists. "Damn — that's the end of it for me . . . ! So soon . . . Pop . . ."

"I'll drive you to Doc Miller's, Les," Charlie Reynolds said briskly. "Then home. You other people better stay here . . ."

Charlie had a baffled, subdued look, when he returned an hour later. "I thought his mother would chew my ear, sure," he said. "She didn't. She was just polite. That was worse. She's small — not much color. Of course she was scared, and mad clean through. Know her?"

"I guess we've all seen her around," Nelsen answered. "Widow. Les was in one of my classes during my first high school year. He was a senior, then. They haven't been in Jarviston more than a few years. I never heard where they came from . . ."

Warily, back at the shop, the Bunch told Paul what had happened.

For once his pale eyes flashed. "You Bright Boys," he said. "Especially you, Ramos . . . ! Well, I'm most to blame. I let him hang around, because he was so doggone interested. And *driven* — somehow. Lucky nothing too bad happened. Last August, when you romantics got serious about space, I made him prove he was over twenty-one . . ."

They sweated it out, expecting ear-burning phone calls, maybe legal suits. Nothing happened. Nelsen felt relieved that Lester was gone. One dangerous link in a chain was removed. Contempt boosted his own arrogant pride of accomplishment. Then pity came, and anger for the sneers of Jig Hollins. Then regret for a fallen associate.

The dozen Archers were delivered — there would be a spare, now. The Bunch continued building equipment, they worked out in the motordrome, they drilled at donning their armor and at inflating and rigging a bubb. Gimp Hines exercised with fierce, perspiring doggedness on a horizontal bar he had rigged in the back of the shop. He meant to compensate for his bad leg by improving his shoulder muscles.

Most of the guys still figured that Charlie Reynolds would solve their money problem. But in late November he had a bad moment. Out in front of Hendricks', he looked at his trim automobile. "It's a cinch I can't use it Out There," he chuckled ruefully and un-prompted. Then he brightened. "Nope — selling it wouldn't bring one tenth enough, anyhow. I'll get what we need — just got to keep trying . . . I don't know why, but some so-called experts are saying that off-the-Earth enterprises have been overextended. That makes finding a backer a bit tougher than I thought."

"You ought to just take off on your own, Reynolds," Jig Hollins suggested airily. "I'll bet it's in your mind. The car would pay for that. Or since you're a full-fledged nuclear engineer, some company on the Moon might give you a three year contract and send you out free in a comfortable vehicle. Or wouldn't you like to be tied that long? I wouldn't. Maybe I could afford to be an independent, too. Tough on these shoestring boys, here, but is it *our* fault?"

Hollins was trying to taunt Reynolds. "You're tiresome, Jig," Reynolds said without heat. "Somebody's going to poke you some-time . . ."

Next morning, before going to classes at Tech, Frank Nelsen, with the possibility of bitter disappointment looming in his own mind, spotted Glen Tiflin, the switch blade tosser, standing on the corner, not quite opposite the First National Bank. Tiflin's mouth was tight and his eyes were narrowed.

Nelsen felt a tingle in his nerves — very cold.

"Hi — what cooks, Tif?" he said mildly.

"To you it's which?" Tiflin snapped.

Nelson led him on. "Sometimes I think of all the dough in that bank," he said.

"Yeah," Tiflin snarled softly. "That old coot, Charlie Reynolds' grandpa, sitting by his vault door. Too obvious, though — here. Maybe in another bank — in another town. We could get the cash we need. Hell, though — be cavalier — it's just a thought."

"You damned fool!" Nelsen hissed slowly.

It was harder than ever to like Tiflin for anything at all. But he did have that terrible, star-reaching desperation. Nelsen had quite a bit of it, himself. He knew, now.

"Get up to Tech, Tif," he said like an order. "If you have a chance, tell my math prof I might be a little late . . ."

That was how Frank Nelsen happened to face J. John Reynolds, who, in a question of progress, would still approve of galley slaves. Nelsen had heard jokes like that laughed about, around Jarviston. J. John, by reputation, was all hard business.

Nelsen got past his secretary.

"Young man — I hope you have something very special to say."

There was a cold, amused challenge in the old man's tone, and an implication of a moment of casual audience granted generously, amid mountains of more important affairs.

Nelsen didn't waver. The impulse to do what he was doing had come too suddenly for nervousness to build up. He hadn't planned what to say, but his arguments were part of himself.

"Mr. Reynolds — I'm Frank Nelsen, born here in Jarviston. Perhaps you know me on sight. I believe you are acquainted with Paul Hendricks, and you must have heard about our group, which is aiming at space, as people like ourselves are apt to be doing, these days. We've made fair progress, which proves we're at least earnest, if not dedicated. But unless we wait and save for years, we've come about as far as we can, without a loan. Judging from the success of previous earnest groups, and the development of resources and industries beyond the Earth, we are sure that we could soon pay you back, with considerable interest."

J. John Reynolds seemed to doze, hardly listening. But at the end his eyes opened, and sparks of anger — or acid humor — seemed to dance in them.

"I know very well what sort of poetic tomfoolery you are talking about, Nelsen," he said. "I wondered how long it would be before one of you — other than my grandson with his undiluted brass, and knowing me far too well in one sense, anyway — would have the gall to come here and talk to me like this. You'd probably be considered a minor, too, in some states. Dealing with you, I could even get into trouble."

Nelsen's mouth tightened. "I came to make a proposition and get an answer," he responded. "Thank you for your no. It helps clear the view."

"Hold on, Nelsen," J. John growled. "I don't remember saying no. I said 'gall,' intending it to mean guts. That's what young spacemen need, isn't it? They've almost got to be *young*, so legal viewpoints about the age at which competence is reached are changing. Oh, there is plenty of brass among your generation. But it fails in peculiar places. I was waiting for one place where it didn't fail. Charlie, my grandson, doesn't count. It has never taken him any courage to talk to me any way he wants."

This whole encounter was still dreamlike to Frank Nelsen.

"Then you are saying yes?"

"I might. Do you foolishly imagine that my soul is so completely sour milk that in youth I couldn't feel the same drives that you feel, now, for the limited opportunity there was, then? But under some damnable pressure toward conformity, I took a desk job in a bank. I am now eighty-one years old . . . How much does your 'Bunch' need — at minimum, mind you — for the opportunity to ride in space-armor till the rank smell of their bodies almost chokes them, for developing weird allergies or going murdering mad, but, in the main, doing their best, anyway, pathfinding and building, if they've got the guts? Come on, Nelsen — you must know."

"Fifty thousand," Frank answered quickly. "There are still eleven in our group."

"Yes . . . More may quit along the way . . . Here is *my* proposition: I would make funds available for your expenses up to that amount — from my personal holdings, separate from this bank. The amount due from each individual shall be ten percent of whatever his gains or earnings are, off the Earth, over a period of ten years, but he will not be required to pay back any part of the original loan. This is a high-risk, high-potential profit arrangement for me — with an experimental element. I will ask for no written contract — only a verbal promise. I have found that people are fairly honest, and I know that, far in space, circumstances become too complicated to make legal collections very practical, anyway, even if I ever felt inclined to try them . . . Now, if — after I see your friends, whom you will send to me for an interview and to give me their individual word, also, I decide to make my proposition effective — will you, yourself, promise to abide by these terms?"

Nelsen was wary for a second. "Yes — I promise," he said.

"Good. I am glad you paused to think, Nelsen. I am not fabulously rich. But having more or less money hardly matters to me at this late date, so I am not likely to try to trap you. Yet there is still a game to play, and an outcome to watch — the future. Now get out of here before you become ridiculous by saying more than a casual thanks."

"All right — thanks. Thank you, sir . . ."

Nelsen felt somewhat numb. But a faint, golden glow was increasing inside his mind.

Tiflin hadn't gone up to Tech. He was still waiting on the street corner. "What the hell, Frank?" he said.

"I think we've got the loan, Tif. But he wants to see all of us. Can you go in there, be polite, say you're a Bunch member, make a promise, and — above all — avoid blowing your top? Boy — if you queer this . . . !"

Tiflin's mouth was open. "You kidding?"

"No!"

Tiflin gulped, and actually looked subdued. "Okay, Frank. Be cavalier. Hell, I'd croak before I'd mess this up . . . !"

By evening, everybody had visited J. John Reynolds, including Charlie Reynolds and Jig Hollins. Nelsen got the backslapping treatment.

Charlie sighed, rubbed his head, then grinned with immense relief. "That's a load off," he said. "Glad to have somebody else fix it. Congrats, Frank. I wonder if Otto has got any champagne to go with the hotdogs . . . ?"

Otto had a bottle — enough for a taste, all around. Eileen kissed Frank impulsively. "You ought to get *real* smart," she said.

"Uh-huh," he answered. "Now let's get some beer — more our speed."

But none of them overdid the beer either . . .

Just after New Year's they had eight bubbs completed, tested, folded carefully according to government manuals, and stowed in an attic they had rented over Otto's place. They had seven ionics finished and stored. More parts and materials were arriving. The air-restorers were going to be the toughest and most expensive to make. They were the really vital things to a spaceman. Every detail had to be carefully fitted and assembled. The chlorophane contained costly catalytic agents.

A winter of hard work was ahead, but they figured on a stretch of clear sailing, now. They didn't expect anyone to shake their morale, least of all a nice, soft-spoken guy in U.S.S.F. greys. Harv Diamond was the one man from Jarviston who had gotten into the Space Force. He used to hang around Hendricks'.

He dropped in on a Sunday evening, when the whole Bunch was in the shop. They were around him at once, like around a hero, shouting and questioning. There were mottled patches on his hands, and he wore dark glasses, but he seemed at ease and happy.

"There have been some changes in the old joint, huh, Paul?" he said. "So you guys are one of the outfits building its own gear . . . Looks pretty good . . . Of course you can get some bulky supplies cheaper on the Moon, because everything from Earth has to be boosted into space against a gravity six times as great as the lunar, which raises the price like hell. Water and oxygen, for instance. Peculiar, on the dry, almost airless Moon. But roasting water out of lunar gypsum rock is an easy trick. And oxygen can be derived from water by simple electrolysis."

"Hell, we know all that, Harv," Ramos laughed.

So Harv Diamond gave them the lowdown on the shortage of girls — yet — in Serenitatis Base, on the Moon. Just the same, it was growing like corn in July, and was already a pretty good leave-spot, if you liked to look around. Big vegetable gardens under sealed, stellene domes. Metal refineries, solar power plants, plastic factories and so forth, already in operation . . . But there was nothing like Pallastown, on little Pallas, out in the Asteroid Belt . . . Mars? That was the heebie-jeebie planet.

Gimp asked Harv how much leave he had on Earth.

"Not long, I guess," Harv laughed. "I've got to check back at the Force Hospital in Minneapolis tomorrow . . ."

But right away it was evident that his thoughts had been put on the wrong track. His easy smile faded. He gasped and looked kind of surprised. He hung onto Paul's old swivel chair, in which he was sitting, as if he was suddenly terribly afraid of falling. His eyes closed tight, and there was a funny gurgle in his throat.

The Bunch surrounded him, wanting to help, but he half recovered.

"Even a good Space Force bubb, manufactured under rigid government specifications, can tear," he said in a thick tone. "If some jerk, horsing around with another craft, bumps you even lightly. Compartmentation helps, but you can still be unlucky. I was fortunate — almost buttoned into my Archer Six, already. *But did you ever see a person slowly swell up and turn purple, with frothy bubbles forming under the skin, while his blood boils in the Big Vacuum?* That was my buddy, Ed Kraft . . ."

Lieutenant Harvey Diamond gasped. Huge, strangling hiccups came out of his throat. His eyes went wild. The Kuzaks had to hold him, while Mitch Storey ran to phone Doc Miller. A shot quieted Diamond somewhat, and an ambulance took him away.

That incident shook up the Bunch a little. A worse one came on a Tuesday evening, when not everybody was at the shop.

The TV was on, showing the interior of the *Far Side*, one of those big, comparatively luxurious tour bubbs that take rubbernecks that can afford it on a swing around the Moon. The *Far Side* was just coming into orbit, where tending skip gliders would take off the passengers for grounding at the New Mexico spaceport. Aboard the big bubb you could see people moving about, or sitting with drinks on curved benches. A girl was playing soft music on a tiny, lightweight piano.

There wasn't any sign of trouble except that the TV channel went dead for a second, until a stand by commercial with singing cartoon figures cut in.

But Frank Nelsen somehow put his hands to his head, as if to protect it.

Mitch Storey, with a big piece of stellene in his brown mitts, stood up very straight.

Gimp, at a bench, handed a tiny capacitor to Eileen, and started counting, slow and even. "One — two — three — four — five — "

"What's with you slobs?" Jig Hollins wanted to know.

"Dunno — we're nuts, maybe," Gimp answered. "Ten — eleven — twelve — "

Charlie Reynolds and Paul Hendricks were alert, too.

Then a big, white light trembled on the thin snow beyond the windows, turning the whole night landscape into weird day. The tearing, crackling roar was delayed. By the time the sound arrived, all of the stellene in the *Far Side* must have been consumed. It had no resistance to atmospheric friction at five miles per second, or faster. There were just the heavier metallic details left to fall and burn. Far off, there was a thumping crash that seemed to make the ground sag and recover.

"Here we go!" Charlie Reynolds yelled.

In his and Hollins' cars, they got to the scene of the fragment's fall, two miles out of town, by following a faint, fading glow. They were almost the first to reach the spot. Tiflin and Ramos, who had been working on their jobs, came with their boss, along with a trailing horde of cars from town.

Flashlights probed into the hot impact pit in the open field, where the frozen soil had seemed to splash like a liquid. Crumpled in the hole was a lump of half-fused sheet steel, wadded up like paper. It was probably part of the *Far Side*'s central hub. Magnesium and aluminum, of which the major portions had certainly been made, were gone; they could never have endured the rush through the atmosphere.

Ramos got down into the pit. After a minute, he gave a queer cry, and climbed out again. His mitten smoked as he opened it, to show something.

"It must have been behind a heavy object," he said very seriously, not like his usual self at all. "That broke the molecular impact with the air — like a ceramic nose cone. Kept it from burning up completely."

The thing was a lady's silver compact, from which a large piece had been fused away. A bobbypin had gotten welded to it.

Old Paul Hendricks cursed. Poor Two-and-Two moved off sickly, with a palm clamped over his mouth.

Eileen Sands gasped, and seemed about to yell. But she got back most of her poise. Women have nursed the messily ill and dying, and have tended ghastly wounds during ages of time. So they know the messier side of biology as well as men.

Ramos gave the pathetic relic to a cop who was trying to take charge.

"Somebody must have goofed bad on the *Far Side*, for it to miss orbit like that," Ramos grated. "Or was something wrong, before-hand? Their TV transmitter went out — we were watching, too, at the garage . . . You can see the aurora — the Northern Lights . . . Those damn solar storms might have loused up instruments . . . ! But who'll ever know, now . . . ?"

The Kuzaks, who had been to an Athletic Association meeting at Tech, had grabbed a ride out with the stream of cars from town. Both looked grim. "No use hanging around here, Charlie," Art urged. "Let's get back to the shop."

Before he drove off, Jig Hollins tried to chuckle mockingly at everybody, especially Charlie Reynolds. "Time to think about keep-ing a nice safe job in the Jarviston powerhouse — eh, Reynolds? And staying near granddad?"

"We're supposed not to be children, Hollins," Charlie shot back at him from his car window. "We're supposed to have known long ago that these things happen, and to have adjusted ourselves to our chances."

"Ninnies that get scared first thing, when the facts begin to show!" Tiflin snarled. "Cripes — let's don't be like soft bugs under boards!"

"You're right, Tif," Frank Nelsen agreed, feeling that for once the ne'er-do-well — the nuisance — might be doing them all some good. Frank could feel how Tiflin shamed some of the quiver out of his own insides, and helped bring back pride and strength.

The *Far Side* disaster had been pretty disturbing, however. And next day, Thursday, the blue envelopes came to the members of the Bunch. A printed card with a typed-in date, was inside each: "Re-port for space-fitness tests at Space-Medicine Center, February 15th . . ."

"Just a couple of weeks!" Two-and-Two was moaning that night. "How'll I get through, with my courses only half-finished. You've gotta help me some more, people! With that stinking math . . . !"

So equipment building was almost suspended, while the Bunch crammed and sweated and griped and cursed. But maybe now some of them wouldn't care so very much if they flunked.

Two loaded automobiles took off for Minneapolis on the night before the ordeal. The Bunch put up at motels to be fresh the next morning. Maybe some of them even slept.

At the Center, there were more forms to fill out. Then complete physicals started the process. Next came the written part. Right off, Frank Nelsen knew that this was going a familiar way, which had happened quite often at Tech: Struggle through a tough course, hear dire promises of head-cracking questions and math problems in the final quiz. Then the switch — the easy letdown.

The remainder of the tests proceeded like assembly-line operations, each person taking each alone, in the order of his casual position in the waiting line.

First there was the dizzying, mind-blackening centrifuge test, to see if you could take enough Gs of acceleration, and still be alert enough to fit a simple block puzzle together.

Then came the free fall test, from the top of a thousand foot tower. A parachute-arrangement broke your speed at the bottom of the track. As in the centrifuge, instruments incorporated into the fabric of a coverall suit with a hood, were recording your emotional and bodily reactions. The medics wanted to be sure that your panic level was high and cool. Nelsen didn't find free fall very hard to take, either.

Right after that came the scramble to see how fast you could get into an Archer, unfold and inflate a bubb and rig its gear.

"That's all, Mister," the observer with the camera told Nelsen in a bored tone.

"Results will be mailed to your home within twelve hours — Mr. Nelsen," a girl informed him as she read his name from a printed card.

So the Bunch returned tensely to Jarviston, with more time to sweat out. Everybody looked at Gimp Hines — and then looked away. Even Jig Hollins didn't make any comments. Gimp, himself, seemed pretty subdued.

The small, green space-fitness cards were arriving at Jarviston addresses in the morning.

Near the end of the noon hour, Two-and-Two Baines was waving his around the Tech campus, having gone home to look, as of course everybody else who could, had also done. "Cripes! — Hi-di-ho — here it is!" he was yelling at the frosty sky, when Frank came with his own ticket.

The Kuzaks had theirs, and were calm about it. Eileen Sands' card was tucked neatly into her sweater pocket, as she joined those who were waiting for the others on the front steps of Tech's Carver Hall.

Ramos had to make a noise. "See what Santa brought the lady! But he didn't forget your Uncle Miguel, either — see! We're in, kid — be happy. Yippee!"

He tried to whirl her in some crazy dance, but Gimp was swinging along the slushy walk on his crutches. His grin was a mile wide. Mitch Storey was with him, looking almost as pleased.

"Guess legs don't count, Out There," Gimp was saying. "Or patched tickers, either, as long as they work good! I kind of figured on it . . . Hey — I don't want to ride anybody's shoulders, Ramos — cut it out . . . ! We won't know about Charlie and Jig till tonight, when they come to Paul's from their jobs. But I don't think that there's any sweat for them, either . . . Only — where's Tif? He should be back by now from where he lives with his father . . ."

Tiflin didn't show up at Hendricks' at all that evening, or at his garage job either. Ramos phoned from the garage to confirm that.

"And he's not at home," Ramos added. "The boss sent me to check. His Old Man says he doesn't know where Tif is and cares less."

"Just leave Tif be," Mitch Storey said softly.

"Maybe that's best, at that," old Paul growled. "Only I hope the darned idiot doesn't cook himself up another jam . . ."

They all knew then, for sure, what had happened. Right now, Glen Tiflin was wandering alone, somewhere, cursing and suffering. As likely as not, he'd start hitchhiking across the country, to try to get away from himself . . . Somewhere the test instruments — which had seemed so lenient — had tripped him up, spotting the weakness that he had tried to fight. Temper, nerves — emotional instability. So there was no green card for Tif, to whom space was a kind of Nirvana . . .

The Bunch worked on with their preparations. Things got done all right, but the fine edge of enthusiasm had dulled. Jig Hollins flung his usual remarks, with their derisive undertone, around for a couple of weeks. Then he came into the shop with a girl who had a pretty, rather blank face, and a mouth that could twist with stubborn anger.

"Meet Minnie," Jig said loudly. "She is one reason why I have decided that I've had enough of this kid stuff. I gave it a whirl — for kicks. But who, with any sense, wants to go batting off to Mars or the Asteroids? That's for the birds, the crackpots. Wife, house, kids — right in your own home town — that's the only sense there is. Minnie showed me that, and we're gonna get married!"

The Bunch looked at Jig Hollins. He was swaggering. He was making sour fun of them, but in his eyes there were other signs, too.

A pleading: Agree with me — back me up — quit! Don't see through me — it's not so, anyhow! Don't say I'm hiding behind a skirt . . . Above all, don't call me yellow! I'm *not* yellow, I tell you! I'm tough Jig Hollins! You're the dopes! . . .

Frank Nelsen spoke for the others. "We understand, Jig. We'll be getting you a little wedding present. Later on, maybe we'll be able to send you something really good. Best of luck . . ."

They let Jig Hollins and his Minnie go. They felt their contempt and pity, and their lifting, wild pride. Maybe Jig Hollins, wise guy and big mouth, boosted their own selves quite a bit, by contrast.

"Poor sap," Joe Kuzak breathed. "Who's he kidding — us or himself, or neither . . . ?"

Soon Eileen began to show symptoms: Sighs. A restlessness. Sudden angry pouts that would change as quickly to the secret smiles of reverie, while she hummed a soft tune to herself, and rose on her toes, dancing a few steps. Speculative looks at Nelsen, or the other guys around her. Maybe she envied men. Her eyes would narrow thoughtfully for a second. Then she might look scared and very young, as if her thoughts frightened her. But the expression of determined planning would return.

After about ten days of this, Gimp asked, "What's with you, Eileen? You don't usually say much, but now there must be something else."

She tossed down a fistful of waste with which she had been wiping her hands — she had been cementing segments of the last of the ten bubbs they would make — more than they needed, now, but spares might be useful.

"Okay, all," she said briskly. "You should hear this, without any further delay. I'm clearing out, too. Reasons? Well — at least since Tif flunked his emotional I've been getting the idea that possibly I've been playing on a third-rate team. No offense, please — I don't really believe it's so, and if it isn't so you're tough enough not to be hurt. Far worse — I'm a girl. So why am I trying to do things in a man's way, when there are means that are made for me? I'm all of twenty-two. I've got nobody except an aunt in Illinois. Meanwhile, out in New Mexico, there's a big spaceport, and a lot of the right people who can help me. I'll bet I can get where you want to go, before you do. Tell Mr. J. John Reynolds that he can have my equipment — most of which he paid for. But perhaps I'll still be able to give him his ten percent."

"Eileen! Cripes, what are you talking about?" This was Ramos yelping, as if the clown could be hurt, after all.

"I don't mean anything so bad, Fun Boy," she said more gently.

"Lots of men are remarkably chivalrous. But no arguments. Now that I have declared my intentions, I'll pick up and pull out of here this minute — taking some pleasant memories with me, as well as a space-fitness card. You're all good, plodding joes — honest. But there'll be a plane west from Minneapolis tomorrow."

She was getting into her blazer. Even Ramos saw that arguments would be futile. Frank Nelsen's throat ached suddenly, as if at sins of omission. But that was wrong. Eileen Sands was too old for him, anyhow.

"So long, you characters," she said. "Good luck. Don't follow me outside. Maybe I'll see you, someplace."

"Right, Eileen — we'll miss yuh," Storey said. "And we better sure enough see you that someplace!"

There were ragged shouts. "Good luck, kid. So long, Eileen . . ."

She was gone — a small, scared, determined figure, dressed like a boy. On her wrist was a watch that might get pawned for a plane ticket.

Ramos was unbelievably glum for days. But he worked harder building air-restorers than most of the Bunch had ever worked before. "We're hardcore, now — we'll last," he would growl. "Final, long lap — March, April and May — with no more interruptions. In June, when our courses at Tech are finished, we'll be ready to roll . . ."

That was about how it turned out. Near the end of May, the Bunch lined up in the shop, the ten blastoff drums they had made, including two spares. The drums were just large tubes of sheet magnesium, in which about everything that each man would need was compactly stowed: Archer Five, bubb, sun-powered ionic drive motor, air-restorer, moisture-reclaimer, flasks of oxygen and water, instruments, dehydrated foods, medicines, a rifle, instruction manuals, a few clothes, and various small, useful items. Everything was cut to minimum, to keep the weight down. The lined up drums made a utilitarian display that looked rather grim.

The gear was set out like this, for the safety inspectors to look at during the next few days, and provide their stamp of approval.

The blastoff tickets had also been purchased — for June tenth.

"Well, how do you think the Bunch should travel to New Mexico, Paul?" Frank Nelsen joshed.

"Like other Bunches, I guess," Paul Hendricks laughed. "A couple of moving vans should do the trick . . ."

III

On June first, ten days before blastoff, David Lester came back to the shop, sheepishness, pleasure and worry showing in his face.

"I cleared up matters at home, guys," he said. "And I went to Minneapolis and obtained one of these." He held up the same kind of space-fitness card that the others had.

"The tests are mostly passive," he explained further. "Anybody can be whirled in a centrifuge, or take a fall. That is somewhat simpler, in its own way, than clinging to a careening motor scooter. Though I do admit that I was still almost rejected . . . ! So, I'll join you, again — if I'm permitted? I understand that my old gear has been completed, as a spare? Paul told me. Of course I'm being crusty, in asking to have it back, now?"

"Uh-uh, Les — I'm sure that's okay," Ramos grunted. "Right, fellas?"

The others nodded.

A subdued cheerfulness seemed to possess Lester, the mamma's boy, as if he had eased and become less introverted. The Bunch took him back readily enough, though with misgivings. Still, the mere fact that a companion could return, after defeat, helped brace their uncertain morale.

"I'll order you a blastoff ticket, Les," Frank Nelsen said. "In one of the two GOs — ground-to-orbit rockets — reserved for us. The space is still there . . ."

David Lester had won a battle. He meant to win through, completely. Perhaps some of this determination was transmitted to the others. Two-and-Two Baines, for example, seemed more composed.

There wasn't much work to do during those last days, after the equipment had been inspected and approved, the initials of each man painted in red on his blastoff drum, and all the necessary documents put in order.

Mitch Storey rode a bus to Mississippi, to say goodbye to his folks. The Kuzaks flew to Pennsylvania for the same reason. Likewise, Gimp Hines went by train to Illinois. Ramos rode his scooter all the way down to East Texas and back, to see his parents and a flock of younger brothers and sisters. When he returned, he solemnly gave his well-worn vehicle to an earnest boy still in high school.

"No dough," Ramos said. "I just want her to have a good home."

Those of the Bunch who had families didn't run into any serious last minute objections from them about their going into space. Blasting out was getting to be an accepted destiny.

There was a moment of trouble with Two-and-Two Baines about a kid of eight years named Chippie Potter, who had begun to hang around Hendricks' just the way Frank Nelsen had done, long ago. But more especially, the trouble was about Chippie's fox terrier, Blaster.

"The lad of course can't go along with us, Out There, on account of school and his Mom," Two-and-Two said sentimentally, on one of those final evenings. "So he figures his mutt should go in his place. Shucks, maybe he's right! A lady mutt first made it into orbit, ahead of any people, remember? And we ought to have a mascot. We could make a sealed air-conditioned box and smuggle old Blaster. Afterwards, he'd be all right, inside a bubb."

"You try any stunt like that and I'll shoot you," Frank Nelsen promised. "Things are going to be complicated enough."

"You always tell me no, Frank," Two-and-Two mourned.

"I know something else," said Joe Kuzak — he and his tough twin had returned to Jarviston by then, as had all the others who had visited their homes. "There's a desperate individual around, again. Tiflin. He appealed his test — and lost. Kind of a good guy — someways . . ."

The big Kuzaks, usually easy and steady and not too comical, both had a certain kind of expression, now — like amused and secretive gorillas. Frank wasn't sure whether he got the meaning of this or not, but right then he felt sort of sympathetic to Tiflin, too.

"I didn't hear anything; I won't say or do anything," he laughed.

Afterwards, under the pressure of events, he forgot the whole matter.

It would take about thirty-six hours to get to the New Mexico spaceport. Calculating accordingly, the Bunch hoisted their gear aboard two canvas-covered trucks parked in the driveway beside Hendricks', just before sundown of their last day in Jarviston.

People had begun to gather, to see them off. Two-and-Two's folks, a solid, chunky couple, looking grave. David Lester's mother, of course, seeming younger than the Bunch remembered her. Make-up brought back some of her good-looks. She was more Spartan than they had thought, too.

"I have made up a basket of sandwiches for you and your comrades, Lester," she said.

Otto Kramer was out with free hotdogs, beer and Pepsi, his face sad. J. John Reynolds, backer of the Bunch, had promised to come down, later. Chief of Police, Bill Hobard, was there, looking grim, as if he was half glad and half sorry to lose this passel of law-abiding but worrisome young eccentrics. There were various cynical and curious loafers around, too. There were Chippie Potter and his mutt — a more wistful and worshipping pair would have been hard to imagine.

Sophia Jameson, one of Charlie Reynolds' old flames, was there. Charlie had sold his car and given away his wardrobe, but he still managed to look good in a utilitarian white coverall.

"Well, we had a lot of laughs, anyway, you big ape!" Sophia was saying to Charlie, when Roy Harder, the mailman with broken-down feet, shuffled up, puffing.

"One for you, Reynolds," he said. "Also one for you, Nelsen. They just came — ordinarily I wouldn't deliver them till tomorrow morning. But you see how it is."

A long, white envelope was in Frank Nelsen's hands. In its upper left-hand corner was engraved:

UNITED STATES SPACE FORCE
RECRUITING SECTION
WASHINGTON, D.C.

"Jeez, Frankie — Charlie — you made it — open 'em, quick!" Two-and-Two said.

Frank was about to do so. But everybody knew exactly what was inside such an envelope — the only thing that was ever so enclosed, unless you were already in the Force. An official summons to report, on such and such a date and such and such a place, for examination.

For a minute Frank Nelsen suffered the awful anguish of indecision over a joke of circumstance. Like most of the others, he had tried to get into the Force. He had given it up as hopeless. Now, when he was ready to move out on his own, the chance came. Exquisite irony.

Frank felt the lift of maybe being one of — well — the Chosen. To wear the red, black and silver rocket emblem, to use the finest equipment, to carry out dangerous missions, to exercise authority in space, and yet to be pampered, as those who make a mark in life are pampered.

"*Que milagro!* — holy cow!" Ramos breathed. "Charlie — Frankie — congratulations!"

Frank saw the awed faces around them. They were looking up to him and Charlie in a friendly way, but already he felt that he had kind of lost them by being a little luckier. Or was this all goof ball sentiment in his own mind, to make himself feel real modest?

So maybe he got sentimental about this impoverished, ragtag Bunch that, even considering J. John Reynolds' help, still were pulling themselves up into space almost literally by their own bootstraps. He had always belonged to the Bunch, and he still did. So perhaps he just got sore.

Charlie's and his eyes met for a second, in understanding.

"Thanks, Postman Roy," Charlie said. "Only you were right the first time. These letters shouldn't be delivered until your next trip around, tomorrow morning."

They both handed the envelopes back to Roy Harder.

The voices of their Bunch-mates jangled in a conflicting chorus.

"Ah — yuh damn fools!" Two-and-Two bleated.

"Good for them!" Art Kuzak said, perhaps mockingly.

"Hey — they're us — they'll stay with us — shut up — didn't we lose enough people, already?" Gimp said.

Frank grinned with half of his mouth. "We always needed a name," he remarked. "How about *The Planet Strappers*? Hell — if the chair-borne echelon of the U.S.S.F. is so slow and picky, let 'em go sit on a sunspot."

"I need some white paint and a brush, Paul," Ramos declared, running into the shop.

In a couple of minutes more, the name for the Bunch was crudely and boldly lettered on the sides of both trucks.

"Salute your ladies, shake hands with your neighbors, and then let's get moving," Charlie Reynolds laughed genially.

And so they did. Old Paul Hendricks, born too soon, blinked a little as he grinned, and slapped shoulders. "On your way, you lucky tramps . . . !"

There were quick movements here and there — a kiss, a touch of hands, a small gesture, a strained glance.

Frank Nelsen blew a kiss jauntily to Nance Codiss, the neighbor girl, who waved to him from the background. "So long, Frank . . ." He wondered if he saw a fierce envy showing in her face.

Miss Rosalie Parks, his high school Latin teacher, was there, too. Old J. John Reynolds appeared at the final moment to smile dryly and to flap a waxy hand.

"So long, sir . . . Thanks . . ." they all shouted as the diesels of the trucks whirred and then roared. J. John still had never been around the shop. It was only Frank who had seen him regularly, every week. It might have been impertinent for them to say that they'd make him really rich. But some must have hoped that they'd get rich, themselves.

Frank Nelsen was perched on his neatly packed blastoff drum in the back of one of the trucks, as big tires began to turn. Near him, similarly perched, were Mitch Storey, dark and thoughtful, Gimp Hines with a triumph in his face, Two-and-Two Baines biting his lip, and Dave Lester with his large Adam's apple bobbing.

So that was how the Bunch left Jarviston, on a June evening that smelled of fresh-cut hay and car fumes — home. Perhaps they had chosen this hour to go because the gathering darkness might soften their haunting suspicions of complete folly before an adventure so different from the life they knew — neat streets, houses, beds, Saturday nights, dances, struggling for a dream at Hendricks' — that even if they survived the change, the difference must seem a little like death.

Seeking the lifting thread of magical romance again, Frank Nelsen looked up at the ribbed canvas top of the truck. "Covered wagon," he said.

"Sure — Indians — boom-boom," Two-and-Two chuckled, brightening. "Wild West . . . Yeah — *wild* — that's a word I kind of like."

Up ahead, in the other truck, Ramos and Charlie Reynolds had begun to sing a funny and considerably ribald song. They made lots of lusty, primitive noise. When they were finished, Ramos, still in a spirit of humor, corned up an old Mexican number about disappointed love.

> "*Adios, Mujer —*
> *Adios para siempre —*
> *Adios . . .*"

Ramos wailed out the last syllable with lugubrious emphasis.

"Always it's girls," Dave Lester managed to chuckle. "I still don't see how they expect to find many, Out There."

"If our Eileen has — or will — make it, she won't be the first — or last," Frank offered, almost mystically.

"Hey — I was right about the word, *wild*," Two-and-Two mused. "Yeah — we're all just plum-full of wanting to be wild. Not *mean* wild, mostly — constructive wild, instead. And, damn, we'll *do* it . . . ! Cripes — we ought to come back to old Paul's place in June, ten years from now, and tell each other what we've accomplished."

"Damn — that's a fine idea, Two-and-Two!" David Lester

piped up. "I'll suggest it to the other guys, first chance I get . . . !"

Of course it was another piece of callow whistling in the dark, but it was a buildup, too. Coming home at a fixed, future time, to compare glittering successes. Eldorados found and exploited, cities built, giant businesses established, hearts won, real manhood achieved past staggering difficulties. But they all had to believe it, to combat the icy sliver of dread concerning an event that was getting very near, now.

Mitch Storey sat with his mouth organ cupped in his hands. He began to make soft, musing chords, tried a fragment of Old Man River, shifted briefly to a spiritual, and wound up with some eerie, impromptu fragments, partly like the drums and jingling brass of old Africa, partly like a joyful battle, partly like a lonesome lament, and then, mysteriously like absolute silence.

Storey stopped, abashed. He grinned.

"Reaching for Out There, Mitch?" Frank Nelsen asked. "Music of your own, to tell about space? Got any words for it?"

"Nope," Mitch said. "Maybe it shouldn't have any words. Anyhow, the tune doesn't come clear, yet. I haven't been — There."

"Maybe some more of Otto's beer will help," Frank suggested. "Here — one can, each, to begin." For once, Frank had an urge to get slightly pie-eyed.

"High's a good word," he amended. "High and sky! Mars and stars!"

"Space and race, nuts and guts!" Lester put in, trying to belong, and be light-minded, like he thought the others were, instead of a scared, pedantic kid. He slapped the blastoff drum under him, familiarly, as if to draw confidence from its grim, cool lines.

The whole Bunch was quite a bit like that, for a good part of the night, shouting lustily back and forth between the two trucks, laughing, singing, wise-cracking, drinking up Otto Kramer's Pepsi and beer.

But at last, Gimp Hines, remembering wisdom, spoke up. "We're supposed to be under mild sedation — a devil-killer, a tranquilizer — for at least thirty hours. It's in the rules for prospective ground-to-orbit candidates. We're supposed to be sleeping good. Here goes my pill — down, with the last of my beer . . ."

Faces sobered, and became strained and careful, again. The guys on the trucks bedded down as best they could, among their gaunt equipment. Soon there were troubled snores from huddled figures that quivered with the motion of the vehicles. The mottled Moon rode high. Big tires whispered on damp concrete. Lights blinked past. The trucks curved around corners, growled up grades, highballed down. There were pauses at all-night drive-ins, coffees misguidedly drunk in a blurred, fur-tongued half wakefulness that seemed utterly bleak. Oh, hell, Frank Nelsen thought, wasn't it far better to be home in bed, like Jig Hollins?

At grey dawn, there was a breakfast stop, the two truck drivers and their relief man grinning cynically at the Bunch. Then there was more country, rolling and speeding past. Wakefulness was half sleep, and vice-versa. And the hours, through the day and another night, dwindled toward blastoff time, at eleven o'clock tomorrow morning.

When the second dawn came, the Bunch were all tautly and wearily alert again, peering ahead, across dun desert. There wasn't much fallout from the carefully developed hydrogen-fusion engines of the GO rockets, but maybe there was enough to distort the genes of the cacti a little, making their forms more grotesque.

Along the highway there were arrows and signs. When the trucks had labored to the top of a ridge, the spaceport installations came into view all at once:

Barbed-wire fences, low, olive-drab gate buildings, guidance tower, the magnesium dome of a powerhouse reactor, repair and maintenance shops, personnel-housing area carefully shielded against radiation by a huge stellene bubble, sealed and air-conditioned, with double-doored entrances and exits. Inside it were visible neat bungalows, lawns, gardens, supermarket, swimming pools, swings, a kid's bike left casually here or there.

The first sunshine glinted on the two rockets and their single, attendant gantry tower, waiting on the launching pad. The rockets were as gaunt as sharks. They might almost have been natural spires on the Moon, or ruined towers left by the extinct beings of Mars. At first they were impersonal and expected parts of the scene, until the numbers, ceramic-enamelled on their striped flanks, were noticed: GO-11 and GO-12.

"They're us — up the old roller coaster!" Charlie Reynolds shouted.

Then everybody was checking his blastoff ticket, as if he didn't remember the number primly typed on it. Frank Nelsen had GO-12. GO — Ground-to-Orbit. But it might as well mean go! glory, or gallows, he thought.

The trucks reached the gate. The Bunch met the bored and cynical reception committee — a half-dozen U.S.S.F. men in radiation coveralls.

Each of the Bunch held his blastoff ticket, his space-fitness and his equipment-inspection cards meekly in sweaty fingers. It was an old story — the unknowing standing vulnerable before the knowing and perhaps harsh.

Nelsen guessed at some of the significance of the looks they all received: Another batch of greenhorns — to conquer and develop and populate the extra-terrestrial regions. They all come the same way, and look alike. Poor saps . . .

Frank Nelsen longed to paste somebody, even in the absence of absolute impoliteness.

The blastoff drums were already being lifted off the trucks, weighed, screened electronically, and moved toward a loading elevator on a conveyor. The whole process was automatic.

"Nine men — ten drums — how come?" one of the U.S.S.F. people inquired.

"A spare. Its GO carriage charge is paid," Reynolds answered.

He got an amused and tired smirk. "Okay, Sexy — it's all right with us. And I hope you fellas were smart enough not to eat any breakfast. Of course we'd like to have you say — tentatively — where you'll be headed, on your own power, after we toss you Upstairs. Toward the Moon, huh, like most fledglings say? It helps a little to know. Some new folks start to scream and get lost, up there. See how it is?"

"Sure — we see — thanks. Yes — the Moon." This was still Charlie Reynolds talking.

"No problem, then, Sexy. We mean to be gentle. Now let's move along, in line. Never mind consulting wristwatches — we've got over four hours left. Final blood pressure check, first. Then the shot, the devil-killer, the wit-sharpener. And try to remember some of what you're supposed to have learned. Relax, don't talk too much, and try not to swallow any live butterflies."

The physician, looking them over, shook his head and made a wry face of infinite sadness, when he came to Gimp and Lester, but he offered no comment except a helpless shrug.

The U.S.S.F. spokesman was still with them. "All right — armor up. Let's see how good you are at it."

They scrambled to it grimly, and still a little clumsily. Gimp Hines had, of course, long ago tailored his Archer to fit that shrunken right leg. Then they just sat around in the big locker room, trying to get used to being enclosed like this, much of the time, checking to see that everything was functioning right, listening to the muffled voices that still reached them from beyond their protecting encasement. They could still have conversed, by direct sound or by helmet-radio, but the devil-killer seemed to subdue the impulse, and for a while caused a dreaminess that shortened the long wait . . .

"Okay — time to move!"

Heavy with their Archies, they filed out into desert sun-glare that their darkened helmets made feeble. They arose in the long climb of the gantry elevator and split into two groups, for the two rockets, according to their GO numbers. It didn't seem to matter, now, who went with whom. Each man had his own private sweating party. The padded passenger compartments were above the blastoff drum freight sections.

"Helmets secure? Air-restorer systems on? Phones working? Answer roll call if you hear me. Baines, George?"

"Here!" Two-and-Two responded, loud and plain in Frank Nelsen's phone, from the other rocket.

"Hines, Walter?"

One by one the names were called . . . "Kuzak, Arthur? . . . Kuzak, Joseph? . . ."

"Okay — the Mystic Nine, eh? Lash down!"

They lay on their backs on the padded floors, and fastened the straps. Gimp Hines, next to Frank, seemed to have discarded his crutches, somewhere.

The inspector swaggered around among them, jerking straps, and tapping shoulders and buttocks straight on the floor padding with a boot toe.

"All right — not good, not too bad. Ease off — shut your eyes, maybe. The next twenty minutes are ours. The rest are yours, except for orders. I hope you remember your jump procedures. Also that there are a lot of wooden nickels Upstairs — in orbit, on the Moon, anyplace. We'll call some of your shots from the ground. Good luck — and Glory help you . . ."

The growl in their phones died away with the muffled footsteps. Doors closed on their gaskets and were dogged, automatically.

Then it was like waiting five minutes more, inside a cannon barrel. There was a buzzing whisper of nuclear exciters. The roar of power cut in. A soft lurch told that the rockets were off the ground — fireborne. The pressure of acceleration mounted. You closed your eyes to make the blackness seem natural, instead of a blackout in your optic nerves, and the threadiness of your mind seem like sleep. But you felt smothered, just the same. Somebody grunted. Somebody gave a thick cry.

Frank Nelsen had the strange thought that, by his body's mounting velocity, enough kinetic energy was being pumped into it to burn it to vapor in an instant, if it ever hit the air. But it was the energy of freedom from gravity, from the Earth, from home — *for* adventure. Freedom to wander the solar system, at last! He tried, still, to believe in the magnificence of it, as the thrust of rocket power ended, and the weightlessness of orbital flight came dizzily.

He didn't consciously hear the order to leave the orbiting GO-12, which was moving only about five hundred feet from it's companion, GO-11. But, like most of the others, he worked his way with dogged purpose through what seemed a fuzzy nightmare.

The doors of the passenger compartments had opened; likewise the blastoff drums had been ejected automatically, and were orbiting free.

Maybe it was Gimp who moved ahead of him. Looking out, Frank saw what was certainly Ramos, already straddling a drum marked with a huge red M.R., riding it like a jaunty troll on a seahorse. He saw the Kuzaks dive for their initialled drums, big men not yet as apt in this new game as in football, but grimly determined to learn fast. The motion was all as silent as a shadow.

Then Frank jumped for his own drum, and found himself turning slowly end-over-end, seeing first the pearl-mist curve that was the Earth, then the brown-black, chalk-smeared sky, with the bright needle points and the corona-winged sun in it. Instinct made him grab futilely outward, for the sense of weightlessness was the same as endless fall. He *was* falling, around the Earth, his forward motion exactly balancing his downward motion, in a locked ellipse, a closed trajectory.

His mind cleared very fast — that must have been another phase of the devil-killer shot coming into action. Controlling panic, he relocated his drum, marked by a splashed red F.N., set his tiny shoulder ionic in operation, and reached back to move its flexible guide, first to stop his spin, then to produce forward motion. He got to the drum, and just clung to it for a moment.

But in the next instant he was looking into the embarrassed, anguished face of a person, who, like a drowning man, had come to hang onto it for dear life, too.

"Frank, I — I even dirtied myself . . ."

"So what? Over there is your gear, Two-and-Two — go get it!" Frank shouted into his phone, the receiver of which was now full of sounds — a moaning grunt, a vast hiccupping, shouts, exhortations.

"Easy, Les," Reynolds was saying. "Can you reach a pill from the rack inside your chest plate, and swallow it? Just float quietly — nothing'll happen. We've got work to do for a few minutes . . . We'll look after you later . . . Cripes, Mitch — he can't take it. Jab the knockout needle right through the sleeve of his Archer, like we read in the manuals. The interwall gum will seal the puncture . . ."

Just then the order came, maddeningly calm and hard above the other sounds in Frank's phone: "All novices disembarked from GOs-11 and -12 must clear four-hundred mile take-off orbital zone for other traffic within two hours."

At once Frank was furiously busy, working the darkened stellene of his bubb from the drum, letting it spread like a long wisp of silvery cobweb against the stars, letting it inflate from the air-flasks to a firm and beautiful circle, attaching the rigging, the fine, radial spoke-wires — for which the blastoff drum itself now formed the hub. To the latter he now attached his full-size, sun-powered ionic motor. Then he crept through the double sealing flaps of the air-lock, to install the air-restorer and the moisture-reclaimer in the circular, tunnel-like interior that would now be his habitation.

He wasn't racing anything except time, but he had worked as fast as he could. Still, Gimp Hines had finished rigging his bubb, minutes ahead of Frank, or anybody else. On second thought, maybe this was natural enough. Here, where there was no weight, his useless leg made no difference — as the space-fitness examiners must have known. Besides, Gimp had talented fingers and a keen mechanical sense, and had always tried harder than anybody.

Ramos was almost as quick. Frank wasn't much farther behind. The Kuzaks were likewise doing all right. Two-and-Two was trailing some, but not very badly.

"Spin 'em!" Gimp shouted. "Don't forget to spin 'em for centrifuge-gravity and stability!"

And so they did, each gripping the rigging at their bubb rims, and using the minute but accumulative thrust of the shoulder ionics of their Archers, to provide the push. The inflated rings turned like wheels with perfect bearings. In the all but frictionless void, they could go on turning for decades, without additional impetus.

"We've made it — we're Out Here — we're all right!" Ramos was shouting with a fierce exultation.

"Shut up, Ramos!" Frank Nelsen yelled back. "Don't ever say that, too soon. Look around you!"

Storey and Reynolds were still struggling with their bubbs. They had been delayed by trying to quiet Dave Lester, who now floated in a drugged stupor, lashed to his blastoff drum.

Slowly, pushed by their shoulder ionics, Gimp, Ramos and Frank Nelsen drifted over to see what they could do for Lester.

He was vaguely conscious, his eyes were glassy, his mouth drooled watery vomit.

"What do you want us to do, Les?" Frank asked gently. "We

could put you back in one of the rockets. You'd be brought back to the spaceport, when they are guided back by remote control."

"I don't know!" Lester wailed in a hoarse voice. "Fellas — I don't know! A little falling is all right . . . But it goes on all the time. I can't stand it! But if I'm sent back — I can't ever live with myself! . . ."

Frank felt the intense anguish of trying to decide somebody else's quandary that might be a life or death matter which would surely involve them all. Damn, weak-kneed kid! How had he ever gotten so far?

"We should have set up his bubb first, put him inside, and spun it to kill that sense of fall!" Gimp said. "We'll do it, now! He should be all right. He *did* pass his space-fitness tests, and the experts ought to know."

With the three of them at it, and with the Kuzaks joining them in a moment, the job was quickly finished.

Meanwhile, the sharp, commanding voice of Ground Control sounded in their phones, again: "GOs-11 and -12 returning to port. Is all in order among delivered passengers? Sound out if true. Baines, George? . . ."

David Lester's name was called just before Frank Nelsen's, and he managed to say, "In order!" almost firmly, creating a damnable illusion, Frank thought. But for a moment, mixed with his anger, Frank felt a strange, almost paternal gentleness, too.

At the end of the roll call, the doors of the GO rockets closed. Stubby wings, useful for the ticklish operation of skip-glide deceleration and re-entry into the atmosphere, slid out of their sheaths. Little, lateral jets turned the vehicles around. Their main engines flamed lightly; losing speed, they dipped in their paths, beginning to fall.

Watching the rockets leave created a tingling sense of being left all alone, at an empty, breathless height from which you could never get down — a height full of dazzling, unnatural sunshine, that in moments would become the dreadful darkness of Earth's shadow.

"Hey — our spare drum — it'll drift off!" Ramos shouted.

The Kuzaks dived to retrieve the cylinder. Others followed. But there was a peculiar circumstance. The friction cover at one of its ends hung open. There was a trailing wisp of stellene — part of the bubb packed inside — and a thin, angry face with rather hysterical eyes, within the helmet of an Archer Five.

"Shhh — it ain't safe for me to come out yet," Glen Tiflin hissed threateningly. "Damn you all — if you dare queer me . . . !"

"Cripes — another Jonah!" Charlie Reynolds growled.

Frank Nelsen looked at the Kuzaks, floating near.

"Well — what could we do?" Joe Kuzak, the gentler twin, whispered. "He came back to Jarviston, to our rooming house, one night. We promised to help him a little. What are you going to do with a character nuts enough about space to armor up and stuff himself inside a blastoff drum? Of course he didn't come that way from home. There's that electronic check of drum contents at the gate of the port. But he was there on a visitor's pass, waiting — having hitchhiked all the way to here. After the electronic check, he figured on stowing away, while the drums were waiting to be loaded. The only thing we did to help was to take a little of the stuff out of the spare drum and stow it in our two drums, to leave him some room. We thought sure he'd be caught, quick. But you can see how he got away with it. Those U.S.S.F. boys at the port don't really give a damn who gets Out Here."

"Okay — I'll buy it," Reynolds sighed heavily. "Good luck with the stunt, Tif."

Tiflin only gave him a poisonous glare, as the nine fragile, gleaming rings, the drifting men and the spare drum, orbited on into the Earth's shadow, not nearly as dark as it might have been because the Moon was brilliant.

"We'd better rig the parabolic mirrors of the ionics to catch the first sunshine in about forty minutes, so we can start moving out of orbit," Ramos said. "We'll have to think of food, sometime, too."

"Food, yet — ugh!" Art Kuzak grunted.

Frank felt the fingers of spasm taking hold of his stomach. Most everybody was getting fall-sick, now, their insides not finding any up or down direction. But the guys wavered back to their bubbs. The shoulder ionics of their Archers, though normally sun-energized, could draw power from the small nuclear batteries of the armor during the rare moments when there could be darkness anywhere in solar space.

The Planet Strappers stood in the rigging of their fragile vehicles, setting the full-sized ionics to produce increased acceleration which would gradually push the craft beyond orbit. Joe Kuzak ran a steel wire from a pivot bolt at the hub of his ring, to tow Tiflin and his drum.

Then everybody crawled into their respective bubbs, most of them needing the centrifugal gravity to help straighten out their fall-sickness.

"My neck is swelling, too," Frank Nelsen heard Charlie Reynolds say. "Lymphatic glands sometimes bog down in the absence of weight. Don't worry if it happens to some of you. We know that it straightens out."

For a few minutes it seemed that they had a small respite in their struggle for adjustment to a fantastic environment.

"Well — I got cleaned up, some — that's better," Two-and-Two said. "But look at the fuzzy lights down on Earth. Hell, is it right for a fella to be looking down on the lights of Paris, Moscow, Cairo, and Rangoon — when he hasn't ever been any farther than Minneapolis?" Two-and-Two sounded fabulously befuddled.

David Lester started screaming again. They had left him alone and apparently unconscious, inside his ring, because all ionics, including his, had had to be set. Then, in the pressure of events, they had almost forgotten him.

"I'll go look," Frank Nelsen said.

Mitch Storey was there ahead of him. Mitch's helmet was off; his dark face was all planes and hollows in the moonlight coming through the thin, transparent walls of the vehicle. "Should we call the U.S.S.F. patrol, Frank?" he asked anxiously. "Have them take him off? 'Cause he sure can't stand another devil-killer."

"We'd better," Frank answered quickly.

But now Tiflin, having deserted his blastoff drum, was coming through the airlock flaps, too. He stepped forward gingerly, along the spinning, ring-shaped tunnel.

"Poor bookworm," he growled in a tone curiously soft for Glen Tiflin. "Think I don't understand how it is? And how do you know if he *wants* to get sent back?"

Mitch had removed Lester's helmet, too. Tiflin knelt. His arm moved with savage quickness. There was the crack of knuckles, in a rubberized steel-fabric space glove, against Lester's jaw. His hysterical eyes glazed and closed; his face relaxed.

For a second of intolerable fury, Frank wanted to tear Tiflin apart.

But Mitch half-grinned. "That might be an answer," he said.

They plopped where they were, and tried to rest until the orbiting cluster of rings emerged from Earth's shadow into blazing sunshine, again. Then Mitch and Frank returned to their own bubbs to check on the acceleration.

It was soon plain that Joe Kuzak's bubb, towing Tiflin's drum, would lag.

"Hell!" Art Kuzak snapped. "Get that character out here to help us inflate and rig his own equipment! We did enough for him! So if the Force notices that there are ten bubbs instead of nine, the extra is still just our spare . . . Hey — Tiflin!"

"Nuts — I'm looking after Pantywaist," Tiflin growled back.

"Awright," Art returned. "So we just cast your junk adrift! Come on, boy!" There was no kidding in the dry tone.

Tiflin snarled but obeyed.

Ions jetting from the Earthward hub-ends of the rotating rings, yielded their steady few pounds of thrust. The gradual outward spiral began.

"Cripes — I'm not sure I can even astrogate to the Moon," Two-and-Two was heard to complain.

"I'll check your ionic setting for you, Two-and-Two," Gimp answered him. "After that the acceleration should continue properly without much attention. So how about you and me taking first watch, while the others ease off a little . . . ?"

Frank Nelsen crept carefully back into his own rotating ring, still half afraid that an armored knee or elbow might go right through the thin, yielding stellene. Prone, and with his helmet still sealed, he slipped into the fog which the tranquilizer now induced in his brain, while the universe of stars, Moon, sun and Earth tumbled regularly around him.

He dreamed of yelling in endless fall, and of climbing over metal-veined chunks of a broken world, where once there had been air, sea, desert and forest, and minds not unlike those of men, but in bodies that were far different. Gurgling thickly, he awoke, and snapped on his helmet phone to kill the utter silence.

Someone muttered a prayer in a foreign tongue:

" . . . *Nuestra Dama de Guadalupe — te pido, por favor . . . Tengo miedo* — I'm scared . . . *Pero pienso mas en ella* — I think more of her. *Mi chula, mi linda* . . . My beautiful Eileen . . . Keep her — "

The prayer broke off, as if a switch was turned. It had been brash Ramos . . . Now there were only some fragments of harmonica music . . .

Frank slipped into the blur, again, awakening at last with Two-and-Two shaking his shoulder. "Hey, Frankie — we're five hours out, by the chronometers — look how small the Earth has got . . . ! We're all gonna have brunch in Ramos' vehicle . . . Know what that goof ball Mex was doing, before? Stripped down to his shorts, and with the spin stopped for zero-G, he was bouncing back and forth from wall to wall inside his bubb! The sun makes it nice and warm in there. Think I might try it, myself, sometime. Shucks, I feel pretty good, now . . . Frankie, ain't you hungry?"

Frank felt limp as a rag, but he felt much better than before, and he could stand some nourishment. "Lead on, Two-and-Two," he said.

Ramos' bubb was spinning once more, but he was wearing just

dungarees. The Bunch — the Planet Strappers — with only their helmets off, were crouched, evenly spaced, around the circular interior of the ring. Dave Lester was there, too — staring, but fairly calm, now. In this curious place, there was a delicious and improbable aroma of coffee — cooked by mirror-reflected sunlight on a tiny solar stove.

"So that's the way it goes," Charlie Reynolds commented profoundly. "We reach out for strangeness. Then we try to make it as familiar as home."

"Stew, warmed in the cans, too," Ramos declared. "Enough for a light one-time-around. I brought the stew along. Hope you birds remember. Then we're back on dehydrates. Hell, except for that weight problem and consequent cost of stuff from Earth, we'd have it made, Out Here. The Big Vacuum ain't so tough — no storms in it, even, to tear our bubbs apart. I guess we won't ever have a bigger adventure than finding out for ourselves that we can get along with space."

"If we had a beef roast, we'd put it in a sealed container of clear plastic," Gimp laughed. "Set it turning, outside the bubb, on a swiveled tether wire. It would rotate for hours like on a spit — almost no friction. Rig some mirrors to concentrate the sun's heat. Space Force men do things like that."

"Shut up — I'm getting *hong*-gry!" Art Kuzak roared.

Ramos poured the coffee in the thin magnesium cups that each of the Bunch had brought. Their squeeze bottles, for zero-G drinking, were not necessary, here. Their skimpy portions of stew were spooned on magnesium plates. Knife and fork combinations were brought out. An apple purée which had been powder, followed the stew. Brunch was soon over.

"That's all for now, folks," Ramos said ruefully.

Tiflin snaked a cigarette out from inside the collar of his Archer.

"Hey!" Reynolds said mildly. "Oxygen, remember? Shouldn't you ask our host, first?"

Ramos had eased up on ribbing Tiflin months ago. "It's okay," he said. "The air-restorers are new."

But Tiflin's explosive nerves, under strain for a long time, didn't take it. He threw down the unlighted fag. He snicked his switch blade from a thigh pocket. For an instant it seemed that he would attack Reynolds. Then the knife flew, and penetrated the thin, taut wall, to its handle. There was a frightening hiss, until the sealing gum between the double layers, cut off the leak.

The Kuzaks had Tiflin helpless and snarling, at once.

"Get a patch, somebody — fix up the hole," Joe, the mild one, growled. "Tiflin — me and my brother helped you. Now we're gonna sit on you — just to make sure your funny business doesn't kill us all. Try anything just *once*, and we'll feed you all that vacuum — without an Archer. If you're a good boy, maybe you'll live to get dumped on the Moon as we pass by."

"Nuts — let's give this sick rat to the Space Force right now." Art Kuzak hissed. "Here comes their patrol bubb."

The glinting, transparent ring with the barred white star was passing at a distance.

"All is well with you novices?" The enquiring voice was a gruff drawl, mingled with crunching sounds of eating — perhaps a candy bar.

"No!" Tiflin whispered, pleading. "I'll watch myself!"

The United Nations patrol was out, too, farther off. Another, darker bubb, with other markings, passed by, quite close. It had foreign lines, more than a bit sinister to the Bunch's first, startled view. It was a Tovie vehicle, representing the other side of the still — for the most part — passively opposed forces, on Earth, and far beyond. But through the darkened transparency of stellene, the armored figures — again somewhat sinister — only raised their hands in greeting.

In a minute, Frank Nelsen emerged from Ramos' ring. Floating free, he stabilized himself, fussed with the radio antenna of his helmet-phone for a moment, making its transmission and reception directional. On the misty, shrinking Earth, North America was visible.

"Frank Nelsen to Paul Hendricks," he said. "Frank Nelsen to Paul Hendricks . . ."

Paul was waiting, all right. "Hello, Frankie. Some of the guys talked already — said you were asleep."

"Hi, Paul — yeah! Terra still looks big and beautiful. We're okay. Amazing, isn't it, how just a few watts of power, beamed out in a thin thread, will reach this far, and lots farther? Hey — will you open and shut your front door? Let's hear the old customer's bell jingle . . . Best to you, to J. John, to Nance Codiss, Miss Parks — everybody . . ."

The squeak of hinges and the jingling came through, clear and nostalgically.

"Come on, Frank," Two-and-Two urged. "Other guys would like to talk to Paul . . . Hey, Paul — maybe you could get my folks down to the store to say hello to me on your transmitter. And I guess Les would appreciate it if you got his mother . . ."

When the talk got private, Frank went to Mitch Storey's bubb.

"I wanted to show you," Mitch said. "I brought seeds, and these little plastic tubes with holes in them, that you can string around inside a bubb. The weight is next to nothing. Put the seeds in the tubes, and water with plant food in solution. The plants come up through the holes. Hydroponics. Gotta almost do it, if I'm going way out to Mars without much supplies. Maybe, before I get there, I'll have even ripe tomatoes! 'Cause, with sun all the time, the stuff grows like fury, they say. I'll have string beans and onions and flowers, anyhow! Helps keep the air oxygen-fresh, too. Wish I had a few bumble bees! 'Cause now I'll have to pollinate by hand . . ."

Nope — Mitch couldn't get away from vegetation, even in space.

The Planet Strappers soon established a routine for their journey out as far as the Moon. There were watches, to be sure that none of the bubbs veered, while somebody was asleep or inattentive. Always at hand were loaded rifles, because you never knew what kind of space-soured men — who might once have been as tame as neighbors going for a drive on Sundays with their families — might be around, even here.

Neither Kuzak slept, if the other wasn't awake. They were watching Tiflin, whose bubb rode a little ahead of the others. He was ostracized, more or less.

Everybody took to Ramos' kind of exercise, bouncing around inside a bubb — even Lester, who was calmer, now, but obviously strained by the vast novelty and uncertainty ahead.

"I gave you guys a hard time — I'm sorry," he apologized. "But I hope there won't be any more of that. The Bunch will be breaking up, soon, I guess — going here and there. And if I get a job at Serenitatis Base, I think I'll be okay."

Frank Nelsen hoped that he could escape any further part of Lester, but he wasn't sure that he had the guts to desert him.

It wasn't long before the ionics were shut off. Enough velocity had been attained. Soon, the thrust would be needed in reverse, for braking action, near the end of the sixty hour journey into a circumlunar orbit.

Sleep was a fitful, dream-haunted thing. Food was now mostly a kind of gruel, rich in starches, proteins, fats and vitamins — each meal differently flavored, up to the number of ten flavors, in a manufacturer's attempt to mask the sameness. Add water to a powder — heat and eat. The spaceman's usual diet, while afield . . .

One of the functions of the moisture-reclaimers was a rough joke, or a squeamishness. A man's kidneys and bowels functioned, and precious water molecules couldn't be wasted, here in the dehydrated emptiness. But what difference did it really make, after the sanitary distillation of a reclaimer? Accept, adjust . . .

Decision about employment or activity in the immediate future, was one thing that couldn't be dismissed. And announcements, beamed from the Moon, emphasized it:

"Serenitatis Base, seventeenth month-day, sixteenth hour. (There was a chime) Lunar Projects Placement is here to serve you. Plastics-chemists, hydroponics specialists, machinists, mechanics, metallurgists, miners, helpers — all are urgently needed. The tax-free pay will startle you. Free subsistence and quarters. Here at Serene, at Tycho Station or at a dozen other expanding sites . . ."

Charlie Reynolds sat with Frank Nelsen while he listened. "The lady has a swell voice," said Charlie. "Otherwise, it *sounds* good, too. But I'm one that's going farther. To Venus — just being explored. All fresh, and no man-made booby traps, at least. Maybe they'll even figure out a way to make it rotate faster, give it a reasonably short day, and a breathable atmosphere — make a warmer second Earth out of it . . . Sometimes, when you jump farther, you jump over a lot of trouble. Better than going slow, with the faint-hearts. Their muddling misfortunes begin to stick to you. I'd rather be Mitch, headed for heebie-jeebie Mars, or the Kuzaks, aiming for the crazy Asteroid Belt."

That was Charlie, talking to him — Frank Nelsen — like an older brother. It made a sharp doubt in him, again. But then he grinned.

"Maybe I am a slow starter," he said. "The Moon is near and humble, but some say it's good training — even harsher than space. And I don't want to bypass and miss anything. Oh, hell, Charlie — I'll get farther, soon, too! But I really don't even know what I'll do, yet. Got to wait and see how the cards fall . . ."

Several hours before the rest of the Bunch curved into a slow orbit a thousand miles above the Moon, Glen Tiflin set the ionic of his bubb for full acceleration, and arced away, outward, perhaps toward the Belt.

"So long, all you dumb slobs!" his voice hissed in their helmet-phones. "Now I get really lost! If you ever cross my path again, watch your heads . . ."

Art Kuzak's flare of anger died. "Good riddance," he breathed. "How long will he last, alone? Without a space-fitness card, the poor idiot probably imagines himself a big, dangerous renegade, already."

Joe Kuzak's answering tone almost had a shrug in it. "Don't jinx our luck, twin brother," he said. "For that matter, how long will *we* last . . . ? Mex, did you toss Tiflin back his shiv?"

"A couple of hours ago," Ramos answered mildly.

Everybody was looking down at the Moon, whose crater-pocked ugliness and beauty was sparsely dotted with the blue spots of stellene domes, many of them housing embryo enterprises that were trying to beat the blastoff cost of necessities brought from Earth, and to supply spacemen and colonists with their needs, cheaply.

The nine fragile rings were soon in orbit. One worker-recruiting rocket and several trader-rockets — much less powerful than those needed to achieve orbit around Earth — because lunar gravity was only one-sixth of the terrestrial — were floating in their midst. On the Moon it had of course been known that a fresh Bunch was on the way. Even telescopes could have spotted them farther off than the distance of their 240,000 mile leap.

Frank Nelsen's tongue tasted of brassy doubt. He didn't know where he'd be, or what luck, good or bad, he might run into, within the next hour.

The Kuzaks were palavering with the occupants of two heavily-loaded trader rockets. "Sure we'll buy — if the price is right," Art was saying. "Flasks of water and oxygen, medicines, rolls of stellene. Spare parts for Archies, ionics, air-restorers. Food, clothes — anything we can sell, ourselves . . ."

The Kuzaks must have at least a few thousand dollars, which they had probably managed to borrow when they had gone home to Pennsylvania to say goodbye.

Out here, free of the grip of any large sphere, there was hardly a limit to the load which their ionics could eventually accelerate sufficiently to travel tremendous distances. Streamlining, in the vacuum, of course wasn't necessary, either.

Now a small, sharp-featured man in an Archie, drifted close to Ramos and Frank, as they floated near their bubbs. "Hello, Ramos, hello, Nelsen," he said. "Yes — we know your names. We investigate, beforehand, down on terra firma. We even have people to snap photographs — often you don't even notice. We like guys with talent who get out here by their own efforts. Shows they got guts — seriousness! But now you've arrived. We are Lunar Projects Placement. We need mechanics, process technicians, administrative personnel — anything you can name, almost. Any bright lad with drive enough to learn fast, suits us fine. Five hundred bucks an Earth-week, to start, meals and lodging thrown in. Quit any time you want. Plenty of different working sites. Mines, refineries, factories, construction . . ."

"Serenitatis Base?" Ramos asked almost too quickly, Frank thought. And he sounded curiously serious. Was this the Ramos who should be going a lot farther than the Moon, anyway?

"Hell, yes, fella!" said the job scout.

"Then I'll sign."

"Excellent . . . You, too, guy?" The scout was looking at Frank. "And your other friends?"

"I'm thinking about it," Frank answered cagily. "Some of them aren't stopping on the Moon, as you can see."

Mitch Storey was lashing a few flasks of oxygen and water to the rim of his bubb, being careful to space them evenly for static balance. He didn't have the money to buy much more, even here.

The Kuzaks were preparing two huge bundles of supplies, which they intended to tow. Reynolds was also loading up a few things, with Two-and-Two helping him.

"I'm all set, Frank!" Two-and-Two shouted. "I'm going along with Charlie, maybe to crash the Venus exploration party!"

"Good!" Frank shouted back, glad that this large, unsure person had found himself a leader.

Now he looked at Gimp Hines, riding the spinning rim of his ring with his good and bad leg dangling, an expectant, quizzical, half-worried look on his freckled face.

But Dave Lester was more pathetic. He had stopped the rotation of his bubb. He looked down first at the pitted, jagged face of the Moon, with an expression in which rapture and terror may have been mingled, glanced with the hope of desperation toward the job scout, and then distractedly continued dismantling the rigging of his vehicle, as if to repack it in the blastoff drum for a landing.

"Hey — hold on, Les!" Two-and-Two shouted. "You gotta know where you're going, first!"

"Make up your mind, Nelsen," said the job scout, getting impatient. "We handle just about everything lunar — except in the Tovie areas. Without us, you're just a lost, fresh punk!"

But another man had approached from another lunar GO rocket, which had just appeared. He had a thin intellectual face, dark eyes, trap mouth, white hair, soft speech that was almost shy.

"I'm Xavier Rodan," he said. "I search out my own employees. I do minerals survey — for gypsum, bauxite — anything. And site survey, for factories and other future developments. I also have connections with the Selenographic Institute of the University of Chicago. It is all interesting work, but in a rather remote region, I'm afraid — the far side of the Moon. And I can pay only three hundred a week. Of course you can resign whenever you wish. Perhaps you'd be interested — Mr. Nelsen, is it?"

Frank had an impulse to jump at the chance — though there was a warning coming to him from somewhere. But how could you ever know? You would always have to go down to that devils' wilderness to find out.

"I'll try it, Mr. Rodan," he said.

"Selenography — that's one of my favorite subjects, sir!" David Lester burst out, making a gingerly leap across the horrible void of spherical sky — stars in all directions except where the Moon's bulk hung. "Could I — too?" His trembling mouth looked desperate.

"Very well, boy," Rodan said at last. "A hundred dollars for a week's work period."

Frank was glad that Lester had a place to go — and furious that he would probably have to nursemaid him, after all.

Gimp Hines kept riding the rim of his ring like a merry-go-round, his face trying to show casual humor and indifference over ruefulness and scare. "Nobody wants me," he said cheerfully. "It's just prejudice and poor imagination. Well — I don't think I'll even try to prove how good I am. Of course I could shoot for the asteroids. But I'd like to look around Serenitatis Base — some, anyway. Will fifty bucks get me and my rig down?"

"Talk to our pilot, Lame Fella," said the job scout. "But you must be suicidal nuts to be around here at all."

The others leapt to help Nelsen, Ramos, Gimp and Lester strip and pack their gear. Ramos' and Gimp's drums were loaded into the job scout's rocket. Nelsen's and Lester's went into Rodan's.

Gloved hands clasped gloved hands all around. The Bunch, the Planet Strappers, were breaking up.

"So long, you characters — see you around," said Art Kuzak. "It won't be ten years, before you all wind up in the Belt."

"Bring back the Mystery of Mars, Mitch!" Frank was saying.

"When you get finished Mooning, come to Venus, Lover Lad," Reynolds told Ramos. "But good luck!"

"Jeez — I'm gonna get sentimental," Two-and-Two moaned. "Luck everybody. Come on, Charlie — let's roll! I don't want to slobber!"

"I'll catch up with you all — watch!" Gimp promised.

"So long, Frank . . ."

"Yeah — over the Milky Way, Frankie!"

"*Hasta luego*, Gang." This was all Ramos, the big mouth, had to say. He wasn't glum, exactly. But he was sort of preoccupied and impatient.

The five remaining rings — a wonderful sight, Frank thought —

began to move out of orbit. Ships with sails set for far ports. No — mere ships of the sea were nothing, anymore. But would all of the Bunch survive?

Charlie Reynolds, the cool one, the most likely to succeed, waved jauntily and carelessly from his rotating, accelerating ring. Two-and-Two wagged both arms stiffly from his.

Mitch Storey's bubb, lightest loaded, was jumping ahead. But you could hear him playing *Old Man River* on his mouth organ, inside his helmet.

The Kuzaks' bubbs, towing massive loads, were accelerating slowest, with the ex-gridiron twins riding the rigging. But their rings would dwindle to star specks before long, too.

The job scout's rocket, carrying Ramos and Gimp, began to flame for a landing at Serene.

In the airtight cabin of Xavier Rodan's vehicle, Frank Nelsen and David Lester had read and signed their contracts and had received their copies.

Rodan didn't smile. "Now we'll go down and have a look at the place I'm investigating," he said.

IV

Frank Nelsen's view of empire-building on the Moon was brief, all encompassing, and far too sketchy to be very satisfying, as Rodan — turned about in his universal-gimbaled pilot seat — spiraled his battered rocket down backwards, with the small nuclear jets firing forward in jerky, tooth-cracking bursts, to check speed further.

It was necessary to go around the abortive sub-planet that had always accompanied the Earth, almost once, to reduce velocity enough for a landing.

Thus, Nelsen glimpsed much territory — the splashed, irregular shape of Serenitatis, the international base on the mare, the dust sea of the same name; the radiating threads of trails and embryo highways, the ever-widening separation of isolated domes and scattered human diggings and workings faintly scratched in the lunar crust, as, at a still great height, Frank's gaze swept outward from the greatest center of human endeavor on the Moon.

It was much the same around Tycho Station, except that this base was smaller, and was built in a great, white-rayed crater, whose walls were pierced by tunnels for exit and entry.

The Tovie camp, glimpsed later, and only at the distant horizon, seemed not very different from the others, except for the misleading patterns of camouflage. That the Tovies should have an exclusive center of their own was not even legal, according to U.N. agreements. But facts were facts, and what did anyone do about them?

Frank was not very concerned with such issues just then, for there was an impression that was overpowering: The slightness of the intrusion of his kind on a two thousand-something miles-in-diameter globe of incredible desert, overlapping ring-walls, craters centered in radiating streaks of white ash, mountain ranges that sank gradually into dust, which once, two billion years ago, after probable ejection from volcanoes, had no doubt floated in a then palpable atmosphere. But now, to a lone man down there, they would be bleak plains stretching to a disconcertingly near horizon.

Frank Nelsen's view was one of fascination, behind which was the chilly thought: This is my choice; here is where I will have to live for a short while that can seem ages. Space looks tame, now. Can I make it all right? Worse — *how about Lester?*

Frank looked around him. Like Rodan, Lester and he had both pivoted around in their gimbaled seats — to which they had safety-strapped themselves — to face the now forward-pointing stern jets.

Rodan, looking more trap-mouthed than before, had said nothing further as he guided the craft gingerly lower. Lester was biting his heavy lip. His narrow chin trembled.

A faint whisper had begun. As far back as the 1940s, astronomers had begun to suspect that the Moon was, after all, not entirely airless. There would be traces of heavy gases — argon, neon, xenon, krypton, and volcanic carbon dioxide. It would be expanded far upward above the surface, because the feeble lunar gravity could not give it sufficient weight to compress it very much. So it would thin out much less rapidly with altitude than does the terrestrial atmosphere. From a density of perhaps 1/12,000th of Earth's sea level norm at the Moon's surface, it would thin to perhaps 1/20,000th at a height of eighty miles, being thus roughly equivalent in density to Earth's gaseous envelope at the same level! And at this height was the terrestrial zone where meteors flare!

This theory about the lunar atmosphere had proven to be correct. The tiny density was still sufficient to give the Moon almost as effective an atmospheric meteor screen as the Earth's. The relatively low velocity needed to maintain vehicles in circumlunar orbits, made its danger to such vehicles small. It could help reduce speed for a landing; it caused that innocuous hiss of passage. But it could sometimes be treacherous.

Frank thought of these things as the long minutes dragged. Perhaps Rodan, hunched intently over his controls, had reason enough, there, to be silent . . .

The actual landing still had to be made in the only way possible on worlds whose air-covering was so close to a complete vacuum as this — like a cat climbing down a tree backwards. With flaming jets still holding it up, and spinning gyros keeping it vertical, the rocket lowered gradually. The seats swung level, keeping their occupants right side up. There was a hovering pause, then the faint jolt of contact. The jet growl stopped; complete silence closed in like a hammer blow.

"Do you men know where you are?" Rodan asked after a moment.

"At the edge of Mare Nova, I think," Frank answered, his eyes combing the demons' landscape beyond the thick, darkened glass of the cabin's ports.

The dazzling sun was low — early morning of two weeks of daylight. The shadows were long, black shafts.

"Yes — there's Tower Rock," Lester quavered. "And the Arabian Range going down under the dust of the plain."

"Correct," Rodan answered. "We're well over the rim of the Far

Side. You'll never see the Earth from here. The nearest settlement is eight hundred miles away, and it's Tovie at that. This is a really remote spot, as I intimated before."

He paused, as if to let this significant information be appreciated. "So that's settled," he went on. "Now I'll enlighten you about what else you need to know . . . Come along."

Frank Nelsen felt the dust crunch under the rubberized boot-soles of his Archer. There was a brief walk, then a pause.

Rodan pointed to a pit dynamited out of the dust and lava rock, and to small piles of grayish material beside six-inch borings rectangularly spaced over a wide area.

"There is an extensive underlying layer of gypsum, here," he said. "The water-bearing rock. A mile away there's an ample deposit of graphite — carbon. Thus, there exists a complete local source of hydrogen, oxygen and carbon, ideal for synthesizing various hydrocarbonic chemicals or making complicated polyethylene materials such as stellene, so useful in space. Lead, too, is not very far off. Silicon is, of course, available everywhere. There'll be a plant belonging to Hoffman Chemicals here, before too long. I was prospecting for them, for a site like this. Actually I was very lucky, locating this spot almost right away — which is fortunate. They think I'm still looking, and aren't concerned . . ."

Rodan was quiet for a moment before continuing. The pupils of his eyes dilated and contracted strangely.

"Because I found something else," he went on. "It was luck beyond dreams, and it must be my very own. I intend to investigate it thoroughly, even if it takes years! Come along, again!"

This time the walk was about three hundred yards, past three small stellene domes, the parabolic mirrors of a solar-power plant, a sun-energized tractor, and onward almost to the mountain wall, imbedded in the dust of the mare. There Frank noticed a circular, glassy area.

Strips of magnesium were laid like bridging planks across chunks of lava, and in the dust all around were countless curious scrabbled marks.

Rodan stood carefully on a magnesium strip, and looked back at Nelsen and Lester, his brows crinkling as if he was suspicious that he had already told them too much. Frank Nelsen became more aware of the heavy automatic pistol at Rodan's hip, and felt a tingling urge to get away from here and from this man — as if a vast mistake had been made.

"It is necessary for you to be informed about *some* matters," Rodan said slowly. "For instance, unless it is otherwise disturbed, a footprint, or the like, will endure for millions of years on the Moon — as surely as if impressed in granite — because there is no weather left to rub it out. You will be working here. I am preserving some of these markings. So please walk on these strips, which Dutch and I have laid down."

Rodan indicated a large, Archer-clad man, who also carried an automatic. He had the face of a playful but dangerous mastiff. He was hunkered down in a shallow pit, scanning the ground with a watch-sized device probably intended for locating objects hidden just beneath the surface, electronically. Beside him was a screen-bottomed container, no doubt meant for sifting dust.

"Greetings, Novices!" he gruffed with genial contempt. But his pale eyes, beyond the curve of his helmet, had a masked puzzlement, as if something from the lunar desolation had gotten into his brain, leaving the realization of where he was, permanently not altogether clear to him.

Rodan pulled a shiny object from his thigh pouch, and held it out in a gloved palm for his new employees to peer at.

"One of the things we found," he remarked. "Incomplete. If we could, for instance, locate the other parts . . ."

Frank saw a little cylinder, with grey coils wrapped inside it — a power chamber, perhaps, to be lined with magnetic force, the only thing that could contain what amounted to a tiny twenty-million degree piece of a star's hot heart. It was a familiar principle for releasing and managing nuclear power. But the device, perhaps part of a small weapon, was subtly marked by the differences of another technology.

"I believe I have said enough," Rodan stated with a thin smile. "Though some facts will be unavoidably obvious to you, working here. But at least I will let you figure them out for yourselves, since you are well-informed young men, by your own statement." Here Rodan looked hard at the pale, unsteady Lester. "We will go back, now, so I can show you the camp, its routine, and your place in it. We have three domes — garden and living quarters, with a work-shop and supply dome between them . . ."

Quarters proved to be okay — two bunks and the usual compact accessories.

"Leave your Archers in the lockers outside your door — here are your keys," Rodan suggested. "Helen will have a meal ready for you in the adjacent dining room. Afterwards, take a helpful tran-quilizer, and sleep. No work until you awaken. I shall leave you, now . . ."

It was a good meal — steak cultured and grown in a nourishing solution, on the Moon, perhaps at Serene, much as Dr. Alexis Carrel had long ago grown and kept for years a living fragment of a chicken's heart. Potatoes, peas and tomatoes, too — all had become common staples in hydroponic gardens off the Earth.

"What do you make of what Rodan was talking about, Les?" Frank asked conversationally.

But David Lester was lost and vague, his food almost untouched. "I — I don't know!" he stammered.

Scared and embittered further by this bad sign, Frank turned to Helen. "And how are you?" he asked hopefully.

"I am all right," she answered, without a trace of encouragement.

She was in jeans, maybe she was eighteen, maybe she was Rodan's daughter. Her face was as reddened as a peasant's. It was hard to tell that she was a girl at all. She wasn't a girl. It was soon plain that she was a zombie with about ten words in her vocabulary. How could a girl have gotten to this impossible region, anyway?

Now Frank tried to delay Lester's inevitable complete crackup by encouraging his interest in their situation.

"It's big, Les," he said. "It's got to be! An expedition came here to investigate the Moon — it couldn't be any more recently than sixty million years ago, if it was from as close as Mars, or the Asteroid Planet! Two adjacent worlds were competing, then, the scientists know. Both were smaller than the Earth, cooled faster, bore life sooner. Which sent the party? I saw where there rocket ship must have stood — a glassy, spot where the dust was once fused! . . . From all the markings, they must have been around for months. Nowhere else on the Moon — that I ever heard of — is there anything similar left. So maybe they did most of their survey work by gliding, somehow, above the ground, not disturbing the dust . . . I think the little indentations we saw look Martian. That would be a break! Mars still has weather. Archeological objects wouldn't stay new there for millions of years, but here they would! Rodan is right — he's got something that'll make him famous!"

"Yes — I think I'll have a devil-killer and hit the sack, Frank," Lester said.

"Oh — all right," Frank agreed wearily. "Me, likewise."

Frank awoke naturally from a dreamless slumber. After a breakfast of eggs that had been a powder, Lester and he were at the diggings, sifting dust for the dropped and discarded items of an alien visitation.

Thus Frank's job began. In the excitement of a hunt, as if for ancient treasure, for a long time, through many ten hour shifts,

Frank Nelsen found a perhaps unfortunate Lethe of forgetfulness for his worries, and for the mind-poisoning effects of the silence and desolation in this remote part of the Moon.

They found things, thinly scattered in the ten acre area that Rodan meant tediously to sift. The screws and nuts, bright and new, were almost Earthly. But would anyone ever know what the little plastic rings were for? Or the sticks of cellulose, or the curved, wire device with fuzz at the ends? But then, would an off-Earth being ever guess the use of — say — a toothbrush or a bobbypin?

The metal cylinders, neatly cut open, might have contained food — dried leaf-like dregs still remained inside. There were small bottles made of pearly glass, too — empty except for gummy traces. They were stoppered with a stuff like rubber. There were also crumpled scraps, like paper or cellophane, most of them marked with designs or symbols.

After ten Earth-days, in the lunar afternoon, Frank found the grave. He shouted as his brushing hands uncovered a glassy, flexible surface.

Rodan took charge at once. "Back!" he commanded. Then he was avidly busy in the pit, working as carefully as a fine jeweler. He cleared more dust away, not with a trowel, not with his gloved fingers, but with a little nylon brush.

The thing was like a seven-pointed star, four feet across. And was the ripped, transparent casing of its body and limbs another version of a vacuum armor? The material resembled stellene. As in an Archer, there were metal details, mechanical, electronic, and perhaps nuclear.

In the punctured covering, the corpse was dry, of course — stomach, brain sac, rough, pitted skin, terminal tendrils — some coarse, some fine, almost, as thread, for doing the most delicate work, half out of protecting sheaths at the ends of its arms or legs.

In the armor, the being must have walked like a toe dancer, on metal spikes. Or it might even have rolled like a wheel. The bluish tint of its crusty body had half-faded to tan. Perhaps no one would ever explain the gaping wound that must have killed the creature, unless it had been a rock fall.

"Martian!" Lester gasped. "At least we know that they were like this!"

"Yes," Rodan agreed softly. "*I'll* look after *this* find."

Moving very carefully, even in the weak lunar gravity, he picked up the product of another evolution and bore it away to the shop dome.

Frank was furious. This was his discovery, and he was not even allowed to examine it.

Still, something warned him not to argue. In a little while, his treasure hunter's eagerness came back, holding out through most of that protracted lunar night, when they worked their ten hour periods with electric lamps attached to their shoulders.

But gradually Frank began to emerge from his single line of attention. Knowing that Lester must soon collapse, and waiting tensely for it to happen, was part of the cause. But there was much more. There was the fact that direct radio communication with the Earth, around the curve of the Moon, was impossible — the Tovies didn't like radio-relay orbiters, useful for beamed, short-wave messages. They had destroyed the few unmanned ones that had been put up.

There were the several times when he had casually sent a slender beam of radio energy groping out toward Mars and the Asteroid Belt, trying to call Storey or the Kuzaks, and had received no answer. Well, this was not remarkable. Those regions were enormous beyond imagining; you had to pinpoint your thread of tiny energy almost precisely.

But once, for an instant, while at work, he heard a voice which could be Mitch Storey's, call "Frank! Frankie!" in his helmet phone. There was no chance for him to get an instrument-fix on the direction of the incoming waves. And of course his name, Frank, was a common one. But an immediate attempt to beam Mars — yellow in the black sky — and its vicinity, produced no result.

His trapped feeling increased, and nostalgia began to bore into him. He had memories of lost sounds. Rodan tried to combat the thick silence with taped popular music, broadcast on very low power from a field set at the diggings. But the girl voices, singing richly, only made matters worse for Frank Nelsen. And other memories piled up on him: Jarviston, Minnesota. Wind. Hay smell, car smell. Home . . . Cripes . . . ! Damn . . . !

Lester's habit of muttering unintelligibly to himself was much worse, now. Frank was expecting him to start screaming at any minute, Frank hadn't tried to talk to him much, and Lester, more introverted than ever, was no starter of conversations.

But now, at the sunrise — S.O.B., was it possible that they had been here almost a month? — Frank at the diggings, indulged in some muttering, himself.

"Are you all right, Frank?" Lester asked mildly.

"Not altogether!" Frank Nelsen snapped dryly. "How about you?"

"Oh, I believe I'm okay at last," Lester replied with startling brightness. "I was afraid I wouldn't be. I guess I had an inferiority complex, and there was also something to live up to. You see, my dad was here with the original Clifford expedition. We always agreed that I should become a space-scientist, too. Mom went along with that — until Dad was killed, here . . . Well, I'm over the hump, now. You see, I'm so interested in everything around me, that the desolation has a cushion of romance that protects me. I don't see just the bleakness. I imagine the Moon as it once was, with volcanoes spitting, and with thundrous sounds in its steamy atmosphere. I see it when the Martians were here — they surely visited Earth, too, though there all evidence weathered away. I even see the Moon as it is, now, noticing details that are easy to miss — the little balls of ash that got stuck together by raindrops, two billion years ago. And the pulpy, hard-shelled plants that you can still find, alive, if you know where to look. There are some up on the ridge, where I often go, when offshift. Carbon dioxide and a little water vapor must still come out of the deep crack there . . . Anyhow, they used to say that a lonesome person — with perhaps a touch of schizophrenia — might do better off the Earth than the more usual types."

Frank Nelsen was surprised as much by this open, self-analytical explanation, and the clearing up of the family history behind him, as by the miracle that had happened. Cripes, was it possible that, in his own way, Lester was more rugged than anybody else of the old Bunch? Of course even Lester was somewhat in wonder, himself, and had to talk it all out to somebody.

"Good for you, Les," Nelsen enthused, relieved. "Only — well, skip it, for now."

Two work periods later, he approached Rodan. "It will take months to sift all this dust," he said. "I may not want to stay that long."

The pupils of Rodan's eyes flickered again. "Oh?" he said. "Per contract, you can quit anytime. But I provide no transportation. Do you want to walk eight hundred miles — to a Tovie station? On the Moon it is difficult to keep hired help. So one must rely on practical counter-circumstances. Besides, I wouldn't want you to be at Serenitatis Base, or anywhere else, talking about my discovery, Nelsen. I'm afraid you're stuck."

Now Nelsen had the result of his perhaps incautious test statement. He knew that he was trapped by a dangerous tyrant, such as might spring up in any new, lawless country.

"It was just a thought, sir," he said, being as placating as he dared, and controlling his rising fury.

For there was something that hardened too quickly in Rodan.

He had the fame-and-glory bug, and could be savage about it. If you wanted to get away, you had to scheme by yourself. There wasn't only Rodan to get past; there was Dutch, the big ape with the dangling pistol.

Nelsen decided to work quietly, as before, for a while . . . There were a few more significant finds — what might have been a nuclear-operated clock, broken, of course, and some diamond drill bits. Though the long lunar day dragged intolerably, there was the paradox of time seeming to escape, too. Daylight ended with the sunset. Two weeks of darkness was no period for any moves. At sunup, a second month was almost finished! And ten acres of dust was less than half-sifted . . .

In the shop and supply dome, David Lester had been chemically analyzing the dregs of various Martian containers for Rodan. In spare moments he classified those scarce and incredibly hardy lunar growths that he found in the foothills of the Arabian Range. Some had hard, bright-green tendrils, that during daylight, opened out of woody shells full of spongy hollows as an insulation against the fearsome cold of night. Some were so small that they could only be seen under a microscope. Frank's interest, here, however, palled quickly. And Lester, in his mumbling, studious preoccupation, was no companionable antidote for loneliness.

Frank tried a new approach on Helen, who really was Rodan's daughter.

"Do you like poetry, Helen? I used to memorize Keats, Frost, Shakespeare."

They were there in the dining room. She brightened a little. "I remember — some."

"Do you remember clouds, the sound of water? Trees, grass . . . ?"

She actually smiled, wistfully. "Yes. Sunday afternoons. A blue dress. My mother when she was alive . . . A dog I had, once . . ."

Helen Rodan wasn't quite a zombie, after all. Maybe he could win her confidence, if he went slow . . .

But twenty hours later, at the diggings, when Dutch stumbled over Frank's sifter, she reverted. "I'll learn you to leave junk in my way, you greenhorn squirt!" Dutch shouted. Then he tossed Frank thirty feet. Frank came back, kicked him in his thinly armored stomach, knocked him down, and tried to get his gun. But Dutch grabbed him in those big arms. Helen was also pointing a small pistol at him.

She was trembling. "Dad will handle this," she said.

Rodan came over. "You don't have much choice, do you, Nelsen?" he sneered. "However, perhaps Dutch was crude. I apologize for him. And I will deduct a hundred dollars from his pay, and give it to you."

"Much obliged," Frank said dryly.

After that, everything happened to build his tensions to the breaking point.

At a work period's end, near the lunar noon, he heard a voice in his helmet-phone. "Frank — this is Two-and-Two . . . ! Why don't you ever call or answer . . . ?"

Two-and-Two's usually plaintive voice had a special quality, as if he was maybe in trouble. This time, Frank got a directional fix, adjusted his antenna, and called, "Hey, Two-and-Two . . . ! Hey, Pal — it's me — Frank Nelsen . . . !"

Venus was in the sky, not too close to the sun. But still, though Nelsen called repeatedly, there was no reply.

He got back to quarters, and looked over not only his radio but his entire Archer. The radio had been fiddled with, delicately; it would still work, but not in a narrow enough beam to reach millions of miles, or even five hundred. An intricate focusing device had been removed from a wave guide.

That wasn't the worst that was wrong with the Archer. The small nuclear battery which energized the moisture-reclaimer, the heating units, and especially the air-restorer — not only for turning its pumps but for providing the intense internal illumination necessary to promote the release of oxygen in the photosynthetic process of the chlorophane when there was no sun — had been replaced by a chemical battery of a far smaller active life-span! The armor locker! Rodan had extra keys, and could tamper and make replacements, any time he considered it necessary.

Lester had wandered afield, somewhere. When he showed up, Nelsen jarred him out of his studious preoccupations long enough for them both to examine his armor. Same, identical story.

"Rodan made sure," Frank gruffed. "That S.O.B. put us on a real short tether!"

David Lester looked frightened for a minute. Then he seemed to ease.

"Maybe it doesn't make any difference," he said. "Though I'd like to call my mother . . . But I'm doing things that I like. After a while, when the job is finished, he'll let us go."

"Yeah?" Frank breathed.

There was the big question. Nelsen figured that an old, corny pattern stuck out all over Rodan. Personal glory emphasized to a point where it got beyond sense. And wouldn't that unreason be more likely to get worse in the terrible lunar desert than it ever would on Earth?

Would Rodan ever release them? Wouldn't he fear encroachment on his archeological success, even after all his data had been made public? This was all surmise-prediction, of course, but his extreme precautions, already taken, did not look good. On the Moon there could easily be an arranged accident, killing Lester, and him — Frank Nelsen — and maybe even Dutch. Rodan's pupils had that nervous way of expanding and contracting rapidly, too. Nelsen figured that he might be reading the signs somewhat warpedly himself. Still . . . ?

At the end of another shift, Nelsen took a walk, farther than ever before, up through a twisted pass that penetrated to the other side of the Arabian Mountains. He still had that much freedom. He wanted to think things out. In bitter, frustrating reversal of all his former urges to get off the Earth, he wanted, like a desperate weakling, to be back home.

Up beyond the Arabians, he saw the tread marks of a small tractor vehicle in a patch of dust. There was a single boot print. A short distance farther on, there was another. He examined them with a quizzical excitement. But there weren't any more. For miles, ahead and behind, unimpressable lava rock extended.

Another curious thing happened, only minutes later. A thousand miles overhead, out of reach of his sabotaged transmitter, one of those around the Moon tour bubbs, like the unfortunate *Far Side*, was passing. He heard the program they were broadcasting. A male voice crooned out what must be a new, popular song. He had heard so few new songs.

> "Serene . . .
> Found a queen . . .
> And her name is Eileen . . ."

Nelsen's reaction wasn't even a thought, at first; it was only an eerie tingle in all his flesh. Then, realizing what his suspicion was, he listened further, with all his nerves taut. But no explanation of the song's origin was given . . . He even tried futilely to radio the pleasure bubb, full of Earth tourists. In minutes it had sunk behind the abrupt horizon, leaving him with his unanswered wonder.

Girls, he thought, in the midst of his utter solitude. All girls, to love and have . . . Eileen? Cripes, could it be little old Eileen Sands, up on her ballet-dancing toes, sometimes, at Hendricks', and humming herself a tune? Eileen who had deserted the Bunch, meaning to approach space in a feminine way? Holy cow, had even *she* gotten *that* far, so fast?

Suddenly the possibility became a symbol of what the others of the Bunch must be accomplishing, while here he was, trapped, stuck futilely, inside a few bleak square miles on the far side of Earth's own satellite!

So here was another force of Frank Nelsen's desperation.

He made up his mind — which perhaps just then was a bit mad.

With outward calm he returned to camp, slept, worked, slept and worked again. He decided that there was no help to be had from Lester, who was still no man of action. Better to work alone, anyway.

Fortunately, on the Moon, it was easy to call deadly forces to one's aid. Something as simple as possible, the trick should be. Of course all he wanted to do was to get the upper hand on Rodan and Dutch, take over the camp, get the missing parts of his radio and Archer, borrow the solar tractor, and get out of here. To Serenitatis Base — Serene.

His only preparation was to sharpen the edges of a diamond-shaped trowel used at the diggings, with a piece of pumice. Then he waited.

Opportunity came near sundown, after a shift. Rodan, Dutch, and he had come into the supply and shop dome, through its air-lock. Lester and Helen — these two introverts had somehow discovered each other, and were getting along well together — were visible through the transparent wall, lingering at the diggings.

Nelsen saw Rodan and Dutch unlatch the collars of their helmets, preparatory for removing them, as they usually did if they stayed here a while, to pack new artifacts or stow tools. Nelsen made as if to unlatch his collar, too. But if he did it, the gasket would be unsealed, and his helmet would no longer be airtight.

Now! — he told himself. Or would it be better to wait fourteen more Earth-days, till another lunar dawn? Hell no — that would be chickenish procrastination. Rodan and Dutch were a good ten feet away from him — he was out of their reach.

With the harmless-looking trowel held like a dagger, he struck with all his might at the stellene outer wall of the dome, and then made a ripping motion. Like a monster gasping for breath, the imprisoned air sighed out.

Taking advantage of the moment when Rodan's and Dutch's hands moved in life-saving instinct to reseal their collars, Frank Nelsen leaped, and then kicked twice, as hard as he could, in rapid succession. At Dutch's stomach, first. Then Rodan's.

They were down — safe from death, since they had managed to

re-latch their collars. But with a cold fury that had learned to take no chances with defeat, Nelsen proceeded to kick them again, first one and then the other, meaning to make them insensible.

He got Dutch's pistol. He was a shade slow with Rodan. "You won't get anything that is mine!" he heard Rodan grunt.

Frank managed to deflect the automatic's muzzle from himself. But Rodan moved it downward purposefully, lined it up on a box marked dynamite, and fired.

Nelsen must have thrown himself prone at the last instant, before the ticklish explosive blew. He saw the flash and felt the dazing thud, though most of the blast passed over him. Results far outstripped the most furious intention of his plan, and became, not freedom, but a threat of slow dying, an ordeal, as the sagging dome was torn from above him, and supplies, air-restorer equipment, water and oxygen flasks, the vitals and the batteries of the solar-electric plant — all for the most part hopelessly shattered — were hurled far and wide, along with the relics from Mars. The adjacent garden and quarters domes were also shredded and swept away.

Dazed, Nelsen still got Rodan's automatic, picked himself up, saw that Dutch and Rodan, in armor, too, had apparently suffered from the explosion no worse than had he. He glanced at the hole in the lava rock, still smoking in the high vacuum. Most of the force of the blast had gone upward. He looked at Helen's toppled tomatoes and petunias — yes, petunias — where the garden dome had been. Oddly, they didn't wilt at once, though the little water in the hydro-ponic troughs was boiling away furiously, making frosty rainbows in the slanting light of the sun. Fragments of a solar lamp, to keep the plants growing at night, lay in the shambles.

Rodan and Dutch were pretty well knocked out from Frank Nelsen's footwork. Now Dave Lester and Helen Rodan came running. Lester's face was all stunned surprise. Helen was yelling.

"I saw you do it — you — murderer!"

When she kneeled beside her father, Frank got her gun, too. He felt an awful regret for a plan whose results far surpassed his intentions, but there was no good in showing it, now. Someone had to be in command in a situation which already looked black.

"Frank — I didn't suppose — " Lester stammered. "Now — what are we going to do?"

"All that we can do — try to get out of here!" Frank snapped back at him.

With some shreds of stellene, he tied Dutch's arms behind his back, and lashed his feet together. Then he pulled Helen away from Rodan.

"Hold her, Les," he ordered. "Maybe I overplayed my hand, but just the same, I still think I'm the best to say what's to be done and maybe get us out of a jam, and I can't have Helen or Rodan or anybody else doing any more cockeyed things to screw matters up even worse than they are."

Nelsen trussed Rodan up, too, then searched Rodan's thigh pouch and found a bunch of keys.

"You come along with me, Les and Helen," he said. "First we'll find out what we've got left to work with."

He investigated the rocket. That the blast had toppled it over, wasn't the worst. When he unlocked its servicing doors, he found that Rodan had removed a vital part from the nuclear exciters of the motors. His and Lester's blastoff drums were still in the freight compartment, but the ionics and air-restorers had been similarly rendered unworkable. Their oxygen and water flasks were gone. Only their bubbs were intact, but there was nothing with which to inflate them.

When Frank examined the sun-powered tractor, he found that tiny platinum plates had been taken from the thermocouple units. It was clear that, with paranoid thoroughness, Rodan had concentrated all capacity to move from the camp's vicinity in himself. He had probably locked up the missing items in the supply dome, and now the exploding dynamite had ruined them.

Exploring the plain, Nelsen even found quite a few of the absent parts, all useless. Only one oxygen flask and one water flask remained intact. Here was a diabolical backfiring of schemes, all around.

Returning to Rodan and Dutch, he examined their Archers through their servicing ports. Rodan's was as the manufacturer intended it. But Dutch's was jimmied the same as his and Lester's.

Nelsen swung Helen around to face him, and unlatched a port at her Archer's shoulder.

"He put even you on a short string, kid," he pronounced bitterly, after a moment. "Well, at least we can give you his nuclear battery for a while, and let him have his chemical cell back."

Helen seemed about to attack him. But then her look wavered; confusion and pain came into her face.

Nelsen was aware that he was doing almost all of the talking, but maybe this had to be.

"So we've got a long walk," he said. "Toward the Tovie settlement. In Archers of mostly much-reduced range. Whose fault the situation is, can't change anything a bit. This is a life-or-death proposition, with lasting-time the most important factor.

So let's get started. Has anybody got any suggestions to increase our chances?"

Both Rodan and Dutch had come to. Rodan said nothing. His look was pure poison.

Dutch sneered. "Smart damn kid you are, huh, Nelsen? *You think!* Wait till you and your mumblin' crackpot pal get out there! I'll watch both of you go bust, squirt!"

Lester seemed not to hear these remarks. "All that gypsum, Frank," he said. "The water-and-oxygen mineral. But this is for real. There's no gimmick — no energy-source — to release it and save us . . ."

Frank Nelsen untied Rodan's and Dutch's feet, and, at pistol point, ordered them to move out ahead. From the charts he knew the bearing — straight toward the constellation Cassiopeia, at this hour, across an arm of Mare Nova, then along a pass that cut through the mountains. Eight hundred hopeless miles . . . ! Well, how did he know, really? How much could a human body take? How fast could they go? How long would the chemical batteries actually last? What breaks *might* appear?

They loped along, even Rodan hurrying. They made a hundred miles in the hours before darkness. With just Helen's shoulder lamp showing the way, they continued onward through the mountains.

Was there truly much to tell, in that slow, losing struggle? Nelsen attached the oxygen flask to his air system for a while, relieving the drain on his battery. Then he gave the flask to Lester. Later he began to move the nuclear battery around to all the Archers, to conserve all of the other batteries a little. Soon they filled the drinking-water tanks of their armor, so that they could discard the flask, whose slight weight seemed to have tripled.

After twenty hours, the power of the chemical batteries began to wane. David Lester, hovering close to Helen, muttered to himself, or to her. Rodan, still marching quite strongly, retreated into an unreality of his own.

"Have another scotch on the rocks, Ralph," he said genially. "I knew I'd make it . . . Nobel Prize . . . Oh, you have no idea what I went through . . . Most of my staff dead . . . But it's over, now, Ralph . . . Another good, stomach-warming scotch . . ."

"Damn, loony squirt's crackin' up!" Dutch screamed suddenly.

He began to run, promptly falling into a volcanic crack, the bottom of which couldn't even be found with the light. Fortunately he wasn't wearing the nuclear battery just then.

Somehow, Lester remained cool. It was as if, with everyone else scared, too, and nobody to show superior courage, he had found himself.

The batteries waned further. The cold of the inky lunar night — much worse than that of interplanetary space, where there is practically always sunshine, began to bite through the insulation of the Archers, and power couldn't be wasted on the heating coils.

Worst was the need for rest. They all lay down at last, except Frank Nelsen, who moved around, clipping the nuclear battery into one Archer for a minute, to freshen the air, and then into another. It was the only trick — or gimmick — that they found. After a while, Lester made the rounds, while Nelsen rested.

They got a few more miles by swapping batteries in quick succession. But the accumulating carbon dioxide in the air they breathed, made them sleepier. They had to sit down, then lie down. Frank figured that they had come something over a quarter of the eight hundred miles. This was about the end of Frank Nelsen, would-be Planet Strapper from Jarviston, Minnesota. Well — his coffin would be a common one — an Archer Five . . . Somehow, he thought of a line from Kipling: "If you can keep your head when all about you are losing theirs and blaming it on you . . ."

He tried to clip the nuclear battery back in Helen's armor, again. She *might* make the remaining five hundred-something miles, alone . . . ! He just barely managed to accomplish it . . . There was still a little juice, from his chemical cell, feeding his helmet phone . . . Now, he thought he heard someone singing raucously one of those improvised doggerel songs of spacemen and Moonmen . . . Folklore, almost . . .

> "If this god damn dust
> Just holds its crust,
> I'll get on to hell
> If my gear don't bust . . ."

"Hey!" Nelsen gurgled thickly into his phone. "Hey . . ." Then it was as if he sort of sank . . .

Hell was real, all right, because, with needles in his eyes and all through his body, Nelsen seemed to be goaded on by imps to crawl, in infinite weariness, through a hot steel pipe, to face Old Nick himself — or was it somebody he'd met before?

Maybe he asked, because he got an answer — from the grinning, freckled face bending over him, as he lay, armorless, on a sort of pallet, under the taut stellene roof of a Moontent.

"Sure Frankie — me, Gimp Hines, the itinerant trader and repairman of the lunar wilderness . . . What a switch — didn't think *you'd* goof! The Bunch — especially Two-and-Two — couldn't contact you. So I was sort of looking, knowing about where you'd be. Just made it in time. Les and the girl, and that ornery professor-or-whatever, are right here, too — still knocked out with a devil-killer. You've been out twenty hours, yourself. I'll fill you in on the news. Just shut up and drink up. Good Earth whiskey — a hundred bucks just to shoot a fifth into orbit."

Frank gulped and coughed. "Thanks, Gimp." His voice was like pumice.

"Shut up, I said!" Gimp ordered arrogantly. "About me — first. When I got to Serene, I could have convinced them I was worth a job. But I'm independent. I hocked my gear, bought some old parts, built myself a tractor and trailer, loaded it with water, oxygen, frozen vegetables, spare parts, cigarettes, pin-up pictures, liquor and so forth, and came traveling. I didn't forget tools. You'd be astonished by what you can sell and fix — and for what prices — out in the isolated areas, or what you can bring back. I even got a couple of emeralds as big as pigeon eggs. I'm getting myself a reputation, besides. What difference does just one good leg make — at only one-sixth Earth grav? You still hop along, even when you don't ride. And everywhere I go, I leave that left boot print behind in the dust, like a record that could last a thousand ages. I'm getting to be Left Foot, the legend."

Nelsen cleared his throat, found his voice. "Cocky, aren't you, Pal?" he chuckled. So another thing was happening in reverse from what most people had expected. Gimp Hines was finding a new, surer self, off the Earth.

"It's all right, Gimp," Nelsen added. "I figured that I saw your tracks and your tractor tread marks, up in the hills, just before I decided to break away from Rodan . . ."

Then he was telling the whole story.

"Yes, I was there," Gimp said at the end. "I missed you on the first pass, prospected for a couple of Earth-days, found a small copper deposit. High ground gave me a good position to receive short-wave messages — thought I heard your voices a couple of times. So I doubled back, and located what is left of Rodan's camp, and yours and Les' initialed blastoff drums, which I've brought along in my trailer. Lucky a trader needs an atom-powered tractor that can move at night. I followed your tracks, though going through rough country, you were screened from my radio calls until I was almost on you. Though on my first pass, when you were still in camp, I guess I could have reached you by bouncing a beam off a mountain top, had I known . . . Well, it doesn't matter, now. I'm out of stock, again, and full of money — got to head back to Serene . . . You were trying for the Tovie station, eh?"

"What else could we do?"

"I see what you mean, Frank. If you could have made it, and missed getting shot by some trigger-happy guard — where a frontier isn't even supposed to exist — they probably would have held you for a while, and then let you go."

"About the rest of the Bunch?" Frank Nelsen prompted.

"The Kuzaks got to the Belt okay — though they had to fight off some rough and humorous characters. Storey reached his Mars. Charlie Reynolds and Two-and-Two got to Venus, and hooked up with the exploring expedition. Tiflin? Who knows?"

"Ramos?"

"Ah — a real disappointing case, Frank. Darn wild idiot who ought to be probing the farther reaches of the solar system, got himself a job in a chemical plant in Serene. A synthesizing retort exploded. He was burned pretty bad. Just out of the hospital when I last left. It was on account of a woman that he was on the Moon at all."

"Eileen, the Queen of Serene? Gimp! — is *that* so, too?"

"Yep — sort of. Our Eileen. Back in Jarviston, Ramos found out that she was there. She's a good kid. Even admits that she hasn't got much competition, on a mostly — yet — masculine world . . . Well, I guess we start rolling, eh? I didn't want to jolt any of you poor sick people, so I camped. Let's get you all into Archers, for which I have a few spare parts left. Then, after we roll up this sealed, air-conditioned tent of a familiar material, we can be on our way."

"Just let's watch Rodan — that's all," Frank Nelsen warned.

"Sure — we'll keep him good and dopey with a tranquilizer . . ."

They aroused Dave Lester and Helen Rodan, helped them armor up, explained briefly what the situation was, stuffed Xavier Rodan into his Archer, and climbed with him into the sealable cab of the tractor. Here they could all remove their helmets.

After several hours of bumping over rugged country, with the tractor's headlights blazing through the star-topped blackness, they reached a solid trail over a mare. Then they could zip along, almost like on a highway. There were other rough stretches, but most of the well selected route was smooth. Half the time, Nelsen drove, while Gimp rested or slept. They ate spaceman's gruel, heated on a little electric stove. And after a certain number of hours, they climbed over the side of the Moon, and made their own sunrise. After that, the going seemed easier.

Gimp and Frank were just about talked out, by then. Helen

Rodan looked after her slumbering father. Otherwise, she and Lester seemed wrapped up in each other. Frank hardly listened to the few words they exchanged. They kept peering eagerly and worriedly along the trail, that wound past fantastic scenery.

Nelsen was eager and tense, himself. Serene, he was thinking with gratitude. Back to some of civilization. Back to freedom — if there wasn't too much trouble on account of all that had happened. Speeding along, they passed the first scattered domes, a hydroponic garden, an isolated sun-power plant.

It was another hour before they reached the checking-gate of one of the main airlocks. Frank Nelsen didn't try any tricks before the white-armored international guards.

"There have been some difficulties," he said. "I think you will want all of our names."

"I am Helen Rodan," Helen interrupted. "My father, Xavier Rodan, here, is sick. He needs a hospital. I will stay with him. These are our friends. They brought us all the way from Far Side."

Within the broad airlock compartment, Lester also got down from the tractor. "I'll stay, too," he said. "Go ahead, Frank. You and Gimp have had enough."

"A moment," gruffed one of the guards with a slight accent. "We shall say who shall do what — passing this lock. Difficulties? Very well. Names, and space-fitness cards, please, from everybody. And where you will be staying, here in Serene . . ."

Gimp and Frank got permission to pass the lock after about fifteen minutes. Without Helen and Les agreeing to stay, it might have been tougher. They spoke their thanks. For the time being, Frank was free to breathe open air under big, stellene domes. But he didn't know in what web of questioning and accusation he might soon be entangled.

Looking back to his first action against Rodan — with a sharpened trowel that had pierced the wall of a stellene dome — eventually leading up to Dutch's death, and very nearly precipitating his own demise and that of his other companions, he wondered if it wouldn't be regarded as criminal. Now he wasn't absolutely sure, himself, that it hadn't been criminal — or Moon-mad. Yet he didn't hate Xavier Rodan any less.

"The S.O.B. might just get sent to a mental hospital — at the worst," Gimp growled loyally. "Well, come on, Frank — let's forget it, ditch our Archies at the Hostel, get a culture steak, and look around to see what you've missed . . ."

So that was how Frank Nelsen began to get acquainted with Serene — fifteen thousand population, much of it habitually transient; a town of vast aspirations, careful discipline, little spotless cubicles for living quarters, pay twenty dollars a day just for the air you breathe, Earth-beer twenty dollars a can, a dollar if synthesized locally. Hydroponic sunflowers, dahlias, poppies, tomatoes, cabbages, all grown enormous in this slight gravity. New chemical-synthesis plants, above ground and far below; metal refineries, shops making electronic and nuclear devices, and articles of fabric, glass, rubber, plastic, magnesium. A town of supply warehouses and tanks around a great space port; a town of a thousand unfinished enterprises, and as many paradoxes and inconveniencies. No water in fountains, water in toilets only during part of an Earth-day. English, French, Spanish, German, Greek and Arabic spoken, to mention a few of the languages. An astronomical observatory; a selenographic museum, already open, though less than half completed. And of course it was against the law not to work for more than seventy-two consecutive hours. And over the whole setup there seemed to hang the question: Can Man really live in space, or does his invasion of it signal his final downfall?

At a certain point, Nelsen gave up trying to figure out all of the aspects of Serene. Of course he and Gimp had one inevitable goal. There was a short walk, Gimp hopping along lightly; then there was an elevator ride downward, for the place, aggressively named *The First Stop*, was nestled cozily in the lava-rock underlying the dust of Mare Serenitatis.

It had an arched interior, bar, stage, blaring jukebox, tables, and a shoulder-to-shoulder press of tough men, held in curious orderliness in part by the rigid caution needed in their dangerous and artificial existences, in part by the presence of police, and in part perhaps by a kind of stored-up awe and tenderness for girls — all girls — who had been out of their lives for too long. In a way, it was a crude, tawdry joint; but it was not the place that Frank and Gimp — or even many of the others — had come to see.

Eileen Sands was there, dancing crazy, swoopy stuff, possible at lunar gravity, as Frank and Gimp entered. Her costume was no feminine fluff; cheesecake, of which she presumably didn't have much, was not on display, either. Dungarees, still? No, not quite. Slender black trousers, like some girls use for ballet practice, instead.

Maybe she wasn't terribly good, or sufficiently drilled, yet, in her routines. But she had a pert, appealing face, a quick smile; her hair was brushed close to her head. She was a cute, utterly bold pixy to remember smiling at you — just you — like a spirit of luck and love, far out in the thick silence.

Her caper ended. She was puffing and laughing and bowing —

and maybe sweating, some, besides. The clapping was thunderous. She came out again and sang *Fire Streak* in a haunting, husky voice.

Meanwhile, a barman touched Frank's and Gimp's shoulders. "Hines and Nelsen? She has spotted you two. She wants to see you in her quarters."

"Hi, lads," she laughed. "Beer for old times? . . . You look like hell, Frank. Brief me on the missing chapter. You had everybody scared."

"Uh-uh — you first, Your Majesty," Nelsen chuckled in return.

She wrinkled her nose at him. "Well, I got here. There was a need. Somebody decided that I was the best available talent. This is the first step. Maybe I'll have my own spot — bigger and better. Or get back to my own regular self, working Out There with the men."

Maybe it was bad taste, but Nelsen felt like teasing. "Ever hear of a person named Miguel Ramos?"

That didn't bother her. She shrugged. "Still around, though I hope not for long, the buffoon! Who could ever put up with a show-off small boy like that for more than ten minutes? Besides, he's wasting himself. Why should he pick me for a bad influence . . . ? Now, your chapter, Frank."

He told her the story, briefly.

At last she said, "Frank, you must be spiritually all jammed up. Gimp is set, I know . . ."

In a few minutes more, Eileen introduced him to a girl. Jennie Harper had large dark eyes, and a funny, achy sort of voice. Gimp disappeared discreetly with his date. Frank and Jennie sat at a table in a private booth, high up in the arches of *The First Stop*, and watched Eileen do another number.

Jennie explained herself. "I'm another one. I've got to go where the heroes go. That's me — Frankie, is it? So I'm here . . ."

She had a perfume. While he was Rodan's prisoner for two and a half months, there were special things that had driven him almost wild. Now he made hints, inevitably.

"I don't need Eileen to tell me you're a good guy, Frank," she said with a small, warm smile. "We're just entertainers. They wouldn't let us be anything else — here . . ."

It hardly mattered what else they said. Maybe it was fifteen hours later that Frank Nelsen found himself walking along a stellene-covered causeway, looking for Left Foot Gimp Hines. He had memories of a tiny room, very neat and compact, with even a single huge rose in a vase on the bed table. But the time had a fierce velvet-softness that tried to draw him to it forevermore. It was like the grip of home, and the lost Earth, and the fear that he would chicken out and return.

He found Gimp, who seemed worried. "You might get stuck, here, on account of Rodan," he said. "Even I might. We'd better go see."

Nelsen had bitter, vengeful thoughts of Rodan being set at liberty — with himself the culprit.

The official at the police building was an American — a gruff one, but human. "I got the dope from the girl, Nelsen," he said. "And from Lester. You're lucky. Rodan confessed to a murder — another employee — just before he hired you. Apparently just before he made his discovery. He was afraid that the kid would try to horn in. Oh, he's not insane — not enough to escape punishment, anyhow. Here the official means of execution is simple exposure to the vacuum. Now, if you want to leave Serene, you'd better do so soon, before somebody decides to subpoena you as a witness . . ."

Frank felt a humbled wonder. Was Rodan really accountable, or was it the Moon and space, working on people's emotions?

Leaving the building, Frank and Gimp found Dave Lester and Helen Rodan entering. They talked for a moment. Then Lester said:

"Helen's had lots of trouble. And we're in love. What do we do, guys?"

"Dunno — get married?" Nelsen answered, shrugging. "It must happen here, too. Oh, I get it — living costs, off the Earth, are high. Well — I've got what Helen's father paid me. Of course I have to replace the missing parts of my equipment. But I'll loan you five hundred. Wish it could be more."

"Shucks, I can do better," Gimp joined in. "Pay us sometime, when you see us."

"I — I don't know . . ." Lester protested worriedly, like an honest man.

But Gimp and Frank were already shelling out bills, like vagabonds who happened to be flush.

"Poor simpletons," Gimp wailed facetiously afterwards, when they had moved out of earshot. "Even here, it happens. But that's worse. And if her Daddy had stayed human, she might almost have been an heiress . . . Well, come on, Frank. I've got my space gear out of hock, and my tractor sold. And an old buddy of ours is waiting for us at a repair and outfitting shop near the space port. I hope we didn't jump the gun, assuming you want to get out into the open again, too?"

"You didn't," Nelsen answered. "You sure you don't want to

look at Rodan's site — see if we can find any more Martian stuff?"

Gimp looked regretful for a second. "Uh-uh — it's jinxed," he said.

Ramos, scarred, somewhat, along the neck and left cheek, and a bit stiff of shoulder, was rueful but very eager. Frank's gutted gear was out of the blastoff drum, and spread around the shop. Most of it was already fixed. Ramos had been helping.

"Well, Frankie — here's one loose goose who is really glad to be leaving Luna," he said. "Are the asteroids all right with you for a start?"

"They are," Nelsen told him.

"Passing close to Mars, which is lined up orbitally along our route," Gimp put in. "Did you beam Two-and-Two and Charlie on Venus?"

"Uh-huh — they're just kind of bored," Ramos said. "I even got Storey at the Martian Survey Station. But he's going out into those lousy thickets, again. Old Paul, in Jarviston, sounds the same. Can't get him right now — North America is turned away . . . I couldn't pinpoint the Kuzaks in the Belt, but that's not unusual."

"I'll finance a load of trade stuff for them," Gimp chuckled. "We ought to be able to move out in about five hours, eh?"

"Should," Ramos agreed. "Weapons — we might need 'em this trip — and everything else is about ready."

"So we'll get a good meal, and then buy our load," Frank enthused.

He felt the texture of his deflated bubb. The hard lines of deep-space equipment quickened his pulses. He forgot the call of Earth. He felt as free and easy as a hobo with cosmic dust in his hair.

Blastoff from Serene's port, even with three heavily loaded trader rockets, was comparatively easy and inexpensive.

Out in orbit, three reunited Bunch members inflated and rigged their bubbs. For Nelsen it seemed an old, splendid feeling. They lashed the supplies from the trader rockets into great bundles that they could tow.

Before the rockets began to descend, the trio of beautiful, fragile rings, pushed by ions streaming from their centers, started to accelerate.

V

"It's the life of Reilly, Paul," Ramos was beaming back to Jarviston, Minnesota, not many hours after Frank Nelsen, Gimp Hines and he started out from the Moon, with their ultimate destination — after the delivery of their loads of supplies to the Kuzaks — tentatively marked in their minds as Pallastown on Pallas, the Golden Asteroid.

Ramos was riding a great bale, drawn by his spinning and still accelerating ring, to the hub of which it was attached by a thin steel cable, passed through a well-oiled swivel bolt. One of his booted feet was hooked under a bale lashing, to keep him from drifting off in the absence of weight. He held a rifle casually, but at alert, across his knees. Its needle-like bullets were not intended to kill. They were tiny rockets that could flame during the last second of a long flight, homing in on a target by means of a self-contained and marvelously miniaturized radar guidance system. Their tips were anesthetic.

The parabolic antenna mounted on the elbow of Ramos' Archer, swung a tiny bit, holding the beam contact with Paul Hendricks automatically, after it was made. Yet Ramos kept his arm very still, to avoid making the slender beam swing wide. Meanwhile, he was elaborating on his first statement:

" . . . Not like before. No terrestrial ground-to-orbit weight problem to beat, this trip, Paul. And we've got some of about everything that the Moon could provide, thanks to Gimp, who paid the bill. Culture steak in the shadow refrigerators. That's all you need, Out Here, to keep things frozen — just a shadow . . . We've got hydroponic vegetables, tinned bread, chocolate, beer. We've got sun stoves to cook on. We've got numerous luxury items not meant for the stomach. We're living high for a while, anyhow. Of course we don't want to use up too much of the fancy stuff. Tell Otto Kramer about us . . ."

Frank Nelsen and Gimp Hines, who were riding the rigging of their respective bubbs, which were also hauling big bales of supplies, were part of the trans-spatial conversation, too. There was enough leakage from Ramos' tightened beam, here at its source, for them to hear what he said.

But when, after a moment, Paul Hendricks answered from the distance, "Easy with the talk, fella — over-interested people might be listening," they suddenly forgot their own enthusiasms. They realized. Their hides tingled unpleasantly.

Ramos' dark face hardened. Still he spoke depreciatingly. "Shucks, Paul, this is a well-focused beam. Besides it's pointing Earthward and sunward; not toward the Belt, where most of the real mean folks are . . ." But he sounded defensive, and very soon he said, "'Bye for now, Paul."

A little later, Frank Nelsen contacted Art Kuzak, out in the Asteroid Belt, across a much greater stretch of space. He thought he was cautious when he said, "We're riding a bit heavy — for you guys . . ." But after the twenty minute interval it took to get an answer back over ten light-minutes of distance traversed twice — 186,000 miles for every second, spanned by slender threads of radio energy which were of low-power but of low-loss low-dispersal, too, explaining their tremendous range — Art Kuzak's warning was carefully cryptic, yet plain to Nelsen and his companions.

"Thanks for all the favors," he growled dryly. "Now keep still, and be *real* thoughtful, Frankie Boy. That also goes for you other two naive boneheads . . ."

Open space, like open, scarcely touched country, had produced its outlaws. But the distances were far greater. The pressures of need were infinitely harsher.

"Yeah, there's a leader named Fessler," Gimp rasped, with his phone turned low so that only his companions could hear him. "But there are other names . . . Art's right. We'd better keep our eyes open and our mouths shut."

Asteroid miners who had had poor luck, or who had been forced to kill to win even the breath of life; colonists who had left Mars after terrible misfortunes, there; adventurers soured and maddened by months in a vacuum armor, smelling the stench of their own unwashed bodies; men flush with gains, and seeking merely to relieve the tensions of their restrained, artificial existences in a wild spree; refugees from rigid Tovie conformism — all these composed the membership of the wandering, robbing, hijacking bands, which, though not numerous, were significant. Once, most of these men had been reasonably well-balanced individuals, easily lost in a crowd. But the Big Vacuum could change that.

Ramos, Hines, and Nelsen had heard the stories. Now, their watchfulness became almost exaggerated. They felt their inexperience. They made no more radio beam contacts. One of them was always on lookout, clutching a rifle, peering all around, glancing every few seconds at the miniaturized radar screen set inside the collar of his helmet. But the spherical sky remained free of any unexplained blip or luminous speck. Fragments of conversations picked up in their phones — widely separated asteroid-miners talking to each other, for the most part — obviously came from far away. There was a U.S.S.F. bubb cruising a few million miles off. Otherwise, the enormous emptiness was safely and perversely empty, all around.

They kept accelerating. For a planned interval, they enjoyed all the good things. They found that masculine guardedness and laziness went well together. They ate themselves full. Like Mitch Storey had once done, they all started hydroponic gardens inside their bubbs. In the pleasant, steamy sun-warmth of those stellene interiors, they bounced back and forth from elastic wall to elastic wall, with gravity temporarily at zero because they had stopped the spin of their bubbs. Thus they loosened their muscles, worked up a sweat. Afterwards they dozed, slept, listened to beamed radio music or taped recordings of their own. They smiled at pin-up pictures, read microfilmed books through a viewer, looked at the growing plants around them.

There was an arrogance in them, because they had succeeded in bringing so much of home out here. There was even a mood like that of a lost, languid beach in the tropics. And how was that possible, with only a thin skin of stellene between them and frigid nothing?

Ramos said just about what he had said — long ago, it seemed, now. "Nuts — the Big Vacuum ain't so tough." But he amended quickly, "Yeah, I know, Frank — don't scowl. When you aren't looking, it can up and kill you. Like with my Uncle José, only worse. He was a powder monkey in Mexico. It got so he thought dynamite was his friend. Well, there wasn't even anything to put in his coffin . . ."

The luxurious interlude passed, and they reverted mostly to Spartan meals of space-gruel, except for some fresh-grown lettuce. Mars became an agate bead, then a hazy sphere with those swirled, almost fluid markings, where the spores of a perhaps sentient vegetable life followed the paths of thin winds, blowing equatorward from the polar caps of hoarfrost.

The three stellene rings bumped lightly on the ten mile chunk of captured asteroidal rock and nickel-iron that was Phobos, Mars' nearer moon. Gravitation was almost nil. There was no need, here, for rockets, to land or take off. The sun-powered ionics were more than enough.

A small observatory, a U.N.-tended between ground-and-orbit rocket port, and a few hydroponic garden domes nestled in the jaggedness were about all that Phobos had — other than the magnificent view of the Red Planet, below.

Gimp Hines' freckled face shone in the ruddy light. "*I'm* going down," he declared. "Just for a few days, to look around near the Survey Station. You guys?"

Ramos shrugged, almost disinterested. "People have been there — some still are. And what good is poking around the Station? But who wants to goof up, going into the thickets? Others have done that, often enough. Me for Pallastown, and maybe lots farther, pal."

Frank Nelsen wasn't that blasé. On the Moon, he had seen some of the old Mars of advanced native technology, now long extinct. But there was also the recent Mars of explorers and then footloose adventurers, wondering what they could find to do with this quiet, pastel-tinted world of tremendous history. Then had come the colonists, with their tractors and their rolls of stellene to make sealed dwellings and covered fields in that thin, almost oxygenless atmosphere.

But their hopes to find peace and isolation from the crowded and troubled Earth by science and hard work even in so harsh a place, had come into conflict with a third Mars that must have begun soon after the original inhabitants had been destroyed. Though maybe it had had its start, billions of years before, on the planets of another star. The thickets had seemed harmless. Was this another, *different* civilization, that had risen at last in anger, using its own methods of allergy, terrible repellant nostalgia, and mental distortions?

Frank felt the call of mystery which was half dread. But then he shrugged. "Uh-uh, Gimp. I'd like to go down, too. But the gravity is twice that of the Moon — getting up and down isn't so easy. Besides, once when I made a stopover in space, after a nice short hop, I got into trouble. I'll pass this one up. I'd like to talk to Mitch Storey, though."

They all tried to reach him, beaming the Survey Station at the edge of Syrtis Major, the great equatorial wedge of blue-green growths on the floor of a vanished ocean, first.

"Mitchell Storey is not around right now," a young man's voice informed them. "He wandered off again, three days ago. Does it often . . . No — we don't know where to reach him . . ."

Widening their beams over the short range of considerably less than four thousand miles, they tried to call Mitch directly. No luck. Contact should have been easy. But of course he could be wandering with his Archer helmet-phone turned off.

Considering the reputation of Mars, Nelsen was a bit worried. But he had a perhaps treacherous belief that Mitch was special enough to take care of himself.

Ramos was impatient. "We'll hook old Mitch on our party line, sometime, Frank," he said. "Right now we ought to get started. Space is still nice and empty ahead, toward the Kuzaks and Pallastown. That condition might not last . . . Gimp, are you honest-to-gosh set on going down to this dried-up, museum-world?"

"Um-hmm. See you soon, though," Gimp answered, grinning. "I'll leave my bubb and my load of supplies up here on Phobos. Be back for it probably in a week. And there'll be a freight-bubb cluster, or something, for me to join up with, and follow you Out . . ."

Nelsen and Ramos left Gimp Hines before he boarded the winged skip-glide rocket that would take him below. Parting words flew back and forth. "See you . . . Take care . . . Over the Milky Way, suckers . . ."

Then they were standing off from Mars and its two moons. During the next several Earth-days of time, they accelerated with all the power that their bubb ionics could wring out of the sunshine, weakened now, with distance. They knew about where to find the Kuzaks. But contact was weeks off. When they were close enough, they could radio safely, checking the exact position of Art's and Joe's supply post. And they knew enough to steer clear of Ceres, the largest Asteroid, which was Tovie-occupied. All the signs were good. They were well-armed and watchful. They should have made the trip without trouble.

Ahead, dim still with distance, but glinting with a pinkish, metallic shine which made it much brighter than it would otherwise have been, was Pallas, which Ramos watched like a beacon.

"El Dorado," he said once, cockily, as if he remembered something from the Spanish part of his background.

They got almost three-quarters across that unimaginable stretch of emptiness before there was a bad sign. It was a catcall — literally — in their helmet phones. "Meow!" It was falsely plaintive and innocuous. It was a maliciously childish promise of trouble.

A little later, there was a chuckle. "Be cavalier, fellas. Watch yourselves. I mean it." The tone had a strange intensity.

Ramos was on lookout, then, with eyes, radar and rifle. But the spoken message had been too brief to get a fix on the direction of its radio waves.

Ramos stiffened. With his phone power turned very low, he said, "Frank — lots of people say 'Be cavalier', nowadays. But that includes one of the old Bunch. The voice *might* match, too."

"Uh-huh — Tiflin, the S.O.B.," Nelsen growled softly.

For ten hours, nothing else happened. Then there were some tiny radar-blips, which could have indicated meteors. Nelsen and Ramos changed the angle of the ion guides of their ionic motors to move their bubbs from course, slightly, and dodge. During the first hour, they were successful. But then there were more blips, in greater numbers.

Fist-sized chunks flicked through their vehicles almost simultaneously. Air puffed out. Their rings collapsed under them — the sealer was no good for holes of such size. At once, the continued spin of the bubbs wound them, like limp laundry, into knots.

While Nelsen and Ramos were trying to untangle the mess, visible specks appeared in the distance. They fired at them. Then something slammed hard into the fleshy part of Nelsen's hip, penetrating his armor, and passing on out, again. The sealing gum in the Archer's skin worked effectively on the needle-like punctures, but the knockout drug had been delivered.

As his awareness faded, Nelsen fired rapidly, and saw Ramos doing the same — until his hand slapped suddenly at his side . . .

After that there was nothing, until, for a few seconds, Frank Nelsen regained a blurred consciousness. He was lying, unarmored, inside a bubb — perhaps his own, which had been patched and reinflated. All around him was loud laughter and talk, the gurgle of liquor, the smells of cooked meat, a choking concentration of tobacco smoke. Music blared furiously.

"Busht out shummore!" somebody was hollering. "We got jackpot — the whole fanshy works! I almost think I'm back in Sputtsberg — wherever hell that is . . . But where's the wimmin? Nothing but dumb, prissy pitchers! Not even *good* pitchers . . . !"

There were guys of all sizes, mostly young, some armored, some not. One with a pimply face stumbled near. Frank Nelsen choked down his fury at the vandalism. He had a blurred urge to find a certain face, and almost thought he succeeded. But everything, including his head, was a fuzzy jumble.

"Hey!" the pimply guy gurgled. "Hey — Boss! Our benefactors — they're half awake! You should shleep, baby greenhorns . . . !"

A large man with shovel teeth ambled over. Frank managed half to rise. He met the blow and gave some of it back. Ramos was doing likewise, gamely. Then Nelsen's head zeroed out again in a pyrotechnic burst . . .

He awoke to almost absolute silence, and to the turning of the whole universe around him. But of course it was himself that was rotating — boots over head. There was a bad smell of old sweat, and worse.

His hip felt numb from the needle puncture. In all except the most vital areas, those slim missiles would not usually cause death, or even serious injury; but soon the wound would ache naggingly.

First, Frank Nelsen hardly knew where he was. Then he understood that he was drifting free in space, in an armor. He thought it was his own until he failed to recognize the scuffed, grimy interior. Even the work shirt he was wearing wasn't the new blue one he had put on, it seemed only hours ago. It was a greasy grey.

Etched into the scratched plastic of the helmet that covered his head, he saw "Archer III — ser. no. 828211." And casually stuck into the gasketted rim of the collar, was a note, penciled jaggedly on a scrap of paper:

"Honest, Greenie, your a pal. All that nice stuff. Thanks a 1,000,000! Couple of my boys needed new Archies, bad. Thanks again. You and your buddy are not having so bad a brake. These old threes been all over hell. They will show you all about Asteroid hopping and mining. So will the load-hauling net and tools. Thanks for the little dough, too. Find your space fitness card in shirt pocket. We don't need it. Have lots of fun. Just remember me as The Stinker."

Frank Nelsen was quivering with anger and scare. He saw that a mended steel net, containing a few items, had got wrapped around him with his turning. He groped for the ion-guide of the ancient shoulder-ionic, and touched a control. Slowly his spin was checked. Meanwhile he untangled himself, and saw what must be Ramos, adrift like himself in a battered Archer Three, doing the same.

Gradually they managed to ion glide over to each other. Their eyes met. They were the butts of a prank that no doubt had been the source of many guffaws.

"Did you get a letter, too, Frank?" Ramos asked. For close communication, the old helmet-phones still worked okay.

"I did," Nelsen breathed. "Why didn't they just knock us off? Alive, we might tell on them."

"Not slow and funny enough, maybe," Ramos answered dolefully. "In these broken-down outfits, we might not live to tell. Besides, even with these notes for clues, who'd ever find out who they are, way out here?"

Nelsen figured that all this was probably the truth. In the Belt, life was cheap. Death got to be a joke.

"There was an ox of a guy with big teeth!" he hissed furiously. "Thought I saw Tiflin, too — the S.O.B.! Cripes, do I always land in the soup?"

"The bossman with the teeth, I remember," Ramos grated. "Tiflin I don't know about. Could be . . . Hell, though — what now?

I suppose we're going in about the same direction and at the same speed as before? Have to watch the sun and planets to make sure. Did they leave us any instruments? Meanwhile, we might try to decelerate. I'd like to get out to Pluto sometime, but not equipped like this."

"We'll check everything — see how bad off they left us," Nelsen said.

So that was what they did, after they had set their decrepit shoulder-ionics to slow them down in the direction of the Belt.

Each of their hauling nets contained battered chisels, hammers, saws for metal, a radiation counter, a beaten-up-looking pistol, some old position-finding instruments, including a wristwatch that had seen much better days to be used as a chronometer. There were also two large flasks of water and two month-supply boxes of dehydrated space-gruel — these last items obviously granted them from their own, now vanished stores. Here was weird generosity — or perhaps just more ghoulish fun to give them the feeble hope of survival.

Now they checked each other's Archer Threes as well as they could while they were being worn. No use even to try to communicate over any distance with the worn-out radio transmitters. The nuclear batteries were ninety-percent used up, which still left considerable time — fortunately, because they had to add battery power to the normally sun-energized shoulder-ionics, in order to get any reasonable decelerating effect out of them. Out here, unlike on the Moon at night, the air-restorers could also take direct solar energy through their windows. They needed current only for their pumps. But the green chlorophane, key to the freshening and re-oxygenation of air, was getting slightly pale. The moisture-reclaimers were — by luck — not as bad as some of the other vital parts.

Ramos touched his needled side. His wry grin showed some of his reckless humor. "It's not utterly awful, yet," he said. "How do you feel?"

Nelsen's hip hurt. And he found that he had an awful hangover from the knockout drug, and the slapping around he had received. "Bad enough," he answered. "Maybe if we ate something . . ."

They took small, sealed packets of dehydrated food in through their chest airlocks, unsleeved their arms, emptied the packets into plastic squeeze bottles from the utensil racks before them, injected water from the pipettes which led to their shoulder tanks, closed the bottles and let the powdered gruel swell as it reabsorbed moisture. The gruel turned out hot all by itself. For it was a new kind which contained an exothermic ingredient. They ate, in the absence of gravity, by squeezing the bottles.

"Guess we'll have to become asteroid-hoppers — miners — like the slob said," Nelsen growled. "Well — I *did* want to try everything . . ."

This was to become the pattern of their lives. But not right away. They still had an incomplete conception of the vast distances. They hurtled on, certainly decelerating considerably, for days, yet, before they were in the Belt. Even that looked like enormous emptiness.

And the brightened speck of Pallas was too far to one side. Tovie Ceres was too near on the other side — left, it would be, if they considered the familiar northern hemisphere stars of Earth as showing "up" position. The old instruments had put them off-course. Still, they had to bear even farther left to try to match the direction and the average orbital speed — about twelve miles per second — of the Belt. Otherwise, small pieces of the old planet, hurtling in another direction — and/or at a different velocity — than themselves, could smash them.

Maybe they thought that they would be located and picked up — the gang that had robbed and dumped them had found them easily enough. But there, again, was a paradox of enormity. Bands might wait for suckers somewhere beyond Mars. Elsewhere, there could be nobody for millions of miles.

They saw their first asteroid — a pitted, mesoderm fragment of nickel-iron from middle-deep in the blasted planet. It was just drifting slightly before them. So they had achieved the correct orbital speed. They ion-glided to the chunk, and began to search clumsily for worthwhile metal. It was fantastic that somebody had been there before them, chiseling and sawing out a grayish material, of which there was a little left that made the needles of their radiation counters swing wildly.

They got a few scraps of the stuff to put into the nets which they were towing.

"For luck," Ramos laughed. "Without it we'll never pay J. John."

"Shut up. Big deal," Nelsen snapped.

"Okay. Shut up it is!" Ramos answered him.

So they stayed silent until they couldn't stand that, either. Everything was getting on their nerves.

Their next asteroids were mere chips a foot long — core fragments of the planet, heavy metals that had sunk deep. No crust material of any normally formed world could ever show such wealth. It gleamed with a pale yellow shine, and made Ramos' sunken eyes light up with an ancient fever, until he remembered, and until Nelsen said:

"Not for the gold, anymore, pal. Common, out here. So it's almost worthless, everywhere. Not much use as an industrial metal. But the osmium and uranium alloyed with it are something else. One hunk for each of our nets. Too bad there isn't more."

The uranium was driving their radiation-counters wild.

"Could we drag it, if there was more?" Ramos growled. "With just sun-power on these lousy shoulder-ionics?"

Everything was going sour, even Ramos. After a long deceleration they were afraid to draw any more power for propulsion from their weakened batteries. They needed the remaining current for the moisture-reclaimers and the pumps of the air-restorers — a relatively much lighter but vital drain. The sunlight was weak way out here. Worse, the solar thermocouples to power the ionics were almost shot. They tried to fix them up, succeeding a little, but using far more time than they had expected. Meanwhile, the changed positions of the various large asteroids, moving in their own individual orbits, lost them any definite idea of where the Kuzaks' supply post was, and the dizzying distance to Pallas, with only half-functioning ionics to get them there, fuddled them in their inexperience.

Soon their big hope was that some reasonable asteroid-hoppers would come within the few thousand mile range of their weakened transmitters. Then they could call, and be picked up.

Mostly to keep themselves occupied, they hunted pay-metal, taking only the very best that they could find, to keep the towage mass down. Right from the start they cut their food ration — a good thing, because one month went, and then two, as near as they could figure. Cripes, how much longer could they last?

Often they actually encouraged their minds to create illusions. Frank would hold his body stiff, and look at the stars. After a while he would get the soothing impression that he was swimming on his back in a lake, and was looking up at the night sky.

Mostly, they were out of the regular radio channels. But sometimes, because of the movement of distant bubb clusters that must be kept in touch, they heard music and news briefly, again. They heard ominous reports from the ever more populous Earth. Now it was about areas of ocean to become boundaried and to be "farmed" for food. Territorial disputes were now extending far beyond the land. Once more, the weapons were being uncovered. Of course there were repercussions out here. Ceres Station was beaming pronouncements, too — rattling the saber.

Nelsen and Ramos listened avidly because it was life, because it was contact with lost things, because it was not dead silence.

Their own tribulations deepened.

"Cripes but my feet stink!" Ramos once laughed. "They must be rotten. They're sore, and they itch something awful, and I can't scratch them, or change my socks, even. The fungus, I guess. Just old athlete's foot."

"The stuff is crawling up my legs," Nelsen growled.

They knew that the Kuzaks, maybe Two-and-Two, Reynolds, Gimp, Storey, must be trying to call them. They kept listening in their helmet-phones. But this time Frank Nelsen knew that he'd gotten himself a real haystack of enormity in which to double for a lost needle. The slender beams could comb it futilely and endlessly, in the hope of a fortunate accident. Only once they heard, "Nelsen! Ra . . ." The beam swept on. It could have been Joe Kuzak's voice. But inevitably, somewhere, there had to be a giving up point for the searchers.

"This is where I came in," Nelsen said bitterly. "Damn these beam systems that are so delicate and important!"

They did pick up the voices of scattered asteroid-hoppers, talking cautiously back and forth to each other, far away. " . . . Got me pinpointed, Ed? Coming in almost empty, this trip. Not like the last . . . Stake me to a run into Pallastown . . . ?" Most of such voices sounded regular, friendly.

Once they heard wild laughter, and what could have been a woman's scream. But it could have been other things, too.

On another occasion, they almost believed that they had their rescue made. Even their worn-out direction and distance finders could place the ten or so voices as originating not much over a hundred miles away. But they checked their trembling enthusiasm just in time. That was sheerest luck. The curses, and the savage, frightened snarls were all wrong. "If we don't catch us somebody, soon . . ."

Out here, the needs could get truly primitive. Oxygen, water, food, repair parts for vital equipment. Cannibalism and blood-drinking could also be part of blunt necessity.

Nelsen and Ramos were fortunate. Twenty miles off was a haze against the stars — a cluster of small mesoderm fragments. Drawing power for their shoulder-ionics from their almost spent nuclear batteries, they glided toward the cluster, and got into its midst, doubling themselves up to look as much like the other chunks as possible. They were like hiding rats for hours, until long after the distant specks moved past.

While he waited, Frank Nelsen's mind fumbled back to the lost phantom of Jarviston, Minnesota, again. To a man named Jig

Hollins who had got married, stayed home. Yellow? Hell . . . ! Nelsen imagined the comforts he might have had in the Space Force. He coaxed up a dream girl — blonde, dark, red-headed — with an awful wistfulness. He thought of Nance Codiss, the neighbor kid. He fumbled at the edge of a vast, foggy vision, where the wanderlust and spacelust of a man, and needs of the expanding race, seemed to blend with his home-love and love-love, and to become, impossibly, a balanced unit . . .

Later — much later — he heard young, green asteroid-hoppers yakking happily about girls and about how magnificent it was, out here.

"Haw-haw," he heard Ramos mock.

"Yeah," Nelsen said thickly. "Lucky for them that they aren't near us — being careless with their beams, that way . . ."

Frank Nelsen sneered, despising these innocent novices, sure that he could have beaten and robbed them without compunction. That far he had come toward understanding the outlaws, the twisted men of the Belt.

Ramos and he seemed to go on for an indefinite period longer. In a sense, they toughened. But toward the last they seemed to blunder slowly in the mind-shadows of their weakening body forces. They had a little food left, and water from the moisture-reclaimers. At zero-gravity, where physical exertion is slight, men can get along on small quantities of food. The sweetish, starchy liquid that they could suck through a tube from the air-restorers — it was a by-product of the photosynthetic process — might even have sustained them for a considerable interval.

But the steady weakening of their nuclear batteries was another matter. The pumps of their air-restorers and moisture-reclaimers were dependent on current. Gradually the atmosphere they breathed was getting worse. But from reports they had read and TV programs they had seen long ago, they found themselves another faint hope, and worked on it. With only solar power — derived through worn-out thermocouple units — to feed their uncertain ionics, they could change course only very slowly, now.

Yet maybe they had used up their bad luck. At last they came to a surface-fragment a couple of hundred yards long. They climbed over its edge. The thin sunshine hit dried soil, and something like corn-stubble in rows. Ahead was a solid stone structure, half flattened. Beside it a fallen trunk showed its roots. Vegetation was charred black by the absolute dryness of space. There was a fragment of a road, a wall, a hillside.

Here, there must have been blue sky, thin, frosty wind. The

small, Mars-sized planet had been far from the sun. Yet perhaps the greenhouse effect of a high percentage of carbon dioxide in its atmosphere and the radioactive heat of its interior had helped warm it. At least it had been warm enough to evolve life of the highest order, eons ago.

Poof had gone the blue sky and this whole world, all in a moment, the scattered pieces forming the asteroids. Accident? More likely it was a huge, interplanetary missile from competing Mars. The Martians had died, too — as surely, though less spectacularly. Radioactive poison, perhaps . . . Here, there had been an instant of unimaginable concussion, and of swift-passing flame. The drying out was soon ended. Then, what was left had been preserved in a vacuum through sixty millions of years.

Frank Nelsen had glimpsed ancient Mars, preserved on the Moon. Now he glimpsed its opponent culture, about which more was generally known.

"It's real," Ramos grunted. "Hoppers find surface-fragments like this, quite often."

Nelsen hardly cared about the archeological aspects just then. Excitement and hope that became certainty, enlivened his dulled brain.

"An energy source," he grated joyfully. "The Big Answer to Everything, out here! And it's always self-contained in their buildings . . ."

They pushed the collapsed and blackened thing with the slender bones, aside. They crept into the flat, horizontal spaces of the dwelling — much more like chinks than the rooms that humans would inhabit. They shoved away soft, multi-colored fabrics spun from glass-wool, a metal case with graduated dials and a lens, baubles of gold and glinting mineral.

In a recess in the masonry, ribboned with glazed copper strips that led to clear globes and curious household appliances, they found what they wanted. Six little oblong boxes bunched together. Their outsides were blue ceramic.

Frank Nelsen and Miguel Ramos began to work gingerly, though the gloves of their old Archer Threes were insulated. Here, sixty million years of stopped time had made no difference to these nuclear batteries, that, because of the universal character of physical laws, almost had to be similar in principle to their own. They had almost known that it would make no difference. There had been no drain of power through the automatic safety switches.

"DC current, huh?" Ramos said, breathing hard of the rotten air in his helmet.

"Yeah — gotta be," Frank answered quickly. "Same as from a thermocouple. Voltage about two hundred. Lots of current, though. Hope these old ionics'll take it."

"We can tap off lower, if we have to . . . Here — I'll fix you, first . . . Grab this end . . ."

They had a sweating two hours of rewiring to get done.

With power available, they might even have found a way to distill and collect the water, usually held in the form of frost, deep-buried in the soil of any large surface-fragment. They might have broken down some of the water electrolytically, to provide themselves with more oxygen to breathe. But perhaps now such efforts were not necessary.

When they switched in the new current, the pumps of their equipment worked better at once. The internal lights of their air-restorers could be used again, augmenting the action of the pale sunshine on the photosynthetic processes of the chlorophane. The air they breathed improved immediately. They tested the power on the shaky ionics, and got a good thrust reaction.

"We can make it — I think," Frank Nelsen said, speaking low and quick, and with the boldness of an enlivened body and brain. "We'll shoot up, out of the Belt entirely, then move parallel to it, backwards — contrary to its orbital flow, that is. But being outside of it, we won't chance getting splattered by any fragments. Probably avoid some slobs, too. We'll decelerate, and cut back in, near Pallas. There'll be a way to find the Kuzak twins."

Ramos chuckled recklessly. "Let's not forget to pack these historical objects in our nets. Especially that camera, or whatever it is. Money in the bank at last, boy . . ."

But after they set out, it wasn't long before they knew that two people were following them. There was no place to hide. And a mocking voice came into their phones.

"Hey, Nelsen . . . Oh, Mex . . . Wait up . . . I've been looking for you for over three months . . ."

They tried first to ignore the hail. They tried to speed up. But their pursuers still had better propulsion. Nelsen gritted his teeth. He felt the certainty of disaster closing in.

"There's just two of them — so far," Ramos hissed. "Maybe here's our chance, Frank, to really smear that rat!" Ramos' eyes had a battle light. "All right, Tiflin — approach. These guns are lined up and loaded."

"Aw — is *that* friendship, Mex?" the renegade seemed to wheedle. But insolently, he and his larger companion came on.

"Toss us your pistols," Ramos commanded, as they drifted

close, checking speed.

Tiflin flashed a smirk that showed that his front teeth were missing. "Honest, Mex — do you expect us to do that? Be cavalier — I haven't even got a pistol, right now. Neither has Igor, here. Come look-see . . . Hi, Frankie!"

"Just stay there," Nelsen gruffed.

Tiflin cocked his head inside the helmet of a brand-new Archer Six, in a burlesqued pose for inspection. He looked bad. His face had turned hard and lean. There were scars on it. The nervous, explosive-tempered kid, who couldn't have survived out here, had been burned out of him. For a second, Nelsen almost thought that the change could be for the good. But it was naive to hope that that could happen. Glen Tiflin had become passive, yielding, mocking, with an air of secret knowledge withheld. What did an attitude like that suggest? Treachery, or, perhaps worse, a kind of poised — and poisonous — mental judo?

Nelsen looked at the other man, who wore a Tovie armor. Tall, starvation-lean. Horse-faced, with a lugubrious, bumpkinish smile that almost had a whimsical appeal.

"Honest — I just picked up Igor — which ain't his real name — in the course of my travels," Tiflin offered lightly. "He used to be a comic back in Eurasia. He got bored with life on Ceres, and sort of tumbled away."

With his body stiff as a stick, Igor toppled forward, his mouth gaping in dismay. He turned completely over, his great boots kicking awkwardly. His angular elbows flapped like crow-wings. He righted himself, looked astonished, then beatifically self-approving. He burped delicately, patted his chest plate, then sniffed in sad protest at the leveled pistols.

Now Nelsen and Ramos cast off the loaded nets they had been towing, and closed in on this strange pair. Nelsen did the searching, while Ramos pointed the guns.

"Haven't even got my shiv anymore, Frankie," Tiflin remarked, casually. "Threw it at a guy named Fessler, once. Missed by an inch. Guess it's still going — round and round the sun, for millions of years. Longest knife throw there ever was."

"Fessler!" Frank snapped. "Now we're getting places, you S.O.B.! The funny character that robbed and dumped Ramos and me, I'll bet. Probably with your help! You know him, huh?"

"*Knew* — for a while — past tense," Tiflin chuckled wickedly. "Nope — it wasn't me that stripped off his armor in space. He wasn't even around, anymore, when you beauties got caught. They come and they go."

"But *you* were around, Tiflin!"

"Maybe not. Maybe I was twenty million miles off."

"Like hell!" Nelsen gritted his teeth, grabbed Tiflin's shoulder, and swung his gloved fist as hard as he could against the thin layer of rubber and wire over Tiflin's stomach. He struck three times.

"Damn you!" Nelsen snarled. "I promised myself I'd get you good, Tiflin! Now tell us what else you and your friends are cooking for us, or by the Big Silence, you'll be a drifting, explosively decompressed mummy!"

Frank Nelsen didn't know till now, after exerting himself, how weak privations had made him. He felt dizzy.

Tiflin's eyes had glazed slightly, as he and Frank did a slow roll, together. He gasped. But that insulting smirk came back.

"Haven't had your Wheaties lately, have you, Frank? Go ahead — hit, knock yourself out. You, too, Mex. I've been slugged before, by big men, in shape . . . ! Could be I'm not cooking anything. Except I notice that you two have found yourselves some very interesting local objects of ancient history, worth a little money. Also, some good, raw metal . . . Well, I suppose you want to get the load and yourselves to the famous twins, Art and Joe. That's easy — with luck. Though the region is a trifle disturbed, right now. But I can tell you where they are. You won't have to fiddle around, hunting."

"Here, hold these guns, Frank. Lemme have a couple of pokes at the slob," Ramos snapped.

"Aw-right, aw-right — who's asking you guys to believe me?" Tiflin cut in. "I'll beam the twins for you — since I'd guess your transmitter won't reach. You can listen in, and talk back through my set. Okay?"

"Let's see what happens — just for kicks," Ramos said softly. "If you're calling some friends to come and get us, or anything, Tif — well, you've had it!"

They watched Tiflin spin and focus the antenna. "Kuzak . . . Kuzak . . . Kuzak . . . Kuzak . . ." he said into his phone. "Missing boys alive and coming to you. Mex and old Guess Which . . . Kicking and independent, but very hungry, I think . . . Put on the coffee pot, you storekeepers . . . Kuzak . . . Kuzak . . . Kuzak . . . Talk up, Frank and Miguel. Your voices will relay through my phone . . ."

"Hi, Art and Joe — it's us," Ramos almost apologized.

"Yeah — we don't quite know yet what Tiflin is pulling. But here we are — if it's you we're talking to . . ."

There was the usual long wait as impulses bridged the light-minutes.

Then Art Kuzak's voice snarled guardedly. "I hear you, Ram and Nel. Come in, if you can . . . ! Tif, you garbage! Someday . . . ! This is all. This is all . . ." The message broke off.

Tiflin smirked. "Third quadrant of the Belt," he said, giving a position in space almost like latitude and longitude on Earth. "About twenty minutes of the thirty-first degree. Three degrees above median orbital plane. Approximately two hundred hours from here. Can Igor and I leave you, now, or do you want us to escort you in?"

"*We'll* escort *you*," Ramos said.

So it was, until, near the end of a long ride, a cluster of bubbs was in view in the near distance, and Ramos and Nelsen could contact Art Kuzak themselves.

"We've got Tiflin and his Tovie pal with us, Art," Frank Nelsen said. "They showed us the way, more or less because we made them. But Tif did give us the right position at the start. A favor, maybe. I don't know. And now he's saying, 'Be cavalier — it might be awkward for me to meet Art and Joe just at present.' Do you want to fix this character's wagon bad enough? Your customers could get mean — if he ever did them dirt."

"Just one thing I've got against Tiflin!" Art snarled back. "Every time I hear his voice, it means trouble. But I've never seen the crumb face-to-face since that Moonhop. Okay, let's not spoil my stomach. Turn him loose. It can't make much difference. Or maybe I'm sentimental about the old Bunch. He was our cracked, space-wild punk."

"Thanks, Art," Tiflin laughed.

In a minute he, and his comic, scarecrow pal who originated from the dark side of trouble, on Earth and out here, too, were fading against the stars.

Nelsen and Ramos, the long-lost, glided in, past some grim hoppers. A bubb and sweet air were around them once more. They shed their stinking Archer Threes. Hot showers — miraculous luxury — played over them. They rubbed disinfectant salves into their fungus-ridden hides.

Then there was a clean, white table, with plates, knives, forks. They had to treat their shrunken stomachs gently — just a little of everything — beer, steak, vegetables, fruit . . . Somewhere during the past, unmarked days Frank Nelsen had gotten to be twenty years old. Only twenty? Well — maybe this was his celebration.

Ramos and he told their story very briefly. Little time was wasted on congratulations for survival or talk of losses long past. The Kuzaks looked leaner and tougher, now, and there were plenty of present difficulties to worry them. Joe Kuzak hurried out to argue with the miners at the raw metal receiving bins and at the store bubbs. Art stayed to explain the present situation.

"Three big loads of supplies were shipped through to us from the Moon," he growled. "We did fine, trading for metal. We sent J. John Reynolds his percentage — a fair fraction of his entire loan. We sent old Paul five thousand dollars. But the fourth and fifth loads of trade stuff got pirated en route. When there's trouble on Earth, it comes out here, too. Ceres, colonized by our socialist Tovie friends of northern Eurasia, helps stir up the bums, who think up plenty of hell on their own. It's a force-out attempt aimed at us or at anybody who thinks our way. After two lost shipments, and a lot of new installations here at the Post, we're about broke, again. Worse, we've got the asteroid-hoppers expecting us to come through with pay for the new metal in their nets, and with stuff they need. Back home, some people used to raise hell about a trifle like a delayed letter. How about a spaceman's reaction, when what is delayed may be something to keep him alive? They could get really annoyed, and kick this place apart."

Art Kuzak blew air up past his pug nose, and continued. "Finance — here we go again, Frank!" he chuckled. "Gimp Hines is helping us. After Mars, he came here without trouble. He's in Pallastown, now, trying to raise some fast cash, and to rush supplies through from there, under Space Force guard. You know he's got a head for commerce as well as science. But our post, here, perhaps isn't considered secure enough to back a loan, anymore."

Art grinned wryly at Nelsen and Ramos. His hint was plain. He had seen the museum pieces that they had brought in.

"Should we, Frank?" Ramos chuckled after a moment.

"Possibly . . . We've got some collateral, Art. Lots more valuable per unit mass than any raw metal, I should think."

"So you might want to work for us?" Art inquired blandly.

"Not 'for'," Nelsen chuckled. "We might say 'with'."

"Okay, Cuties," Art laughed.

Joe Kuzak had just come back into the dwelling and office bubb.

"Don't let my twin sell you any rotten apples, fellas," he warned lightly. "He might be expecting you to transport your collateral to Pallastown. Naturally anybody trying to strangle this Post will be blocking the route. You might get robbed again. Also murdered."

Ramos' gaunt face still had its daring grin. "Frank and I know that," he said. "I'm past bragging. But we've had experience. Now, we might be smart enough to get through. A few more days out there won't hurt. How about it, Frank?"

"Ten hours sleep and breakfast," Frank said. "Then a little camouflage material, new weapons, a pair of Archers in condition — got any left?"

"Five in stock," Joe answered.

"Settled, then?" Art asked.

"Here, it is," Ramos answered, and Nelsen nodded.

It would have been rough going for them to try to sleep in beds. They had lost the habit. They slept inside their new Archer Fives.

Afterwards they painted their armor a dark grey, like chunks of mesoderm stone. They did likewise to the two bundles in which they wrapped their relics.

They were as careful as possible to get away from the post without being observed, visually or by radar. But of course you could never be sure.

Huddled up to resemble stray fragments, they curved out of the Belt — toward the Pole Star, north of its orbital plane. Moving in a parallel course, they proceeded toward Pallastown. The only thing that would seem odd was that they were moving contrary to the general orbital rotation of most of the permanent bodies of the solar system. Of course they and their bundles *might* have been stray meteors from deep in space.

Four watchful, armored figures seemed to notice the peculiarity of their direction, and to become suspicious. These figures seemed too wary for honesty as they approached. They got within twenty-five miles.

Even without the memory that Tiflin might make guesses about what they meant to do, Nelsen and Ramos would have taken no chances. They had to be brutal. Homing darts pierced armor. The four went to sleep.

VI

The asteroid, Pallas, was a chunk of rich core material, two hundred-some miles in its greatest dimension. It had a mottled, pinkish shine, partly from untarnished lead, osmium, considerable uranium, some iron, nickel, silver, copper. The metals were alloyed, here; almost pure, there. There was even a little rock. But thirty-five percent of Pallas' roughly spherical mass was said to be gold.

Gold is not rare at the cores of the worlds, to which most of the heavy elements must inevitably sink, during the molten stage of planetary developments. On Earth it must be the same, though who could dig three thousand miles into a zone of such heat and pressure? But the asteroid world had exploded. Pallas was an exposed and cooled piece of its heart.

Pallas had a day of twenty-four hours because men, working with great ion jets angling toward the stars, had adjusted its natural rate of rotation for their own convenience to match the terrestrial. A greater change was Pallastown.

Frank Nelsen and Miguel Ramos made the considerable journey to it without further incident. Because he was tense with hurry, Nelsen's impressions were superficial: Something like Serene, but bigger and more fantastic. A man weighed only a few ounces, here. Spidery guidance towers could loom impossibly high. There were great storage bins for raw metal brought in from all over the Belt. There were rows of water tanks. As on the Moon, the water came mostly from gypsum rock or occasionally from soil frost, both found on nearby crustal asteroids. Beyond the refineries bulged the domes of the city itself, housing factories, gardens, recreation centers, and sections that got considerably lost and divergent trying to imitate the apartment house areas of Earth.

Frank Nelsen's wonder was hurried and dulled.

Gimp Hines and David Lester were waiting inside the stellene reception dome when Nelsen and Ramos landed lightly at the port on their own feet, with no more braking assistance than their own shoulder-ionics.

Greetings were curiously breathless yet casual, but without any backslapping.

"We'd about given you two up," Gimp said. "But an hour ago Joe Kuzak beamed me, and said you'd be along with some museum stuff . . . Les lives here, now, working with the new Archeological Institute."

"Hi-hi — good to see you guys," Ramos said.

"Likewise. Hello, Les," Frank put in.

While Frank was gripping David Lester's limp, diffident hand, which seemed almost to apologize for his having come so far from home, Gimp teased a little. "So you latched onto Art Kuzak, too. Or was it the other way around?"

Frank's smile was lopsided. "I didn't analyze motives. Art's a pretty good guy. I suppose we just wanted to help Joe and him out. Or maybe it was instinct. Anyhow, what's wrong with latching onto — or being latched onto by — somebody whom you feel will get himself and you ahead, and make you both a buck?"

"Check. Not a darn thing," Gimp laughed. "Now let's go to my hotel and have a look at what you brought in. Did you really examine it, yet?"

"Some — on the way. Not very much," Ramos said. "There's a camera."

In the privacy of Gimp's quarters, the bundles were opened; the contents, some of them dried and gruesome, all of them rather wonderful, were exposed.

David Lester and Gimp Hines were both quietly avid. Lester knew the most about these things, but Gimp's hands, on the strange camera, were more skillful. The cautious scrutiny of dials and controls marked with cryptic numerals and symbols, and the probing of detail parts and their functions, took about an hour.

"What do you think, Les?" Gimp asked.

"I'm not an expert, yet," Lester answered. "But as far as I know, this is the first undamaged camera that has yet been found. That makes it unique. Of course by now, hoppers are bringing in quite a lot of artifacts from surface-asteroids. But there's not much in the way of new principle for our camera manufacturers to buy. Lens systems, shutters, shock mountings, self-developing, integral viewing, projecting and sonic features, all turn out to be similar to ours. It's usually that way with other devices, too. It's as if all their history, and ours, were parallel."

"Well, damn it — let's see what the thing can show!" Ramos gruffed.

In the darkened room, the device threw a rectangle of light on the wall. Then there was shape, motion, and color, kept crystallized from sixty million years before. A cloud, pinked by sunrise, floating high in a thin, expanded atmosphere. Did clouds everywhere in the universe always look much the same? Wolfish, glinting darts, vanishing away. Then a mountainside covered with spiny growths that, from a distance, seemed half cactus and half pine. A road, a field, a dull-hued cylinder pointing upward. Shapes of soft, bluish grey, topped like rounded roofs, unfolding out of a chink, and swaying off in a kind of run — with little clinkings of equipment, for there were sounds, too. Two eyelike organs projecting upward, the pupils clear and watchful. A tendril with a ridged, dark hide, waving what might have been a large, blue flower, which was attached to the end of a metal tube by means of a bit of fibre tied in a granny knot. A sunburst of white fire in the distance . . .

It could have gone on, perhaps for many hours. Reality, with every detail sharp. Parallels with Earthly life. Maybe even sentiment was there, if you only knew how it was shown. But in the differences you got lost, as if in a vivid dream that you couldn't fully understand. Though what was pictured here was certainly from the last beautiful days of a competing planet.

Frank Nelsen's mouth often hung open with fascination. But his own realities kept intruding. They prodded him.

"I hate to break this off," he said. "But a lot of asteroid-hoppers are out at the post, waiting for Ramos and me to bring stuff back. It's a long ride through a troubled region. There's plenty to get arranged beforehand . . . So first, what do we do to realize some quick funds out of these relics?"

Hines terminated the pictured sequence. "Frank — Ramos — I'd keep this camera," he said urgently. "It's a little bit special, at least. History is here, to be investigated. Offers — bids — could come up. Okay — I'm talking about dough, again. Still, who wants to detach himself, right away, from something pretty marvelous, by selling it? I'd dump most of the other things. Getting a loan — the hock-shop approach — is no good . . . Am I telling it right, Les?"

Lester nodded. "More of the same will be brought in. Prices will drop. Archeological Survey has a buying service for museums back home. I've been working for them for a month. I don't claim to love them entirely, but they'll give you the safest break. You should get enough, for your purposes, without the camera. With a load like this, you can see Doc Linford, the boss, any time."

"Right now, then," Frank said.

"Hcy, you impolite slobs!" Ramos laughed. "When do you consult me, co-discoverer and -owner? Awright, skip it — you're the Wizards of Oz. I'll just grab out a few items for my Ma and the kids, and maybe a girl or two I'll meet someplace. You guys might as well do the same."

He took some squares of fabric, silken-soft, though spun from fibre of colored glass. And some wheeled devices, which might have been toys. Lester and Hines picked up only token pieces of the fabric. Frank took a three inch golden ring that glinted with mineral. Except that it looked decorative, he had no idea of its original purpose.

The broken, fine-boned mummy and the other items were appraised and bought in a large room across the city. It was already cluttered with queer fossils and objects. The numbers printed on the two equal checks, and on the cash in their hands, still looked slightly mythical to Nelsen and Ramos, to whom a thousand dollars had seemed a fortune.

Later, at the U.S.S.F. headquarters, he was prepared to argue grimly. Words were in his mind: A vital matter of supply . . . Without an escort, we'll still have to try to get through, alone. You have been informed, therefore, if anything happens, you will be responsible . . .

He didn't have to say anything like this. They knew. Maybe an old bitterness had made him misjudge the U.S.S.F. A young colonel smiled tiredly.

"This has been happening," he said. "We have limited facilities for this purpose. The U.N.S.F. even less. However, an escort is due in, now. We can move out again, with you, in seven hours."

"Thank you, sir," Nelsen responded.

Gimp Hines had the better part of the supplies to be purchased already lined up at the warehouses.

Nelsen counted the money he had left. "Figuring losses and gains, I have no idea how much I owe J. John — if anything," he laughed. "So I'll make it a grand — build up my ego . . . But we owe old Paul more than dough."

"All right, I'm another idiot — I'll mail J. John a similar draft," Ramos gruffed. "Paul's a problem. He can use money, but he never lived for it. And you can't buy a friend. We'll have to rig something."

"Yeah — we will," Gimp said. "Couple of times I forgot J. John. But I lost my shirt on those loads that were lifted off you boneheads. The Kuzaks reimbursed me for half. Do you two want to cover the other half? Aw — forget it! Who's got time to figure all this? That old coot doped himself out a nice catch-dollar scheme, making us promise. Or was it a leg pull on a highly elusive proposition, where big sums and the vastness of space seem to match? Hell — I'm getting mixed up again . . ."

Dave Lester had wandered off embarrassedly, there in the warehouse. But now he returned, clearing his throat for attention.

"Fellas," he said. "Helen and I want you to come out to our apartment, now, for dinner."

"Shucks, that's swell, Les," Ramos responded, suddenly curious.

"Here, also," Nelsen enthused.

"Sure," Gimp said. But his smile thinned.

In this gravity, going to Lester's place was a floating glide rather than a walk. Along a covered causeway, into a huge dome, up a wall with handholds, onto a wispy balcony. Nelsen and Ramos brought liquor and roses.

Much of what followed was painful and familiar — in a fantastic setting. Two young people, recently married, struggling with problems that they hadn't been able to plan for very well.

While his wife was out of earshot, Lester put his hand on the back of a chair constructed entirely of fine golden wire — later it developed that he had made it, do-it-yourself fashion, to be economical — and seemed more intent on holding it down than to rest his hand.

"Gimp . . . Frank . . ." he began nervously. "You helped Helen and me to get married and get set up out here. The Archeological Institute paid our way to Pallastown. But there were other expenses . . . Her — my father-in-law, died by his own hand while still awaiting trial . . . Everything he owned is still tied up . . . Now, well — you know human biology . . . I hope you can wait a little longer for us to begin paying back your loan . . ."

Nelsen had a vagrant thought about how money now had to stand on its own commercial value, rather than rely on the ancient witchcraft of a gold standard. Then he almost suspected that Lester was being devious and clever. But he knew the guy too well.

"Cripes, Les!" he burst out almost angrily. "How about your services, just now, as an archeological consultant? If you won't consider that we might have meant to make you a gift. Pretty soon you'll have us completely confused!"

"What a topic for an evening of fun," Gimp complained. "Hey, Helen — can I mix the drinks?"

"Yes — of course, Mr. Hines. I'll get you the things," she said with apology in her eyes and voice, as if fussy celebrities had descended on her small, unsettled, and poor household.

"On the Moon you were a swell cook, Helen," Frank reminded her.

She flashed a small smile. "It was different, there. Things weighed something, and stayed in place. Here — just breathe hard and you have a kitchen accident. Besides, I had a garden. We'd like one here, but there's no room . . . And in the market . . ."

"Shucks — it's new here to us, too," Ramos soothed. "Riding an Archer in space, at zero-G, is different from this . . ."

Things were a bit less strained, after that, through the skimpy meal, with its special devices, unique to the asteroids and their tiny gravity. Clamps to fasten plates to tables and victuals to plates. Drinking vessels that were half-squeeze bottles. Such equipment was now available in what might once have been called a dime store — but with another price-level.

The visitors made a game of being awkward and inept, together. It was balm for Helen's sensitivity.

"Somebody's got to keep the camera for us, Mex," Frank Nelsen said presently.

"Yeah — I know. Les'll do it for us," Ramos answered. "He's the best, there. He can run through all the pictures — make copies with an ordinary camera . . . See if he can market them. Twenty percent ought to be about right for his cut."

Lester tried to interrupt, but Frank got ahead of him. "We owe Gimp for those loads we lost. Got to cut him into this, as a consultant. You'll be around Pallastown for a while, helping out with this end of the Twin's enterprises, won't you, Gimp?"

Hines grinned. "Probably. Glad you slobs got memories. Glad to be of assistance, anytime. Les is no louse — he'll help old friends. I'll bring him the camera, out of the safe at my hotel, as soon as we leave here . . ."

Lester smiled doubtfully, and then happily. That was how they worked the fabulous generosity of spacemen in the chips on him.

Nelsen, Ramos and Hines escaped soon after that.

"Three hours left. I guess you guys want to get lost — separately," Gimp chuckled. "I'll say so long at the launching catapults, later. I've got some tough guards, fresh from the Moon, who will go along with you. Art and Joe need them . . ."

Frank Nelsen wandered alone in the recreation area. He heard music — *Fire Streak*, *Queen of Serene* . . . He searched faces, looking for an ugly one with shovel teeth. He thought, with an achy wistfulness, of a small hero-worshipping girl named Jennie Harper, at Serene.

He found no one he had ever seen before. In a joint he watched a girl with almost no clothes, do an incredible number of spinning somersaults in mid-air. He thought he ought to find himself a friend — then decided perversely, to hell with it.

He thought of the trouble on Earth, of Ceres, of Tiflin and Igor, of Fanshaw, the latest leader of the Asteroid Belt toughs — the Jolly Lads — that you heard about. He thought about how terribly vulnerable to attack Pallastown seemed, even with its encirclement of outriding guard stations. He thought of Paul Hendricks, Two-and-Two Baines, Charlie Reynolds, Otto Kramer, Mitch Storey, and

Miss Rosalie Parks who was his old Latin teacher.

He thought of trying to beam some of them. But hell, they all seemed so long-lost, and he wasn't in the mood, now. He even thought about how it was, trying to give yourself a dry shave with a worn-out razor, inside an Archer. He thought that sometime, surely, perhaps soon, the Big Vacuum would finish him.

He wound up with a simple sentimental impulse, full of nostalgia and tenderness for things that seemed to stay steady and put. The way he felt was half-hearted apology for human moods in which murder would have been easy. He even had a strange envy for David Lester.

Into the synthetic cellulose lining of a small carton bought at a souvenir shop, he placed the sixty million-year old golden band with its odd arabesques and its glinting chips of mineral. Regardless of its mysterious intentional function, it could be a bracelet. To him, just then, it was only a trinket that he had picked up.

Before he wrapped and addressed the package, he put a note inside:

"Hi, Nance Codiss! Thinking about you and all the neighbors. This might reach you by Christmas. Remember me? Frank Nelsen."

Postage was two hundred dollars, which seemed a trifle. And he didn't quite realize how like a king's ransom a gift like this would seem in Jarviston, Minnesota.

On leaving the post office, he promptly forgot the whole matter, as hard, practical concerns took hold of him, again.

At the loading quays, special catapults hurled the gigantic bales of supplies clear of Pallas. To the Kuzaks, this shipment would now have seemed small, but it was much larger than the loads Ramos and Nelsen had handled before. Gimp and Lester saw them off. Then they were in space, with extra ionics pushing the bales. The guard of six new men was posted. Nelsen wasn't sure that they'd be any good, or whether he could trust them all, but they looked eagerly alert. Riding a mile off was the Space Force patrol bubb.

All through the long journey — beam calls ahead were avoided for added safety — Nelsen kept wondering if he'd find the post in ruins, with what was left of Art and Joe drifting and drying. But nothing like that happened yet, and the shipment was brought through. Business with the asteroid-hoppers was started at once.

When there was a lull, Art Kuzak talked expansively in his office bubb:

"Good work, Frank. Same to you, Ramos — except that I know you're itching with your own ideas, and probably won't be around long. Which is your affair . . . Never mind what anybody says about

Venus, or any other place. The Belt, with its history, its metals, and its possibilities, is the best part of the solar system. Keep your defenses up, your line of communication covered, and you can't help but make money. There are new posts to set up, help to recruit and bring out, stellene plants and other factories to construct. There'll be garden bubbs, repair shops — everything. Time, work, and a little luck will do it. You listening, Frank?"

Nelsen got a bit cagy with Art, again. "Okay, Art — you seem like a formal fella. Mex and I joined up and helped out pretty much as informal company members. But as long as we've put in our dough, let's make it official, in writing and signed. The KRNH Enterprises — Kuzak, Ramos, Nelsen and Hines. The 'H' could also stand for Hendricks — Paul Hendricks."

"I *like* it that way, you suspicious slob," Art Kuzak chuckled.

So another phase began for Nelsen. Offices bored him. Amassing money, per se, meant little to him, except as a success symbol that came out of the life he had known. He figured that a man ought to be a success, even a rough-and-tumble romantic like Ramos, or Joe Kuzak. Or himself, with both distance and home engrained confusingly into his nature.

One thing that Nelsen was, was conscientious. He could choose and stick to a purpose for even longer than it seemed right for him.

Mostly, now, during the long grind of expansion, he was afield. Disturbances on Earth quieted for a while, as had always happened, so far. The Belt responded with relative peace. Tovie Ceres, the Big Asteroid, which, like the others, should have been open to all nations, but wasn't, kept mostly to its own affairs. There were only the constant dangers, natural, human, and a combination. There was always a job — a convoy to meet, a load of supplies to rush to a distant point, Jolly Lads to scare off. Reckless Ramos might be with Nelsen, or Joe Kuzak who usually operated separately, or a few guards, or several asteroid-hoppers, most of whom were tough and steady and good friends to know. Often enough, Nelsen was alone.

At first, KRNH just handled the usual supplies. But when factory and hydroponic equipment began to arrive, Joe Kuzak and Frank Nelsen might be out establishing a new post. There'd be green help, bubbing out from the Moon, to break in. Nelsen would see new faces that still seemed familiar, because they were like those of the old Bunch, as it had been. Grim, scared young men, full of wonder. But the thin stream of the adventurous was thickening, as more opportunities opened. Occasionally there was a young couple. *Oh, no,* you thought. Then — *well, maybe.* That is, if somebody didn't crack up, or get lymph node swellings that wouldn't reduce, and if you didn't have to try to play nursemaid.

Now and then Nelsen was in Pallastown — for business, for relief, for a bit of hell-raising; to see Gimp and the David Lesters. Pretty soon there was an heir in the Lester household. Red, healthy, and male. Cripes — Out Here, too? Okay — josh the parents along. The most wonderful boy in the solar system! Otherwise, matters, there, were much better than before. The camera was in a museum in Washington. The pictures it had contained were on TV, back home. Just another anti-war film, maybe. But impressive, and *different*. The earnings didn't change Nelsen's life much, nor Gimp's, nor Ramos'. But it sure helped the Lesters.

David Lester had resigned from Archeological Survey. He was getting actually sharp. He was doing independent research, and was setting up his own business in Belt antiques.

Frank Nelsen had another reason for coming to Pallastown. Afield, you avoided beam communication, nowadays, whenever you could. Someone might trace your beam to its source, and jump you for whatever you had. But Gimp Hines could tell Nelsen about the absent Bunch members and the old friends, while they both sat in the little KRNH office in Town.

" . . . Paul Hendricks is still the same, Frank. New bunch around him . . . Too bad we can't call him, now — because the Earth is on the far side of the sun. Mitch Storey just vanished into the Martian thickets, during one of his jaunts. Almost a year ago, now . . . I didn't see him when I stopped over on Mars, but he was back at the Station once, after that. Take it easy, Frank. They've looked with helicopters, and even on the ground; you couldn't do any more. I'll keep in touch, to see if anything turns up . . ."

After a minute, Nelsen relaxed, slightly. "Two-and-Two? I guess he's okay — with Charlie Reynolds looking after him?"

"Peculiar about Charlie," Gimp answered, looking awed and puzzled. "Got the news from old J. John, his granddad, when he acknowledged the receipt of our latest draft, by letter. Hold your hat. Charlie got himself killed . . . I'll dig the letter out of the file."

Nelsen sat up very straight. "Never mind," he said. "Just tell me more. Anything can happen."

"Our most promising member," Gimp mused. "He didn't get much. The Venus Expedition had to move some heavy equipment to the top of a mountain, to make some electrostatic tests before a storm. Charlie had just climbed down from the helicopter. A common old lightning bolt hit him. Somebody played *Fire Streak* on the bagpipes — inside a sealed tent — while they buried him. Otherwise, he didn't even get a proper spaceman's funeral. Venus' escape velocity is almost as high as Earth's. Boosting a corpse up into orbit, just for atmospheric cremation, would have been too much of a waste for the Expedition's rigid economy."

Nelsen had never really been very close to Charlie Reynolds, though he had liked the flamboyant Good Guy. Now, it was all a long ways back, besides. Nelsen didn't feel exactly grief. Just an almost mystical bitterness, a shock and an uncertainty, as if he could depend on nothing.

"So what about Two-and-Two?" he growled, remembering how he used to avoid any responsibility for the big, good-hearted lug; but now he felt surer about himself, and things seemed different.

"I guess the Expedition medic had to straighten him out with devil-killers," Hines answered. "He bubbed all the way back to Earth, alone, to see J. John about Charlie. I beamed him, there, before the Earth hid behind the sun. He was still pretty shaken up. Funny, too — Charlie's opportunity-laden Venus has turned out to be a bust, for two centuries, at least, unless new methods, which aren't in sight, yet, turn up. Sure — at staggering expense, and with efforts on the order of fantasy, reaction motors could be set up around its equator, to make it spin as fast as the Earth. Specially developed green algae have already been seeded all over the planet. They're rugged, they spread fast. But it will take the algae about two hundred years to split the carbon dioxide and give the atmosphere a breathable amount of free oxygen, to say nothing of cracking the poisonous formaldehyde."

"Two-and-Two's back in Jarviston, then?" Nelsen demanded.

"No — not anymore — just gimme breath," Hines went on. "He and Charlie had figured another destination of opportunity — Mercury, the planet nearest the sun, everlasting frozen night on one side, eternal, zinc-melting sunshine on the other. But there's the fringe zone between the two — the Twilight Zone. If you can live under stellene, you've got a better place there than Mars might have been. Colonists are going there, to quit the Earth, to get away from it all. Two-and-Two was about to leave for Mercury, when I last spoke to him. By now he's probably almost there. And even under the most favorable conditions, Mercury is hard to beam — too much solar magnetic interference."

"That poor sap," Nelsen gruffed.

"It probably isn't that bad, anymore," Hines commented. "Sometime I might go to Mercury, myself — when I get good and sick of sitting on my tail, here — when I always was a man of action! Mercury does have possibilities — plenty of solar power, certainly; plenty of frozen atmosphere on the dark face. Interesting, Frank . . .

Oh, hell, I forgot — there's a letter here for you. And a package. Just arrived . . . I'll scram, now. Got to go down to the quays. Hold the fort, here, will you?"

Gimp Hines grinned as he left.

Nelsen was glad to be alone. The lonesomeness of the Big Vacuum was getting grimed into him. When he saw the return name and address on the package, and the two hundred-ten dollar postage sticker, he thought, *Cripes — that poor kid — what did I start?* Then the awful wave of nostalgia for Jarviston, Minnesota, hit him, as he fumbled to open the microfilmed letter capsule, and put it in the viewer.

"Hello, Frank — it has to be that, doesn't it, and not Mr. Nelsen, since you've sent me this miraculous bracelet — which I don't dare wear very much, since I don't want to lose an arm to some international — or even interstellar — jewel thief! It makes me feel like the Queen of Something — certainly not Serene, since it implies calmness and repose, which I certainly don't feel — no offense to our Miss Sands, whom I admire enormously. In a very small way I am repaying to you in kind — an item which I made, myself, and which I know that some spacemen use inside their Archers. You see, we are all informed in details. Paul, Otto, Chippie Potter and his dog, and other characters whom you won't remember, send their best greetings. Oh, I've got Stardust fever, too, but I'll yield to my folks' wishes and wait, and learn a profession that will be of some use Out There. May you wear what I'm sending in good health, safety and fortune. Send no more staggering gifts, please — I couldn't stand it — but please do write. Tell me how it really is in the Belt. You simply don't realize how much — "

Nance Codiss' missive rattled along, and the scrawled words got to be like small, happy bells inside Nelsen's skull. His crooked grin came out; he unpacked the sweater — creylon wool, very warm, bright red, a bit crude in workmanship here and there — but imagine a girl bothering, these days! He donned the garment and decided it fit fine.

Then he tried to write a letter:

"Hi, Nance! I've just put it on — first time — beautiful! It'll stay right with me. Thanks. Talk about being staggered . . ."

There he bogged down, some, wondering how much she had changed, wondering just what he ought to say to her, and who these characters that he wouldn't remember, might be. Cripes, how old was she, now? Seventeen? He ended up taking her at her word. He described Pallastown rather heavy-handedly, and bought some microfilm postcards to go along with his missive, as soon as he went out to mail it.

But a few hours later, from deep in space, he looked back at the Town, shining in the distance, and in the blue mood of thinking about Charlie Reynolds, Mitch Storey, and Two-and-Two, he wondered how much longer it, or Nance, or anything else, could last. Then he glanced down at the bright sweater, and chuckled . . .

Unexpectedly, Ramos remained an active member of KRNH Enterprises for over a year. But the end had to come. "I told Art I'd let my dough ride, Frank," he said to Nelsen in the lounge of Post One. "I'll only draw enough earnings to build me a real, deep-space bubb, nuclear-propelled, and with certain extra gadgets. A few guys have tried to follow the unmanned, instrumented rockets, out to the system of Saturn. Nobody got back, yet. I think I know what they figured wrong. The instruments showed — well, skip it . . . I'm going into Town to prepare. It'll take quite a while, so I'll have some fun, too."

Ramos' eyes twinkled with a secret triumph — before the fact.

"You don't argue a fighting rooster out of fighting," Nelsen laughed. "Besides, it wouldn't be Destiny — or any fun — to succeed. So accept the complimentary comparison — if it fits — which maybe it doesn't, you egotistical bonehead. Good luck — *buena suerte, amigo*. I'll look you up in Town, if I get a chance . . ."

Nelsen was always busy to the gills. Progress was so smooth for another couple of years, that the hunch of Big Trouble building up, became a gnawing certainty in his nerves.

Of course there were always the Jolly Lads to watch out for — the extreme individualists, space-twisted and wild. Robbing and murdering could seem easier than digging. Take your loot into Pallastown — who knew you hadn't grubbed it, yourself? Sell it. Get the stink blown off you — forget some terrible things that had happened to you. Have yourself a time. Strike Out again. Repeat . . .

Nelsen knew that, through the months, he had killed defensively at least twice. Once, with a long-range homing bullet — weapons sanctioned by pious and cautious international agreement, were more lethal, now, to match the weapons of the predatory. Once by splitting a helmet with a rifle barrel. When he was out alone, exploring a new post site on a small asteroid, a starved Tovie runaway had jumped him. Maybe he should regret the end of that incident.

Trips to Pallastown were increasingly infrequent. But there was one time when he almost had come specially to see Ramos' new bubb, still under wraps, supposedly. Well — that erratic character had it out on a long test run. Damn him! As usual, time was crowding Nelsen. He had to get back on the job. He had just a couple of hours left.

He wrote a letter to Nance Codiss, answering one of hers — funny, he'd never yet tried to contact her vocally. Being busy, being cautious about using a beam — these were good reasons. Now there was hardly enough spare time to reach twice across the light-minutes. Maybe the real truth was that men got strangely shy in the silences of the Belt.

"Dear Nance: You seem to be making fine headway in your new courses. All the good words, for that . . ."

There were plenty of good words, but he didn't put many of them down. He didn't know if the impulse to write *Darling*, was just his own loneliness, which any girl with a kind word would have filled. He didn't know her, or that part of himself, very well. He kept remembering her as she had been. Then he'd realize that memory wasn't a stable thing to hang onto. Everything changed — how well he had learned that! She was older, now, intelligent, and at school again, studying some kind of medical laboratory technology. Certainly she had become more sophisticated and elusive — her gay letters were just a superficial part of what she must be. And certainly there were dates and boyfriends, and all the usual phases of getting out of step with a mere recollection, like himself. Nelsen had some achy emotions. Should he ask for her picture? Should he send one of himself?

He just scribbled on, ramblingly, as usual. Yep, in a new Archer Seven, you could undo a few clamps, pull a foot up out of a boot, and actually change your socks . . . Inconsequential nonsense like that. He ended by telling her not to worry about any knicknacks he might send — that they came easy, out here. He microposted the letter, and mailed a square of soft glass-silk of many colors.

Then he pronounced a few cuss words, laughed at himself for getting so serious, shrugged, and with the casualness of hopper with his pockets loaded, moved toward the rec area, which was some distance off.

It was night over this part of rapidly growing Pallastown. Moving along a lighted causeway, he saw the man with the shovel teeth. Glory, had *he* managed to survive so long? His mere presence, here, seemed like a signal of the end of peace. Nelsen and Ramos used to practice close-contact tactics at zero-G, in space. So Nelsen didn't even wait for the man to notice him. He leaped, and sped like an arrow, thudding into the guy's stomach with both of his boot heels. Shovel Teeth was hurled fifty yards backward, Nelsen hurtling with him all the way. Unless Nelsen wanted to kill him, there wasn't any more to do. Partial revenge.

He wasn't worried about anybody except the guy's Jolly Lad henchmen. There was nobody close by. Now he did a quick fade, sure that nobody had seen who he was, during the entire episode. No use to call the cops — there were too many uncertainties about the setup in wild, polyglot Pallastown. Nelsen moved on to the rec area.

He didn't go into a garishly splendid place, named *The Second Stop*. Thus, he didn't see its owner, whose identity he had already heard about, of course. Not that he wouldn't have liked to. But there wasn't any time to get involved in a long chat with a woman . . . Nor did he see the tall, skinny, horse-faced comic, known only as Igor, go through slapstick acrobatics that once would have been impossible . . .

By a round-about route he proceeded to the catapults, where Gimp Hines was waiting for him. They had been conversing just a short while ago.

"Did you drop in on Eileen?" Gimp asked right away.

"No. There'll be other occasions," Nelsen laughed. "Someday, if we live, she'll own all the joints in the solar system."

"Uh-huh — I'd bet on it . . . By the way, there's a grapevine yarn around. Somebody kicked Fanshaw — the Jolly Lad big-shot — in the belly. You, perhaps?"

"Don't listen to gossip," Nelsen said primly. "Are you serious about going to Mercury?"

"Of course. There are people to take over my office duties. I'll be on my way in a couple of weeks. I think you'd like to come along, Frank."

Nelsen felt an urge that was like a crying for freedom.

"Sure I would. But I'm bound to the wheel. Cripes, though — watch yourself, fella. Don't *you* get into a mess!"

"Hell — you're the mess specialist, Frank. Fanshaw isn't here for fun. And there's been that new trouble at home . . ."

A Tovie bubb, loaded with people, and a Stateside bubb, both in orbit around the Earth, had collided. No survivors. But there was plenty of blaming and counter-blaming. Another dangerous incident. Glory — with all the massed destructive power there was, could luck really last forever?

Frank Nelsen got back to Post One, okay. But later, riding in to Post Three, just in an Archer Six, with a couple of guards for company, he picked up a long-lost voice, falsely sweet, then savage at the end:

"I'm a Jinx, aren't I, Frankie? A vulture. Nice and cavalier, you are. I bet you hoped I was dead. Okay — Sucker . . . !"

Tiflin didn't even answer when Nelsen tried to beam him.

Nelsen was able to save Post Three. The guards and most of the personnel were experienced and tough. They drove the Jolly Lads back and deflected some chunks of aimed and accelerated asteroid chips, with new defense rockets.

Joe Kuzak, at Post Seven, wasn't so lucky, though Frank had tipped him off. Half of the post was scattered and pirated. Six fellas and the wife of one of them — a Bunch from Baltimore — were just drying shreds that drifted in the wreckage. Big Joe, though he had a rocket chip through his chest, had been able to beat off the attackers, with the help of a few asteroid-hoppers and his novice crew which turned out to be more rugged than some people might have expected.

Frank got to them just as it was over — except for the cursing, the masculine tears of grief and rage, the promises of revenge. Luckily, none of the women had been captured.

Joe Kuzak, full of new antibiotics and coagulants, was still up and around. "So we knocked off a few of them, Frank," he said ruefully in his office bubb. "Several were in Tovie armor. Runaways, or agents? They're crowding us, boy. Hell, what a junk heap this post is going to be, to sort out . . ."

"Get to it," Nelsen commented.

"You've got something in mind?"

"Uh-huh. Coming in, I heard somebody address somebody else as Fan. Fanshaw, that would be. And I kind of remembered his voice, as he cracked out orders. He was with this group. I'm going after him."

"Good night . . . ! I'll send some of my crowd along."

"Nope, Joe. They'd spot two or more guys. One, they won't even believe in. This is a lone-wolf deal. Besides, it's personal . . . Shucks — I don't even think there's a risk . . ."

There, he knew he exaggerated — especially as, huddled up to resemble a small asteroid-fragment, he followed the retreating specks. His only weapon was a rapid-fire launcher, using small rockets loaded only with chemical explosive. He felt a tingle all through him. Scare, all right.

Ahead, as he expected, he saw three stolen bubbs blossom out. There'd be a real pirates' party, like he'd seen, once. They'd have a lookout posted, of course. But the enormity of the Belt made them cocky. Who could ever really police very much of it? One other advantage was that Jolly Lads were untidy. Around the distant bubbs floated a haze of jettisoned refuse. Boxes, wrappings, shreds of stellene. Nelsen had figured on that.

Decelerating, he draped a sheet of synthetic cellulose that he'd brought along, loosely over his armored shape. Then he drifted unobtrusively close. At a half-mile distance, he peered through the telescope sight of his launcher. The bubbs were close together. The lookout floated free. Him, he got first, with a careful, homing shot.

Immediately he fired a burst into each bubb, saw them collapse around their human contents. The men inside were like cats in limp bags, the exits of which could no longer be found. Calmly he picked the biggest lumps of struggling forms, and fired again and again, until there was no more motion left except an even rotation.

He soon located Fanshaw. His unarmored body was bloated and drying, his mouth gaped, his shovel teeth were exposed to the stars and the distant, naked sun. Nelsen had to think back to six dead young men and a girl, to keep from feeling lousy. Had Fanshaw been just another guy invading a region that was too big and terrible for humans?

With something like dread, Nelsen looked for Tiflin, too. But, of course, that worthy wasn't around.

Nelsen picked up some space-fitness cards. Quite a few nations were represented. Joe would have to turn in the cards to the respective authorities. Noting its drift course, Nelsen left the wreckage, and hurried back to Post Seven, before other Jolly Lads could catch up and avenge their pals.

"Fanshaw's groups will fight it out for a new leader, Joe," he said. "That should keep them busy, for a while . . ."

Succeeding months were quieter. But the Tovies had lost no advantage. They had Ceres, the biggest of the asteroids, and their colonies were moving in on more and more others that were still untouched, closing them, against all agreements, to any competition.

The new Archer Seven which Nelsen presently acquired, had a miniature TV screen set in its collar. Afield, he was able to pick up propaganda broadcasts from Ceres. They showed neat, orderly quarters, good food, good facilities, everything done by command and plan. He wondered glumly if that was better for men who were pitted against space. The rigid discipline sheltered them. They didn't have to think in a medium that might be too huge for their brains and emotions. Maybe it was more practical than rough-and-tumble individualism. He had a bitter picture of the whole solar system without a free mind in its whole extent — that is, if another gigantic blowup didn't happen first . . .

Nelsen didn't see Ramos' new bubb, nor did he see him leave

for Saturn and its moons. The guy had avoided him, and gone secretive. But over a year later, the news reached Nelsen at Post Eight. A man named Miguel Ramos had got back, more dead than alive, after a successful venture, alone, to the immediate vicinity of the Ringed Planet. His vehicle was riddled. He was in a Pallastown hospital.

Frank Nelsen delegated his duties, and went to see Ramos. The guy seemed hardly more than half-conscious. He had no hands left. His legs were off at the knee. Frostbite. Only the new antibiotics he had taken along, had kept the gangrene from killing him. There was a light safety belt across his bed. But somehow he knew Nelsen. And his achievement seemed like a mechanical record fixed in his mind.

"Hi, Frank," he whispered hurriedly. "I figured it right. Out there, near Saturn, clusters of particles of frozen methane gas are floating free like tiny meteors. The instrumented rockets didn't run into them, and they were too light to show clearly on radar. But a bubb with a man in it is lots bigger, and can be hit and made like a sieve. That's what happened to those who went first. Their Archers were pierced too. I had mine specially armored, with a heavy helmet and body plating . . . The particles just got my gloves and my legs. Cripes, I got pictures — right from the rim of the Rings! And lots of data . . ."

Ramos showed the shadow of a reckless grin of triumph. Then he passed out.

Later, Nelsen saw the photographs, and the refrigerated box with the clear, plastic sides. Inside it was what looked like dirty, granular snow — frozen water. Which was all it was. Unless the fact that it was also the substance of Saturn's Rings made a difference.

Saturn — another of the great, cold, largely gaseous planets, where it would perhaps always be utterly futile for a man to try to land . . . Ramos, the little Mex who chased the girls. Ramos, the hero, the historical figure, now . . .

Cursing under his breath, Nelsen wandered vaguely to *The Second Stop*. There, he saw what probably every spaceman had dreamed of. Lucette of Paris swimming nude in a gigantic dew-drop — possible where gravity was almost nil. Music played. Beams of colored light swung majestically, with prismatic effects through the great, flattened, shimmering ovoid of water, while Lucette's motions completed a beautiful legend . . .

Two figures moved past Nelsen in the darkened interior. The first one was tall and lean. Then he saw the profile of a lean face with a bent nose, heard a mockingly apologetic "Oh-oh . . ." and didn't quite realize that this was Tiflin, the harbinger of misfortune, before it was too late to collar him. Nelsen followed as soon as he could push his way from the packed house. But pursuit was hopeless in the crowded causeway outside.

A few minutes later, he was in Eileen Sands' apartment. It was not his first visit. Eileen seldom danced or sang, anymore, herself. She was different, now. She wore an evening dress — soft blue, tasteful. Here, she was the cool, poised owner, the lady.

"Tiflin hasn't been around here for a long time, Frank," she was saying. "You know that his buddy entertained for me for a while. I have an interested nature, but Tiflin never gave me anything but wisecracks. There are lots of Tovies around — there's even a center for runaways. I don't ask questions of customers usually. And technically, all I can require of a comic is talent. This Igor had a certain kind. What is the difficulty now?"

Frank Nelsen looked at Eileen almost wearily for a second. "Just that Tiflin is somehow involved with most of the bad luck that I've ever had out here," he said, grimly. "And if Pallastown were destroyed, everybody but the Tovies might as well go home from the Belt. The timing seems to me to be about right. They'd risk it, feeling we're too scared to strike back at home. The Jolly Lads — who are international — could be encouraged to do the job for them."

Sudden hollows showed in Eileen's cheeks. "What are you going to do?" she asked.

"Nothing much for me to do," he answered. "I only happened to notice, while I was coming in to Pallas, that all the guard stations, extending way out, were quietly very alert. But is that enough? Well, if they can't cope with an attack, what good am I? We're vulnerable, here. I guess we just sit tight and wait."

She smiled faintly. "All right — let's. Sit, relax, converse. Stop being the Important Personage for a while, Frank."

"Look who's talking. Okay — what do you know that's new to tell?"

"A few things. I keep track of most everybody."

He took her slender hand, brown in his angular fist, that was pale from his space gloves. "Gimp, first," he said.

"Still on Mercury, with Two-and-Two. Two-and-Two was a bricklayer, a good beginning for a construction man. That seems to be paying off, as colonists move in. Gimp is setting up solar power stations."

"Encouraging information, for once. Here's a hard one — Jig Hollis. The real intelligent man who stayed home. I've envied him for years."

"Hmmm — yes, Frank. Intelligent, maybe — but he never quite believed it, himself. His wife stayed with him, even after he turned real sour and reckless. One night he hit a big oak tree with his car. Now, he is just as dead as if he had crashed into the sun at fifty miles per second. He couldn't take knowing that he was scared to do what he wanted."

"Hell!" Nelsen said flatly.

"Now who else should I gossip about?" Eileen questioned. "Oh, yes — Harv Diamond, hero of our lost youth, who got space fatigue. Well, he recovered and returned to active duty in the U.S.S.F. Which perhaps leaves me with just my own love life to confess." She smiled lightly. "Once there was a kid named Frankie Nelsen, who turned out to be a very conscientious jerk. Since then, there have been scads of rugged, romantic characters on all sides . . . You're going to ask about Miguel Ramos."

She paused, looked unhappy and tired. "The celebrity," she said. "Mashed up. But he'll recover — this time. I've seen him — sent him flowers, sat beside him. But what do you do with a clown like that? Lock him in the closet or look at him through a telescope? Goodbye — hello — goodbye. A kid with gaudy banners flying, if he lives to be forty — which he never will. They'll be giving him artificial hands and feet, and he'll be trying for Pluto. A friend. I guess I'm proud. That's all. Anything else you want to know?"

"Yeah. There was a cute little girl at Serene."

"Jennie Harper. She married one of those singing Moon prospectors. Somebody murdered them both — way out on Far Side."

Frank Nelsen's mouth twisted. "That's enough, pal," he said. "I better go do my sitting tight someplace else. Keep your Archer handy. Thanks, and see you . . ."

Within forty minutes David Lester was showing him some pictures that a hopper had brought in from a vault in a surface-asteroid.

On the screen, great, mottled shapes moved through a lush forest. Thousands of tiny, flitting bat-like creatures — miniature pterodactyls of the terrestrial Age of Reptiles   hovered over a swamp, where millions of insects hung like motes in the light of the low sun. A much larger pterodactyl, far above, glided gracefully over a cliff, and out to sea, its long, beaked head turning watchfully.

"Hey!" Nelsen said mildly, as his jaded mind responded.

Lester nodded. "*They* were on Earth, too — as the Martians must have been — exploring and taking pictures, during the Cretaceous Period. Oh, but there's a perhaps even better sequence! Like the Martians, they had a world-wrecking missile, which they were

building in space. Spherical. About six miles in diameter, I calcu-
late. Shall I show you?"

"No . . . I think I'll toddle over to the offices, Les. Keep wearing
those Archers, people. Glad the kid likes to play in his . . ."

Nelsen had donned his own Seven, with the helmet fastened
across his chest by a strap. At the KRNH office, there was a letter,
which luckily hadn't been sent out to Post Eight. The tone was more
serious than that of any that Nance Codiss had sent before.

"Dear Frank: I'm actually coming your way. I'll be stopping to
work at the Survey Station Hospital on Mars for two months en
route . . ."

He read that far when he heard the sirens and saw the flashes of
defending batteries that were trying to ward off missiles from Pallastown. He latched his helmet in place. He was headed for the
underground galleries when the first impacts came. He saw four
domes vanish in flashes of fire. Then he didn't run anymore. He
had his small rocket launcher, from the office. If they ever came
close enough . . . But of course they'd stay thousands of miles off.
He got to the nearest fallen dome as fast as he could. Everybody had
been in armor, but there were over a hundred dead. Emergency and
rescue crews were operating efficiently.

He glanced around for indications. No explosive, chemical or
nuclear, had yet been used. But there was the old Jolly Lad trick:
Accelerate a chunk of asteroid-material to a speed of several miles
per second by grasping it with your gloved hands, while the shoulder-ionic of your armor was at full power. Start at a great distance,
aim your missile with your body, let it go . . . Impact would be sheer,
blasting incandescence. A few hundred chunks of raw metal could
finish Pallastown . . . Were these just crazy, wild slobs whooping it
up, or real crud provided with a purpose and reward? Either way,
here was the eternal danger to any Belt settlement.

Nelsen could have tried to reach an escape-exit into open
space, but he helped with the injured while he waited for more
impacts to come. There was another series of deflecting flashes
from the defense batteries. Two more domes vanished . . . Then —
somehow — nothing more. Evidently some of the attackers had
been only half hearted, *this time*. Reprieve . . .

Almost four hundred people were dead. It could have been the
whole Town. Then spreading disaster. All Nelsen's friends were
okay. The Posts called in — okay, too. Nelsen waited three days. He
wanted to help defend, if the attack was renewed. But now the
U.N.S.F. was concentrating in the vicinity. For a while, things would
be quiet, Out Here. Just the same, he felt kind of fed up. He felt as if

the end of everything he knew had crept inevitably a little closer.

He beamed Mars — the Survey Station. He contacted Nance. He had known that she should have arrived already. He was relieved. He knew what the region between here and there could be like when there was trouble.

"It's me — Frank Nelsen — Nance," he said into his helmet-phone, as he stood beyond the outskirts of the Town, on the barren, glittering surface of Pallas. "I'm still wearing the sweater. Stay where you are. I've never been on Mars, either. But I'll be there, soon . . ."

His old uncertainties about talking to her evaporated now that he was doing it.

"For Pete's sake — Frank!" he heard her laugh happily, still sounding like the neighbor kid. "Gosh, it's good to hear you!"

He left for Post One, soon after that. Nowadays, it was almost a miniature of the ever more magnificent — if insecure — Pallastown. He kept thinking angrily of Art Kuzak, getting a little overstuffed, it seemed. The hunkie kid, the ex-football player who had become a big commercial and industrial baron of the Belt. Easy living. Cuties around. And poor twin Joe — just another stooge . . .

Nelsen went into the office, his fists clenched overdramatically. "I'm taking a leave, Art — maybe a long one," he said.

Art Kuzak stared at him. "You damned, independent bums — you, too, Nelsen!" he began to growl. But when he saw Nelsen's jaw harden, he got the point, and grinned, instead. "Okay, Frank. Nobody's indispensable. I might do the same when you come back — who knows . . . ?"

Frank Nelsen joined a KRNH bubb convoy — Earthbound, but also passing fairly close to Mars — within a few hours.

VII

Frank Nelsen meant the journey to be vagabond escape, an interlude of to hell with it relief from the grind, and from the increasingly uncertain mainstream of the things he knew best.

He rode with a long train of bubbs and great sheaves of smelted metal rods — tungsten, osmium, uranium 238. The sheaves had their own propelling ionic motors. He lazed like a tramp. He talked with asteroid-hoppers who meant to spend some time on Earth. Several had become almost rich. Most had strong, quiet faces that showed both distance- and home-hunger. A few had broken, and the angry sensitivity was visible.

Nelsen treated himself well. He was relieved of the duty of eternal vigilance by men whose job it was. So, for a while, his purpose was almost successful.

But the memory — or ghost — of Mitch Storey was never quite out of his mind. And, as a tiny, at first telescopic crescent with a rusty light enlarged with lessened distance ahead, the ugly enigma of present-day Mars dug deeper into his brain.

Every twenty-four hours and thirty-eight minutes — the length of the Martian day — whenever the blue-green wedge of Syrtis Major appeared in the crescent, he beamed the Survey Station, which was still maintained for the increase of knowledge, and as a safeguard for incautious adventurers who will tackle any dangerous mystery or obstacle. His object was to talk to Nance Codiss.

"I thought perhaps you and your group had gotten restless and had started out for the Belt already," he laughed during their first conversation.

"Oh, no — a lab technician like me is far too busy here, for one thing," she assured him, her happy tone bridging the distance. "We came this far with a well-armed freight caravan, in good passenger quarters. If we went on, I suppose it would be the same . . . Anyway, for years you didn't worry much about me. Why now, Frank?"

"A mystery," he teased in return. "Or perhaps because I considered Earth safe — instinctively."

But he was right in the first place. It *was* a mystery — something to do with the startling news that she was on the way, that closer friendship was pending. The impulse to go meet her had been his first, almost thoughtless impulse.

He was still glad that she wasn't out between Mars and the Belt, where disaster had once hit him hard. But now he wondered if the Survey Station was any better for anybody, even though it was reputed to be quite secure.

The caravan he rode approached his destination no closer than ten million miles. Taking cautious note of radar data which indicated that space all around was safely empty, he cast off in his Archer with a small, new, professional-type bubb packed across his hips. Inside his helmet he lighted a cigarette — quite an unusual luxury.

It took a long time to reach Phobos. They gave him shots there — new preventative medicine that was partially effective against the viruses of Mars. Descent in the winged rocket was rough. But then he was gliding with a sibilant whistle through a natural atmosphere, again. Within minutes he was at the Station — low, dusty domes, many of them deserted, now, at the edge of the airfield, a lazily-spinning wind gauge, tractors, auto-jeeps, several helicopters.

He stepped down with his gear. Mars was all around him: A few ground-clinging growths nearby — harmless, locally evolved vegetation. Distant, coppery cliffs reflecting the setting sun. Ancient excavations notched them. Dun desert to the east, with little plumes of dust blowing. Through his Archer — a necessary garment here not only because the atmosphere was only one-tenth as dense as Earth-air and poor in oxygen, but because of the microscopic dangers it bore — Nelsen could hear the faint sough of the wind.

The thirty-eight percent of terrestrial gravity actually seemed strong to him now, and made him awkward, as he turned and looked west. Perhaps two miles off, past a barbed-wire fence and what must be an old tractor trail of the hopeful days of colonization, he saw the blue-green edge of Syrtis Major, the greatest of the thickets, with here and there a jutting spur of it projecting toward him along a gully. Nelsen's hide tingled. But his first glimpse was handicapped by distance. He saw only an expanse of low shagginess that might have been scrub growths of any kind.

Dug into the salt-bearing ground at intervals, he knew, were the fire weapons ready to throw oxygen and synthetic napalm — jellied gasoline. Never yet had they been discharged, along this defense line. But you could never be sure just what might be necessary here.

A man of about thirty had approached. "I meet the new arrivals," he said. "If you'll come along with me, Mr. Nelsen . . ."

He was dark, and medium large, and he had a genial way. He looked like a hopper — an asteroid-miner — the tough, level-headed kind that adjusts to space and keeps his balance.

"Name's Ed Huth," he continued, as they walked to the reception dome. "Canadian. Good, international crowd here — however long you mean to stay. Most interesting frontier in the solar system, too. Probably you've heard most of the rules and advice. But here's a paper. Refresh your memory by reading it over as soon as you can. There is one thing which I am required to show everybody who comes here. Inside this peek box. You are instructed to take a good look."

Huth's geniality had vanished.

The metal box was a yard high, and twice as long and wide. It stood, like a memorial, before the reception dome entrance. A light shone beyond the glass-covered slot, as Nelsen bent to peer.

He had seen horror before now. He had seen a pink mist dissolve in the sunshine as a man in armor out in the Belt was hit by an explosive missile, his blood spraying and boiling. Besides, he had read up on the thickets of Mars, watched motion pictures, heard Gimp Hines' stories of his brief visit here. So, at first, he could be almost casual about what he saw in the peek box. There were many ghastly ways for a man to die.

Even the thicket plant in the box seemed dead, though Nelsen knew that plant successors to the original Martians had the rugged power of revival. This one showed the usual paper-dry whorls or leaves, and the usual barrel-body, perhaps common to arid country growths, everywhere. Scattered over the barrel, between the spines, were glinting specks — vegetable, light-sensitive cells developed into actual visual organs. The plant had the usual tympanic pods of its kind — a band of muscle-like tissue stretched across a hollow interior — by which it could make buzzing sounds. Nelsen knew that, like any Earthly green plant, it produced oxygen, but that, instead of releasing it, it stored the gas in spongy compartments within its horny shell, using it to support an animal-like tissue combustion to keep its vitals from freezing during the bitterly frigid nights.

Nelsen also knew that deeper within the thing was a network of whitish pulp, expanded at intervals to form little knobs. Sectioned, under a microscope, they would look like fibred masses of animal or human nerve and brain cells, except that, chemically, they were starch and cellulose rather than protein.

Worst to see was the rigid clutch of monster's tactile organs, which grew from the barrel's crown. It was like a powerful man struggling to uproot a rock, or a bear or an octopus crushing an enemy. It was dark-hole drama, like something from another galaxy. Like some horribly effective piece of sculpture, the tableau in the box preserved the last gasp of an incautious youth in armor.

The tendrils of the thicket plant were furred with erect spines of a shiny, russet color. They were so fine that they looked almost soft. But Nelsen was aware that they were sharper than the hypodermic needles they resembled — in another approach to science. Now, Nelsen felt the tingling revulsion and hatred.

"Of course you know that you don't have to get caught like that poor bloke did," Huth said dryly. "Just not to disinfect the outside of your Archer well enough and then leave it near you, indoors, is sufficient. I was here before there was any trouble. When it came, it was a shambles . . ."

Huth eyed Nelsen for a moment, then continued on another tack. "Biology . . . Given the whole universe to experiment in, I suppose you can never know what it will come up with — or what is possible. These devils — you get to hate them in your sleep. If their flesh — or their methods — were something like ours, as was the case with the original Martians or the people of the Asteroid Planet, it wouldn't seem so bad. Still, they make you wonder: What would you do, if, in your own way, you could think and observe, but were rooted to the ground; if you were denied the animal ability of rapid motion, if you didn't have hands with which to fashion tools or build apparatus, if fire was something you could scarcely use? . . ."

Nelsen smiled. "I *am* wondering," he said. "I promise to do a lot more of it as soon as I get squared away. I could inflate my bubb, and sleep in the yard in it, if I had to. Then, as usual, off the Earth, you'll expect me to earn my breathing air and keep, after a couple of days, whether I can pay instead or not. That's fine with me, of course. There's another matter which I'd like to discuss, but that can be later."

"No sleeping out," Huth laughed. "That's just where people get careless. There are plenty of quarters available since the retreat of settlers almost emptied this world of terrestrial intrusion — except for us here and the die-hard desert rats, and the new, screwball adventurers . . . By the way, if it ever becomes important, the deserts are safe — at least from what you just saw — as you probably know . . ."

Nelsen passed through an airlock, where live steam and a special silicone oil accomplished the all-important disinfection of his Archer, his bubb, and the outside of his small, sealed baggage roll. Armor and bubb he left racked with rows of others.

It wasn't till he got into the reception dome lounge that he saw Nance Codiss. She didn't rush at him. Reserve had dropped over them both again as if in reconsideration of a contact made important too suddenly. He clasped her fingers, then just stood looking at her. Lately, they had exchanged a few pictures.

"Your photographs don't lie, Nance," he said at last.

"Yours do, Frank," she answered with complete poise. "You look a lot less grim and tired."

"Wait," he told her. "I'll be right back . . ."

He went with Ed Huth to ditch his roll in his sleeping cubicle, get cleaned up and change his clothes.

She *was* beautiful, she had grave moods, she was wearing his fabulous bracelet — if only not to offend him. But when he returned, he met two of the girls who had come out to Mars with her — a nurse and another lab technician. They were the bubbly type, full of bravado and giggles for their strange, new surroundings. For a moment he felt far too old at twenty-four for Nance's twenty. He wondered regretfully if her being here was no more than part of his excuse for getting away from the Belt and from the sense of ultimate human disaster building up.

But much of his feeling of separation from her disappeared as they sat alone in the lounge, talking — first about Jarviston, then about here. Nance had available information about the thickets pretty well down pat.

"You can't keep those plants alive here at the Station, Frank," she said quietly. "They make study difficult by dying. It's as if they knew that they couldn't win here. So they retreat — to keep their secrets. But Dr. Pacetti, our head of Medical Research, says that we can never know that they won't find a way to attack us directly. That's what the waiting napalm line is for. I don't think he is exaggerating."

"Why do you say that?" Nelsen asked.

He was encouraging her, of course. But he wasn't being patronizing. Frost tingled in his nerves. He wanted to know her version.

"I'll show you the little museum we have," she replied, her eyes widening slightly. "This is probably old hat to you — but it's weird — it gives you the creeps . . ."

He followed her along a covered causeway to another dome. In a gallery there, a series of dry specimens were set up, inside sealed boxes made of clear plastic.

The first display was centered around a tapered brass tube — perhaps one of the barrels of an antique pair of field glasses. Wrapping it was a spiny brown tendril from which grew two sucker-like organs, shaped like acorn tops. One was firmly attached to the metal. The other had been pulled free, its original position on the barrel marked by a circular area of corrosion. The face of the detached sucker was also shown — a honeycomb structure of waxy vegetable tissue, detailed with thousands of tiny ducts and hairlike feelers.

"Some settler dropped the piece of brass out on a trail in Syrtis Major," Nance explained. "Later, it was found like this. Brass is something that people have almost stopped using. So, it was new to *them*. They wouldn't have been interested in magnesium, aluminum, or stainless steel anymore. The suckers aren't a usual part of them either. But the suckers grow — for a special purpose, Dr. Pacetti believes. A test — perhaps an analysis. They exude an acid, to dissolve a little of the metal. It's like a human chemist working. Only, perhaps, better — more directly — with specialized feelers and sensing organs."

Nance's quiet voice had a slight, awed quaver at the end.

Frank Nelsen nodded. He had examined printed pictures and data before this. But here the impact was far more real and immediate; the impact of strange minds with an approach of their own was more emphatic.

"What else?" he urged.

They stood before another sealed case containing a horny, oval pod, cut open. It had closed around a lump of greenish stone.

"Malachite," Nance breathed. "One kind of copper ore. *They* reduced it, extracted some of the pure metal. See all the little reddish specks shining? It is pretty well established that the process is something like electroplating. There's a dissolving acid — then a weak electric current — from a kind of battery . . . Oh, nobody should laugh, Frank — Dr. Pacetti keeps pointing out that there are electric eels on Earth, with specialized muscle-tissue that acts as an electric cell . . . But this is somewhat different. Don't ask me exactly how it functions — I only heard our orientation lecture, while we toured this museum. But see those small compartments in the thick shells of the pod — with the membranes separating them? All of them contained fluids — some acid, others alkaline. Mixed in with the cellulose of the membranes, you can see both silvery and reddish specks — as if *they* had to incorporate both a conductor and a difference of metals to get a current. At least, that was what was suggested in the lecture . . ."

Frank Nelsen and Nance Codiss moved on from display case to display case, each of which showed another kind of pod cut in half. The interiors were all different and all complicated . . . Membranes with a faint, metallic sheen — laminated or separated by narrow air spaces as in a capacitor, for instance . . . Balls of massed fibre, glinting . . . Curious, spiral formations of waxy tissue . . .

"They use electricity as a minor kind of defense," Nance went on, her tone still low with suppressed excitement that was close to dread. "We know that some of them can give you a shock — if you're fool enough to get so close that you can touch them. And they do emit radio impulses on certain wavelengths. Signals — communication . . . ? As for the rest, perhaps you'd better do your own guessing, Frank. But the difference between us and them seems to be that we *make* our apparatus. They *grow* them, *build* them — with their own living tissue cells — in a way that must be under their constant, precise control. I suppose they even work from a carefully thought-out design — a kind of cryptic blue-print . . . Go along with the idea — or not — as you choose. But our experts suspect that much of what we have here represents research apparatus — physical, chemical, electrical. That *they* may get closer to understanding the ultimate structure of matter than we can, because their equipment is part of themselves, in which they can develop senses that we don't possess . . . Well, I'll skip any more of that. Because the best — or the worst — is still coming. Right here, Frank . . ."

The case showed several small, urn-like growths, sectioned like the other specimens.

Frank Nelsen grinned slightly. "All right — let me tell it," he said. "Because this is something I really paid attention to! Like you imply, their equipment is alive. So they work best with life — viruses, germs, vegetable-allergy substances. These are their in-venting, developing and brewing bottles — for the numerous strains of Syrtis Fever virus. The living molecule chains split off from the inner tissue walls of the bottles, and grow and multiply in the free fluid. At least, that's how I read it."

"And that is where my lab job begins, Frank," she told him. "Helping develop anti-virus shots — testing them on bits of human tissue, growing in a culture bath. An even partially effective anti-virus isn't found easily. And when it is, another virus strain will soon appear, and the doctors have to start over . . . Oh, the need isn't as great, any more, as when the Great Rush away from Mars was on. There are only half a dozen really sick people in the hospital now. Late comers and snoopers who got careless or curious. You've got to remember that the virus blows off the thickets like invisible vapor. There's one guy from Idaho — Jimmy — James Scanlon. Come along. I'll show you, Frank . . ."

He lay behind plastic glass, in a small cubicle. A red rash, with the pattern of frostwork on a Minnesota windowpane in January, was across his lean, handsome face. Maybe he was twenty — Nance's age. His bloodshot eyes stared at terrors that no one else could see.

Nance called softly through the thin infection barrier. "Jimmy!" He moaned a little. "Francy . . ."

"High fever, Frank," Nance whispered. "Typical Syrtis. He wants to be home — with his girl. I guess you know that nostalgia — yearning terribly for old, familiar surroundings — is a major symptom. It's like a command from *them* — to get out of Mars. The red rash is something extra he picked up. An allergy . . . Oh, we think he'll survive. Half of them now do. He's big and strong. Right now, even the nurses don't go in there, except in costumes that are as infection-tight as armor. Later on, when the fever dwindles to chronic intermittence, it will no longer be contagious. Even so, the new laws on Earth won't let him return there for a year. I don't know whether such laws are fair or not. We've got a hundred here, who were sick, and are now stranded and waiting, working at small jobs. Others have gone to the Belt — which seems terrible for someone not quite well. I hope that Jimmy bears up all right — he's such a kid . . . Let's get out of here . . ."

Her expression was gently maternal. Or maybe it was something more?

Back in the lounge, she asked, "What will you do here, Frank?"

"Whatever it is, there is one thing I want to include," he answered. "I want to try to find out just what happened to Mitch Storey."

"Natch. I remember him. So I looked the incident up. He disappeared, deep in Syrtis Major, over three years ago. He had carried a sick settler in — on foot. He always seemed lucky or careful, or smart. After he got lost, his wife — a nurse from here whose name had been Selma Washington — went looking for him. She never was found either."

"Oh?" Nelsen said in mild startlement.

"Yes . . . Talk to Ed Huth. There still are helicopter patrols — watching for signs of a long list of missing people, and keeping tabs on late comers who might turn out to be screwballs. You look as though you might be Ed's type for that kind of work . . . I'll have to go, now, Frank. Duty in half an hour . . ."

Huth was grinning at him a little later. "This department doesn't like men who have a vanished friend, Nelsen," he said. "It makes their approach too heroically personal. On the other hand, some of our lads seem underzealous, nowadays . . . If you can live up to your successful record in the Belt, maybe you're the right balance. Let's try you."

For a week, about all Nelsen did was ride along with Huth in the heli. At intervals, he'd call, "Mitch . . . Mitch Storey . . . !" into his helmet-phone. But, of course, that was no use.

He couldn't say that he didn't see Mars — from a safe altitude of two thousand feet: The vast, empty deserts where, fairly safe from the present dominant form of Martian life, a few adventurers and archeologists still rummaged among the rust heaps of climate control and other machines, and among the blasted debris of glazed ceramic cities — still faintly tainted with radioactivity — where the original inhabitants had died. The straight ribbons of thicket growths, crossing even the deserts, carrying in their joined, hollow roots the irrigation water of the otherwise mythical "canals." The huge south polar cap of hoarfrost melting, blackening the soil with brief moisture, while the frost line retreated toward the highlands. Syrtis, itself, where the trails, once burned out with oxygen and gasoline-jelly to permit the passage of vehicles, had again become completely overgrown — who could hope to stamp out that devilishly hardy vegetation, propagating by means of millions of windblown spores, with mere fire? The broken-down trains of tractors and trailers, now almost hidden. The stellene garden domes that had flattened. Here were the relics left by people who had sought to spread out to safety, to find old goals of freedom from fear.

Several times in Syrtis, Huth and Nelsen descended, using a barren hillock or an isolated spot of desert as a landing area. That was when Nelsen first heard the buzzing of the growths.

Twice, working warily with machetes, and holding their flame weapons ready, they chopped armored mummies from enwrapping tendrils, while little eye cells glinted at them balefully, and other tendrils bent slowly toward them. They searched out the space-fitness cards, which bore old dates, and addresses of next of kin.

In a few more days, Nelsen was flying the 'copter. Then he was out on his own, watching, searching. For a couple of weeks he hangared the heli at once, after each patrol, and Nance always was there to meet him as he did so.

Inevitably the evening came when he said, "We could fly out again, Nance. For an hour or two. It doesn't break any rules."

Those evening rides, high over Syrtis Major, toward the setting sun, became an every other day custom, harmless in itself. A carefully kept nuclear-battery motor didn't conk; the vehicle could almost fly without guidance. It was good to look down at the blue-green shagginess, below . . . Familiarity bred, not contempt, but a decline of dread to the point where it became a pleasant thrill — an overtone to the process of falling in love. Otherwise, perhaps they led each other on, into incaution. Out in the lonely fastnesses of Mars they seemed to find the sort of peace and separation from danger on the hectic Earth that the settlers had sought here.

"We always pass over that same hill," Nance said during one of their flights. "It must have been a beautiful little island in the ancient ocean, when there was that much water. Now it belongs to us, Frank."

"It's barren — we could land," Nelsen suggested quickly.

They visited the hill a dozen times safely, breaking no printed rule. But maybe they shouldn't have come so often to that same place. In life there is always a risk — which is food for a fierce soul. Frank Nelsen and Nance Codiss were fierce souls.

They'd stand by the heli and look out over Syrtis, their gloved fingers entwined. If they couldn't kiss, here, through their helmets, that was merely comic pathos — another thing to laugh and be happy over.

"Our wind-blown hill," Nance chuckled on that last evening. "Looking down over a culture, a history — maybe arguments, lawsuits, jokes, parties; gossip too, for all we know — disguised as a huge briar patch that makes funny noises."

"Shut up — I love you," Nelsen gruffed.

"Shut up yourself — it's you I love," she answered.

The little sun was half sunk behind the Horizon. The 'copter was only a hundred feet away, along the hillcrest. That was when it happened. Two dull, plopping sounds came almost together.

If a thinking animal can use the pressure of a confined gas to propel small missiles, is there any reason why other intelligences can't do the same? From two bottle-like pods the clusters of darts — or long, sharp thorns — were shot. Only a few of them struck their targets. Fewer, still, found puncturable areas and struck through silicone rubber and fine steelwire cloth into flesh. Penetration was not deep, but deep enough.

Nance screamed. Nelsen wasn't at all sure that he didn't scream himself as the first anguish dizzied and half blinded him.

From the start it was really too late. Nelsen was as hardy and determined as any. He tried to get Nance to the 'copter. Less than halfway, she crumpled. With a savage effort of will he managed to drag her a few yards, before his legs refused to obey him, or support him.

His blood carried a virus to his brain about as quickly as it would have carried a cobra's venom. *They* probably could have made such protein-poisons, too; but they had never used them against men, no doubt because something that could spread and infect others was better.

For a while, as the black, starshot night closed in, Nelsen knew, or remembered, nothing at all — unless the mental distortions were too horrible. Then he seemed to be in a pit of stinking, viscous fluid, alive with stringy unknowns that were boring into him . . . Unreachable in another universe was a town called Jarviston. He yelled till his wind was gone.

He had a half-lucid moment in which he knew it was night, and understood that he had a raging fever. He was still clinging to Nance, who clung to him. So instinct still worked. He saw that they had blundered — its black bulk was visible against the stars. Phobos hadn't risen; Deimos, the farther moon, was too small to furnish appreciable light.

Something touched him from behind, and he recoiled, pushing Nance back. He yanked the machete from his belt, and struck blindly . . . Oh, *no!* — you didn't get caught like this — not usually, he told himself. Not in their actual grip! They were too slow — you could always dodge! It was only when you were near something not properly disinfected that you got Syrtis Fever, which was the worst that could happen — wasn't it . . . ?

He heard an excited rhythm in the buzzing. Now he remembered his shoulder-lamp, fumbled to switch it on, failed, and stumbled a few steps with Nance toward the hill. Something caught his feet — then hers. Trying to get her free, he dropped his machete . . .

Huth's voice spoke in his helmet-phone. "We hear you, Nelsen! Hold out . . . We'll be there in forty minutes . . ."

Yeah — forty minutes.

"It's — it's silly to be so scared, Frankie . . ." he heard Nance stammer almost apologetically. Dear Nance . . .

Screaming, he kicked out again and again with his heavy boots, and got both her and himself loose.

It wasn't any good. A shape loomed near them. A thing that must have sprung from *them* — someway. A huge, zombie form — the ugliest part of this night of anguish and distortion. But he was sure that it was real.

The thing struck him in the stomach. Then there was a biting pain in his shoulder . . .

There wasn't any more, just then. But this wasn't quite the end, either. The jangled impressions were like split threads of consciousness, misery-wracked and tenuous. They were widely separated. His brain seemed to crack into a million needle-pointed shards, that made no sense except to indicate the passage of time. A month? A century . . . ?

It seemed that he was always struggling impossibly to get himself and Nance somewhere — out of hot, noisesome holes of suffocation, across deserts, up endless walls, and past buzzing sounds that were mixed incongruously with strange harmonica music that seemed to express all time and space . . . He could never succeed though the need was desperate. But sometimes there was a coolness answering his thirst, or rubbed into his burning skin, and he would seem to sleep . . . Often, voices told him things, but he always forgot . . .

It wasn't true that he came out of the hot fog suddenly, but it seemed that he did. He was sitting in dappled sunshine in an ordinary lawn chair of tubular magnesium with a back and bottom of gaudy fabric. Above him was a narrow, sealed roof of stellene. The stone walls showed the beady fossils of prehistoric Mars. More than probably, these chambers had been cut in the living rock, by the ancients.

Reclining in another lawn chair beside his was Nance, her eyes closed, her face thin and pale. He was frightened — until he remembered, somehow, that she was nearly as well as he was. Beyond her was a doorway, leading into what seemed a small, modern kitchen. There was a passage to a small, neat garden, where Earthly vegetables and flowers grew. It was ceiled with stellene; its walls were solid rock. Looking up through the transparent roof above him, he saw how a thin mesh of fuzzy tendrils and whorls masked this strange Shangri-la.

Nelsen closed his eyes, and thought back. Now he remembered most of what he had been told. "Mitch!" he called quietly, so as not to awaken Nance. "Hey, Mitch . . . ! Selma . . . !"

Mitch Storey was there in a moment — dressed in dungarees and work shirt like he used to be, but taller, even leaner, and unsmiling.

Nelsen got up. "Thanks, Mitch," he said.

Their voices stayed low and intense.

"For nothing, Frank. I'm damned glad to see you, but you still shouldn't have come nosing. 'Cause — I told you why. Looking for you, Huth burned out more than five square miles. And if folks get too smart and too curious, it won't be any good for what's here . . ."

Nelsen felt angry and exasperated. But he had a haunting thought about a lanky colored kid in Jarviston, Minnesota. A guy with a dream — or perhaps a prescient glimpse of his own future.

"What's a pal supposed to do?" he growled. "For a helluva long time you've answered nobody — though everyone in the Bunch must have tried beaming you."

"Sure, Frank . . . Blame, from me, would be way out of line. I heard you guys lots of times. But it was best to get lost — maybe help keep the thickets like they are for as long as possible . . . A while back, I began picking up your voice in my phones again. I figured you were heading for trouble when you kept coming with your girl to that same hill. So I was around, like I told you before . . . Sorry I had to hit you and give you the needle, but you were nuts — gone with Syrtis. Getting you back here, without Huth spotting the old heli I picked up once at a deserted settlers' camp was real tough going. I had to land, hide it and wait, four or five times. And you were both plenty sick. But there are a few medical gimmicks I learned from the thickets — better than those at the Station."

"You've done all right for yourself here, haven't you, Mitch?" Nelsen remarked with a dash of mockery. "All the modern conveniences — in the middle of the forbidden wilds of Syrtis Major."

"Sure, Frank — 'cause maybe I'm selfish. Though it's just stuff the settlers left behind. Anyway, it wasn't so good at the start. I was careful, but I got the fever, too. Light. Then I fell — broke my leg — out there. I thought sure I was finished when they got hold of me. But I just lay there, playing on my mouth organ — an old hymn — inside my helmet. Maybe it was the music — they must have felt the radio impulses of my tooting before. Or else they knew, somehow, that I was on their side — that I figured they were too important just to disappear and that I meant to do anything I could, short of killing, to keep them all right . . . Nope, I wouldn't say that they were so friendly, but they might have thought I'd be useful — a guinea-pig to study and otherwise. For all I know, examining my body may have helped them improve their weapons . . . Anyhow — you won't believe this — 'cause it's sort of fantastic — but you know they work best with living tissue. They fixed that leg, bound it tight with tendrils, went through the steel cloth of my Archer with hollow thorns. The bone knit almost completely in four days. And the fever broke. Then they let me go. Selma was already out looking for me. When I found her, she had the fever, too. But I guess we're immune now."

Storey's quiet voice died away.

"What are you going to do, Mitch? Just stay here for good?"

"What else — if I can? This is better than anything I remember. Peaceful, too. If they study me, I study them — not like a real scientist — but by just having them close around. I even got to know some of their buzzing talk. Maybe I'll have to be their ambassador to human folks, sometime. They *are* from the planets of the stars, Frank. Sirius, I think. Tough little spores can be ejected from one atmosphere, and drift in space for millions of years . . . They arrived after the first Martians were extinct. Now that you're here, Frank, I wish you'd stay. But that's no good. Somebody lost always makes people poke around."

Nelsen might have argued a few points. But for one thing, he felt too tired. "I'll buy it all, your way, Mitch," he said. "I hope Nance and I can get out of here in a couple more days. Maybe I shouldn't have run out on the Belt. Can't run — thoughts follow you. But now — damn it — I want to go home!"

"That's regular, Frank. 'Cause you've got Syrtis. Chronic, now — intermittent. But it'll fade. Same with your girl. Meanwhile, they won't let you go Earthside, but you'll be okay. I'll fly you out, close enough to the Station to get back, any morning before daylight, that you pick . . . Only, you won't tell, will you, Frank?"

"No — I promise — if you think secrecy makes any difference. Otherwise — thanks for everything . . . By the way — do you ever listen in on outside news?"

"Enough. Still quiet . . . And a fella named Miguel Ramos — with nerve-controlled clamps for hands — got a new, special bubb and took off for Pluto."

"No! Damn fool . . . Almost as loony as you are, Mitch."

"Less . . . Wake up, Nance. Dinner . . . Chicken — raised right here . . ."

That same afternoon, Frank Nelsen and Nance Codiss sat in the garden. "If I blur, just hold me tight, Frankie," she said. "Everything is still too strange to quite get a grip on — yet . . . But I'm *not* going home, Frank — not even when it is allowed. I set out — I'm sticking — I'm not turning tail. It's what people have got to do — in space more than ever . . ."

Even when the seizure of fever came, and the sweat gathered on her lips, and her eyes went wild, she gritted her teeth and just clung to him. She had spunk — admirable, if perhaps destructive. "Love yuh," Frank kept saying. "Love yuh, Sweetie . . ."

Two days later, before the frigid dawn, they saw the last of Mitch Storey and his slender, beautiful wife with her challenging brown eyes.

"Be careful that you do right for Mitch and — these *folks*," she warned almost commandingly as the old heli landed in the desert a few miles from the Station. "What would you do — if outsiders came blundering into your world by the hundreds, making trails, killing you with fire? At first, *they* didn't even fight back."

The question was ancient but valid. In spite of his experiences, Nelsen agreed with the logic and the justice. "We'll make up a story, Selma," he said solemnly.

Mitch looked anxious. "Human people will find a way, won't

they, Frank?" he asked. "To win, to come to Mars and live, I mean —
to change everything. Sure — some will be sympathetic. But when
there's practical pressure — need — danger — economics . . . ?"

"I don't know, Mitch," Nelsen answered in the same tone as
before. "Your thickets do have a pretty good defense."

But in his heart he suspected that fierce human persistence
couldn't be stopped — *as long as there were humans left*. Mitch and
his star folk couldn't withdraw from the mainstream of competition — inherent in life — that was spreading again across the solar
system. They could only stand their ground, take their fearful
chances, be part of it.

One of the last things Mitch said, was, "Got any cigarettes,
Frank? Selma likes one, once in a while."

"Sure. Three packs here inside my Archer. Mighty small hospi-
tality gift, Mitch . . ."

After the 'copter drifted away, it seemed that a curtain drew
over Nelsen's mind, blurring the whole memory. It was as though
they had planned that. It was almost as though Mitch, and Selma,
as he had just seen them, were just another mind-fantasy of the
Heebie-Jeebie Planet, created by its present masters.

"Should we believe it?" Nance whispered.

"My cigarettes are gone," Frank told her.

At the Survey Station they got weary looks from Ed Huth. "I
guess I picked a wrong man, Nelsen," he said.

"It looks as though you did, Ed," Frank replied. "I'm really
sorry."

They got worse hell from a little doctor from Italy, whose name
was Padetti. They were asked a lot of questions. They fibbed some,
but not entirely.

"We sort of blanked out, Doctor," Nance told him. "I suppose
we spent most of our time in the desert, living in our Archers. There
were the usual distorted hallucinations of Syrtis Fever. A new strain,
I suspect . . . Four months gone? Oh, no . . . !"

She must have had a time evading his questions for the next
month, while she worked, again, in the lab. Maybe he did divine
half of the truth, at last. Maybe he even was sympathetic toward the
thickets that he was trying to defeat.

Nelsen wasn't allowed to touch another helicopter. During that
month, between brief but violent seizures of the fever, he was
employed as a maintenance mechanic.

Then the news came. There had been an emergency call from
Pallastown. Rescue units were to be organized, and rocketed out in
high-velocity U.N.S.F. and U.S.S.F bubbs. There had been sabotage,

violence. The Town was three-quarters gone, above the surface. Planned attack or — almost worse — merely the senseless result of space-poisoned men kicking off the lid in a spree of hell-raising humor and fun?

Nelsen was bitter. But he also felt the primitive excitement — almost an eagerness. That was the savage paradox in life.

"You still have the dregs of Syrtis Fever," a recruiting physician told him. "But you know the Belt. That makes a big difference . . . All right — you're going . . ."

Nance Codiss didn't have that experience. Her lab background wasn't enough. So she was stuck, on Mars.

Nelsen had been pestering her to marry him. Now, in a corner of the crowded lounge, he tried again.

She shook her head. "You'd still have to leave me, Frank," she told him. "Because that's the way strong people *have* to be — when there's trouble to be met. Let's wait. Let's know a little better where we're at — please, darling. I'll be all right. Contact me when you can . . ."

Her tone was low and tender and unsteady. He hugged her close.

Soon, he was aboard a GO-rocket, shooting up to Phobos to join the assembling rescue team. He wondered if this was the beginning of the end . . .

VIII

Frank Nelsen missed the first shambles at Pallastown, of course, since even at high speed, the rescue unit with which he came did not arrive until days after the catastrophe.

There had been hardly any warning, since the first attack had sprung from the sub-levels of the city itself.

A huge tank of liquid oxygen, and another tank of inflammable synthetic hydrocarbons to be used in the manufacture of plastics, had been simultaneously ruptured by charges of explosive, together with the heavy, safety partition between them. The resulting blast and fountain of fire had jolted even the millions of tons of Pallas' mass several miles from its usual orbit.

The sack of the town had begun at once, from within, even before chunks of asteroid material, man-accelerated and — aimed, had begun to splatter blossoms of incandescence into the confusion of deflating domes and dying inhabitants. Other vandal bands had soon landed from space.

The first hours of trying to regain any sort of order, during the assault and after it was finally beaten off, must have been heroic effort almost beyond conception. Local disaster units, helped by hoppers and citizens, had done their best. Then many had turned to pursuit and revenge.

After Nelsen's arrival, his memory of the interval of acute emergency could have been broken down into a series of pictures, in which he was often active.

First, the wreckage, which he helped to pick up, like any of the others. Pallastown had been like froth on a stone, a castle on a floating, golden crag. It had been a flimsy, hastily-built mushroom city, with a beautiful, tawdry splendor that had seemed out of place, a target shining for thousands of miles.

Haw, haw . . . ! Nelsen could almost hear the coarse laughter of the Jolly Lads, as they broke it up, robbed it, raped it — because they both sneered at its effeteness, and missed what it represented to them . . . Nelsen remembered very well how a man's attitudes could be warped while he struggled for mere survival in an Archer drifting in space.

Yet even as he worked with the others, to put up temporary domes and to gather the bloated dead, the hatred arose in him, and was strengthened by the fury and grief in the grim, strong faces around him. To exist where it was, Pallastown could not be as soft as it seemed. And to the hoppers — the rugged, level-headed ones who deserved the name — it had meant much, though they had visited it for only a few days of fun, now and then.

The Jolly Lads had been routed. Some must have fled chuckling and cursing almost sheepishly, like infants the magnitude of whose mischief has surpassed their intention, and has awed and frightened them, at last. They had been followed, even before the various late-coming space forces could get into action.

Nelsen overheard words that helped complete the pictures:

"I'll get them . . . They had my wife . . ."

"This was planned — you know where . . ."

It was planned, all right. But if Ceres, the Tovie colony, had actually been the instigator, there was evidence that the scheme had gotten out of hand. The excitement of destruction had spread. Stories came back that Ceres had been attacked, too.

"I killed a man, Frank — with this pre-Asteroidal knife. He was after Helen and my son . . ."

This was timid David Lester talking, awed at himself, proud, but curiously ashamed. This made another picture. By luck the Lesters lived in the small above-the-surface portion of Pallastown that had not been seriously damaged.

Frank Nelsen also killed, during a trip to Post One of the KRNH Enterprises, to get more stellene and other materials to expand the temporary encampments for the survivors. He killed two fleeing men coldly and at a distance, because they did not answer his hail. The shreds of their bodies and the loot they had been carrying were scattered to drift in the vacuum, adding another picture of retribution to thousands like it.

Belt Parnay was the name of the leader whom everybody really wanted to get. Belt Parnay — another Fessler, another Fanshaw. That was a curious thing. There was another name and face; but as far as could be told, the personality was very similar. It was as if, out of the darker side of human nature, a kind of reincarnation would always take place.

They didn't get Parnay. Inevitably, considering the enormity of space, many of the despoilers of Pallastown escaped. The shrewdest, the most experienced, the most willing to shout and lead and let others do the dangerous work, had the advantage. For they also knew how to run and hide and be prudently quiet. Parnay was one of these.

Some captives were recovered. Others were found, murdered. Fortunately, Pallastown was still largely a man's city. But pursuit and revenge still went on . . .

Post One was intact. Art Kuzak had surrounded it with a

cordon of tough and angry asteroid-hoppers. It was the same with the other posts, except Five and Nine, which were wiped out.

"Back at last, eh, Nelsen?" Art roared angrily, as soon as Frank had entered his office.

"A fact we should accept, not discuss," Nelsen responded dryly. "You know the things we need."

"Um-hmm — Nelsen. To rescue and restore Pallastown — when it's pure nonsense, only inviting another assault! When we know that dispersal is the only answer. The way things are, everywhere, the whole damned human race needs to be dispersed — if some of it is to survive!"

It made another picture — Art Kuzak, the old friend, gone somewhat too big for his oversized britches, perhaps . . . No doubt Art had had to put aside some grandiose visions, considering the turn that events had taken: Whole asteroids moved across the distance, and put into orbit around the Earth, so that their mineral wealth could be extracted more conveniently. Space resorts established for tourists; new sports made possible by zero-gravity, invented and advertised. Art Kuzak had the gift of both big dreaming and of practice. He'd talked of such things, before.

Nelsen's smirk was wry. "Dispersal for survival. I agree," he said. "When they tried to settle Mars, it was being mentioned. Also, long before that. Your wisdom is not new, Art. It wasn't followed perhaps because people are herding animals by instinct. Anyhow, our side has to hold what it has *really* got — one-fourth of Pallastown above the surface, and considerably more underground, including shops, installations, and seventy per cent of its skilled inhabitants, determined to stay in the Belt after the others were killed or wounded, or ran away. Unless you've quit claiming to be a practical man, Art, you'll have to go along with helping them. You know what kind of materials and equipment are needed, and how much we can supply, better than I do. Or do I have to withdraw my fraction of the company in goods? We'll take up the dispersal problem as soon as possible."

Art Kuzak could only sigh heavily, grin a lopsided grin, and produce. Soon a great caravan of stuff was on the move.

There was another picture: Eileen Sands, the old Queen of Serene in a not-yet-forgotten song, sitting on a lump of yellow alloy splashed up from the surface of Pallas, where a chunk of mixed metal and stone had struck at a speed of several miles per second, fusing the native alloy and destroying her splendid *Second Stop* utterly in a flash of incandescence. Back in Archer, she looked almost as she used to look at Hendricks'. Her smile was rueful.

"Shucks, I'm all right, Frank," she said. "Even if Insurance, with so many disaster-claims, can't pay me — which they probably still can. The boys'll keep needing entertainment, if it's only in a stellene space tent. They won't let me just sit . . . For two bits, though, I'd move into a nice, safe orbit, out of the Belt and on the other side of the sun from the Earth, and build myself a retreat and retire. I'd become a spacewoman, like I wanted to, in the first place."

"I'll bet," Nelsen joshed. "Otherwise, what have you heard and seen? There's a certain fella . . ."

Right away, she thought he meant Ramos. "The damn fool — why ask me, Frank?" she sniffed, her expression sour and sad. "How long has he been gone again, now? As usual he was proposing — for the first few days after he set out. After that, there were a few chirps of messages. Then practically nothing. Anyway, how long does it take to get way out to Pluto and back, even if a whole man can have the luck to make it. And is there much more than half of him left . . . ? For two bits I'd — ah — skip it!"

Nelsen smiled with half of his mouth. "I wanted to know about Ramos, too, Eileen. Thanks. But I was talking about Tiflin."

"Um-hmm — you're right. He and Pal Igor were both around at my place about an hour before we were hit. I called him something worse than a bad omen. He was edgy — almost like he used to be. He said that, one of these days — be cavalier — I was going to get mine. He and Igor eeled away before my customers could break their necks."

Nelsen showed his teeth. "Thanks again. I wondered," he said.

He stayed in Pallastown until, however patched it looked, it was functioning as the center of the free if rough-and-tumble part of the Belt once more — though he didn't know for how long this would be true. Order of one kind had been fairly restored. But out of the disaster, and something very similar on Ceres, the thing that had always been most feared had sprung. It was the fact of opposed organized might in close proximity in the region between Pallas and Ceres. Again there was blaming and counter-blaming, about incidents the exact sources of which never became clear. What each of the space forces, patrolling opposite each other, had in the way of weapons, was of course no public matter, either; but how do you rate two inconceivables? Nor did the threat stay out in the vastness between the planets.

From Earth came the news of a gigantic, incandescent bubble, rising from the floor of the Pacific Ocean, and spreading in almost radioactivity-free waves and ripples, disrupting penned-in areas of food-producing sea, and lapping at last at far shores. Both sides disclaimed responsibility for the blast.

Everybody insisted hopefully that this latest danger would die down, too. Statesmen would talk, official tempers would be calmed, some new working arrangements would be made. But meanwhile, the old Sword of Damocles hung by a thinner hair than ever before. One trigger-happy individual might snap it for good. If not now, the next time, or the next. A matter of hours, days, or years. The mathematics of probabilities denied that luck could last forever. In this thought there was a sense of helplessness, and the ghost of a second Asteroid Belt.

Frank Nelsen might have continued to make himself useful in Pallastown, or he might have rejoined the Kuzaks, who had moved their mobile posts back into a safer zone on the other side of Pallas. But his instincts, now, all pointed along another course of action — the only course that seemed to make any sense just then.

He approached Art Kuzak at Post One. "About deployment," he began. "I've made up some sketches, showing what I'd like the factories to turn out. The ideas aren't new — now they'll spring up all around like thoughts of food in a famine. If anything will approach answering all problems, they will. And KRNH is as well able to put them into effect as anybody . . . So — unless you've got some better suggestions?"

Art Kuzak looked the sketches over shrewdly for half an hour.

"All right, Frank," he said after some further conversation. "It looks good enough. I'll chip in. Whether they're sucker bait or not, these things will sell. Only — could it be you're running away?"

"Perhaps," Nelsen answered. "Or following my nose — by a kind of natural compulsion which others will display, too. Two hundred of these to start. The men going with me will pay for theirs. I'll cover the rest of this batch: You'll be better than I am at figuring out prices and terms for later batches. Just on a hunch, I'll always want a considerable oversupply. Post One's shops can turn them out fast. All they are, mostly, is just stellene, arranged in a somewhat new way. The fittings — whatever can't be supplied now, can follow."

Fifty asteroid-hoppers, ten of them accompanied by wives, went with Nelsen as he started out with a loaded caravan toward an empty region halfway between the orbits of Earth and Mars. Everyone in the group was convinced by yearnings of his own.

Thinking of Nance Codiss, Nelsen planned to keep within beam range of the Red Planet. He had called Nance quite often. She was still working in the Survey Station hospital, which was swamped with injured from Pallastown.

Nelsen could tag all of the fierce drives in him with single words.

Home was the first. After all his years away from Earth, the meaning of the word would have been emphatic in him, even without the recurrent spasms of hot-cold weakness, which, though fading, still legally denied him the relief of going back to old familiar things. Besides, Earth seemed insecure. So he could only try to make home possible in space. Remembering his first trip, long ago, from the Moon to Mars, he knew how gentle the Big Vacuum could sometimes seem, with just a skin of stellene between it and himself. Home was a plain longing, too, in the hard, level eyes around him.

Love. Well, wasn't that part of the first item he had tagged?

Wanderlust. The adventurous distance drive — part of any wild-blooded vagabond male. Here in his idea, this other side of a human paradox seemed possible to answer, too. You could go anywhere. Home went with you. Your friends could go along, if they wished.

Freedom. In the billions of cubic miles could any system ever be big enough to pen you in, tell you what to think or do, as long as you hurt no one? Well — he thought not, but perhaps that remained to be seen.

Safety. Deployment was supposed to be the significant factor, there. And how could you make it any better than it was going to be now? Even if there were new dangers?

The future. There was no staying with the past. The Earth was becoming too small for its expanding population. It was a stifling, dangerous little world that, if the pressures were not relieved, might puff into fire and fragments at any moment during any year. And the era of prospecting and exploration in the Asteroid Belt seemed destined soon to come to an end, in any event.

Frank Nelsen's drives were very strong, after so much had passed around him for so long a time. Thus, maybe he became too idealistic and — at moments — almost fanatically believing, without enough of the saving grain of doubt and humor. The hoppers with him were much like himself   singly directed by what they had lacked for years.

The assembly operation was quickly accomplished, as soon as they were what they considered a safe distance from the Belt. On a greater scale, it was almost nothing more than the first task that Nelsen had ever performed in space — the jockeying of a bubb from its blastoff drum, inflating it, rigging it, spinning it for centrifugal gravity, and fitting in its internal appointments.

Nelsen looked at the fifty-odd stellene rings that they had

broken out of their containers — the others, still packed, were held in reserve. Those that had been freed glistened translucently in the sunlight. Nelsen had always thought that bubbs were beautiful. And these were still bubbs, but they were bigger, safer, more complicated.

A bantam-sized hopper named Hank Janns spoke from beside Nelsen as they floated near each other. "Pop — sizzle — and it's yours, Chief. A prefab, a house, a dwelling. A kitchen, a terrace, a place for a garden, a place for kids, even . . . With a few personal touches, you've got it made. Better than the house trailer my dad used to hook onto the jalopy when I was ten . . . My Alice likes it, too, Chief — that's the *real* signal! Tell your pals Kuzak that this is the Idea of the Century."

Frank Nelsen kind of thought so, too, just then. The first thing he did was to beam the Survey Station on Mars, like he was doing twice a week — to communicate more often would have courted the still dangerous chance of being pinpointed. For similar reasons he couldn't explain too clearly what his project was, but he hoped that he had gotten a picture of what it was like across to his girl.

"Come see for yourself, Nance," he said enthusiastically. "I'll arrange for a caravan from Post One to stop by on Phobos and pick you up. Also — there's my old question . . . So, what'll it be, Nance? Maybe we can feel a little surer of ourselves, now. We can work the rest out. Come and look, hang around — see how everything shakes down, if you'd rather."

He waited for the light-minutes to pass, before he could hear her voice. "Hello, Frank . . ." There was the same eager quaver. "Still pretty jammed, Frank . . . But we know about it here — from Art . . . Some of the Pallastown convalescents will be migrating your way . . . I'll wrangle free and come along . . . Maybe in about a month . . ."

He didn't know quite whether to take her at her word — or whether she was somehow hedging. In the Big Vacuum, the human mind seemed hard put, quite, to know itself. Distances and separations were too great. Emotions were too intense or too stunned. This much he had learned to understand. Perhaps he had lost Nance. But maybe, still — in some bleak, fatalistic way — it would be just as well in the end, for them both.

"Sure, Nance," he said gently. "I'll call again — the regular time . . ."

Right after that he was talking, over a much greater span, to Art Kuzak. "First phase about completed, Art . . . Finger to thumb — in spite of the troubles elsewhere. So let it roll . . . !"

Art Kuzak's reply had an undercurrent of jubilance, as if whatever he knew now was better than he had expected. "Second phase is en route. Joe will be along . . . Don't be surprised . . ."

Joe Kuzak's approach, a few hundred hours later, made a luminous cluster in the sky, like a miniature galaxy. It resolved itself into vast bales, and all of the stellene rings — storage and factory — of Post Three. Also there were over a hundred men and thirty-three wives. Many of them were Pallastown refugees.

Nelsen helped Joe through the airlock of the ring that he had hoped would be his and Nance's. "Bubbtown, huh, Frank?" Joe chuckled. "The idea is spreading faster than we had believed, and we aren't the only ones that have got it. The timing is just right. People are scared, fed up. Out Here — and on Earth, too . . . Most of the guys that are single in this crowd have girls who will be on the way soon. Some of the tougher space-fitness tests are being junked. We're even screening a small batch of runaways from Ceres — to be included in the next load. An experiment. But it should work out. They're just like anybody . . . Art is all of sudden sort of liberal — the way he gets when things seem to break right."

Everything went fine for quite a while. Art Kuzak was out playing his hunches, giving easy terms to those who couldn't pay at once.

"Might as well gamble," he growled from the distance. "Space and terrestrial forces are still poised. If we lose at all, we lose the whole works, anyway. So let's bring them from all around the Belt, from Earth, Venus and from wherever they'll come. Give them a place to work, or let them start their own deal. It all helps . . . You know what I hear? The Tovies are letting men do things by themselves. To hold their own in room as big as this, they have to. Their bosses are over a barrel. Just organized discipline ain't gonna work. A guy has to want things his own way . . ."

In a more general view, doubts were sneaking up on Frank Nelsen, though as far as KRNH was concerned, he had started the ball rolling. "We'll keep our fingers crossed," he said.

It was only a couple of Earth-days later that another member of the old Bunch showed up. "I had to bubb all the way from Mercury to Post One to get your location from Art, Frankie," he complained. "Cripes — why didn't anybody ever try to beam Gimp and me, anymore? Solar radiation ain't *that* hard to get past . . . So I had to come sneak a look for myself, to see what the Big Deal on the grapevine is."

"We left the back door unlatched for you, Two-and-Two," Nelsen laughed. "And you crept in quietly. Swell to see you."

Sitting showered and in fresh clothes on Frank Nelsen's

sundeck, any changes in Two-and-Two Baines were less evident than one might have supposed. His eyes had a much surer, farther look. Otherwise he was still the same large hulk with much the same lugubrious humor.

"Mercury's okay, Frankie," he said. "About four thousand people are living in the Twilight Zone, already. I could show you pictures, but I guess you know. Whole farms and little towns under stellene. Made me some dough doing lots of the building. Could have been more, but who cares? Oh, Gimp'll be along out here sometime, soon. He was putting up another solar powerhouse. But he's beginning to say, what the hell, the future ain't there, or on any planet . . . So this is how it's gonna be, huh? With some additions, sure. Factories, super markets, cornfields, pig farms, parks, playgrounds, beauty parlors, all encased in stellene, and orbiting in clusters around the sun, eh . . . ? 'Hey, Pop!' some small fry will say to his old man. 'Gimme ten bucks, please, for an ice cream cone down at the soda bubb?' And his mom'll say to his dad, 'George, Dear — is the ionocar nice and shiny? I have to go play bridge with the girls over in Nelsenville . . .' No, I'm not ribbing you, Frankie. It'll be kind of nice to hear that type of talk, again — if they only include a place for a man to be a little bit himself."

Two-and-Two (George) Baines sighed rapturously and continued. "Figure it out to the end, Frankie. No planets left — all the materials in them used up to build these bubbtowns. There'll be just big shining, magnificent rings made up of countless little floating stellene houses all around the sun. A zillion people, maybe more. Gardens, flowers, everything beautiful. Everybody free to move anywhere. Uh-uh — I'm not making fun, Frankie. I'm joining in with all the relief and happiness of my heart. Only, it'll be kind of sad to see the old planets go — to be replaced by a wonderful super-suburbia. Or maybe we should say, superbia."

Nelsen burst out laughing, at last. "You sly slob . . . ! Anyhow, *that* extreme is millenniums off — if it has a chance of happening, at all. Even so, our descendants, if any, will be going to the stars by then. There won't be any frustration of their thirst for danger . . . Just as there isn't any, now, for us. Except that we can keep our weapons handy, and hope . . . Me — I'm a bit bored with adventure, just at present."

"So am I," Two-and-Two affirmed fervently. "Now, have you got me a job, Frankie?"

"There'll be something," Nelsen answered him. "Meanwhile, to keep from feeling regimented by civilization, you could take your rocket launcher and join the perimeter watchers that range out a thousand miles . . ."

Nance Codiss arrived a week later, with a group of recent Pallastown convalescents. Bad signs came with her, but that fact got lost as she hugged Nelsen quickly there in the dwelling he had set up with the thought it would be their home. At once she went on a feminine exploring expedition of the prefab's interior, and its new, gleaming appointments. Kitchen, living room, sundeck. Nelsen's garden was already well along.

"Like the place?" he asked.

"Love it, Frank," she answered quietly.

"It could have been more individual," he commented. "But we were in a hurry. So they are all identical. That can be fixed, some, soon. You're thinking about improvements?"

Her eyes twinkled past the shadow in her expression. "Always some," she laughed. Then her face went solemn. "Let them ride, for now, Frank. It's all wonderful and unbelievable. Hug me again — I love you. Only — all this is even more fantastically new to me than it is to you. Realize that, please, Frank. I'm a month late in getting here and I'm still groping my way. A little more time — for us both . . . Because you might be fumbling, some, too."

Her tone was gentle. He saw that her eyes, meeting his, were honest and clear. He felt the careful strength behind them, after a moment of hurt. There was no rushing, one-way enthusiasm that might easily burn out and blow up in a short time.

He held her close. "Sure, Nance," he said.

"You probably know that our group from Mars was followed, Frank. I hope I'm not a jinx."

"Of course you're not. Somebody would have followed — sometime. We're watching and listening. Just keep your Archer handy . . ."

The faint, shifting blips in the radar screens was an old story, reminding him that certain things were no better than before, and that some were worse. Somewhere there were other bubbtowns. There were policing space forces, too. But for millions of miles around, this cluster of eight hundred prefabs and the numerous larger bubbs that served them, were all alone.

Nelsen looked out from his sundeck, and saw dangerous contrasts. The worst, perhaps, was a spherical bubble of stellene. Inside it was a great globe of water surrounded by air — a colossal dewdrop. Within it, a man and two small boys — no doubt father and sons from Pallastown, were swimming, horsing around, having a swell time — only a few feet from nothing. Nelsen spoke softly into his radio-phone. "Leland — close down the pool . . ."

It wasn't long before the perimeter watch, returning from a patrol that had taken them some distance out, brought in a make-shift dwelling bubb made from odds and ends of stellene. They had also picked up its occupant, a lean comic character with an accent and a strange way of talking.

"Funny that you'd turn up, here — Igor, is it?" Nelsen said dryly.

Igor sniffed, as if with sorrow. He had been roughed up, some. "Very funny — also simple. You making a house, so I am making a house for this identical purpose. People from Ceres are already being here; in consequence, I am also arriving. Nobody are saying what are proper doing and thinking — so I am informed. I am believing — okay, Igor. When being not true, I am going away again."

The tone was bland. The pale eyes looked naive and artless, except, perhaps, for a hard, shrewd glint, deep down.

Joe Kuzak was present. "We searched him, Frank," he said. "His bubb, too. He's clean — as far as we can tell. Not even a weapon. I also asked him some questions. I savvy a little of his real lingo."

"I'll ask them over," Nelsen answered. "Igor — a friend named Tiflin wouldn't be being around some place, would he?"

The large space comedian didn't even hesitate. "I am thinking not very far — not knowing precisely. Somebody more is being here, likewise. Belt Parnay. You are knowing this one? Plenty Jollies — new fellas — not having much supplies — only many new rocket launchers they are receiving from someplace. You are understanding this? Bad luck, here, it is meaning."

Nelsen eyed the man warily, with mixed doubt and liking. "I don't think you can be going away again, right now, Igor," he said. "We don't have a jail, but a guard will be as good . . ."

The watch didn't give the alarm for several hours. Three hisses in the phones, made vocally. Then one, then two more. North, second quadrant, that meant. Direction of first attack. Ionic drives functioned. The cluster of bubbs began to scatter further. Nelsen knew that if Igor had told the truth, the outlook was very poor. Too much deployment would thin the defenses too much. And against new, homing rockets — if Parnay really had them — it would be almost useless. A relatively small number of men, riding free in armor, could smash the much larger targets from almost any distance.

Nelsen didn't stay in his prefab. Floating in his Archer, he could be his own, less easily identifiable, less easily hit command post, while he fired his own homing missiles at the far-off radar specks of the attackers. He ordered everyone not specifically needed inside the bubbs for some defense purpose to jump clear.

In the first half-minute, he saw at least fifty compartmented prefabs partly crumple, as explosives tore into them. A dozen, torn open, were deflated entirely. The swimming pool globe was punctured, and a cloud of frosty vapor made rainbows in the sunshine, as the water boiled away. Far out, Nelsen saw the rockets he and his own men had launched, sparkling soundlessly, no doubt scoring, some, too.

The attackers didn't even try to get close yet. Far greater damage would have to be inflicted, before panic and disorganization might give them sufficient advantage. But such damage would take only minutes. Too much would reduce the loot. So now there was a halt in the firing, and another component of fear was applied. It was a growling, taunting voice.

"Nelsen! And all of you silly bladder-brains . . . ! This is Belt Parnay . . . ! Ever hear of him? Come back from hell, eh? Not with just rocks, this time! The latest, surest equipment! Want to give up, now, Nelsen — you and your nice, civilized people? Cripes, what will you cranks try next? Villages built in nothing and on nothing! Thanks, though. Brother, what a blowout this is gonna provide!"

Parnay's tone had shifted, becoming mincingly mocking, then hard and joyful at the end.

Maybe he shouldn't have suggested so plainly what would happen — unless something was done, soon. Maybe he shouldn't have sounded just a little bit unsure of himself under all his bluff. Because Nelsen had made preparations that matched a general human trend. Now, he saw a condition that fitted in, making an opportunity . . . So he began to taunt Parnay back.

"We've got a lot of the latest type rockets to throw, too, Parnay. You'd have quite a time, trying to take us. But there's more . . . Just look behind you, Parnay. And all around. Not too far. Who's silly? Who's the jerk? Some new guys are in your crowd, I hear? Then they won't have much against them — they aren't real outlaws. Do you think they want to keep following you around, stinking in their armor — when what we've got is what they're bound to want, right now, too? They can hear what I'm saying, Parnay. Every one of them must have a weapon in his hands. Why, you stupid clown, you're in a trap! We will give them what they need most, without them having to risk getting killed. In space, there'll have to be a lot of things forgotten, but not for you or for the rough old-timers with you . . . Come on, you guys out there. There's a folded bubb right here waiting for each of you. Take it anywhere you want — away from here, of course . . . Parnay — big, important Belt Parnay — are you still alive . . . ?"

Nelsen had his own sneering tone of mockery. He used it to best advantage — but with fear in his heart. Plenty of his act was only counter-bluff. But now, as he paused, he heard Two-and-Two Baines' mournful voice continue the barrage of persuasion.

"Flowers, Parnay? We ain't got many, yet. But you won't care . . . Fellas — do you want to keep being pushed around by this loud mouth who likes to run and lets you sweat for him, because he's mostly alone and needs company? Believe me, I know what it's like out there, too. At a certain point, all you really want is something a little like home. And the Chief ain't kidding. It was all planned. Try us and see. Send a couple of guys in. They'll come out with the proof . . ."

Other voices were shouting. "Wake up, you suckers . . . ! You'll never take us, you stupid slobs . . . ! Come on and try it, if that's what you want to be . . ."

What happened, could never have happened so quickly if Parnay's doubtless considerably disgruntled following hadn't been disturbed further by intrigue beforehand. Nelsen heard Parnay roar commands and curses that might have awed many a man. But then there was a cluster of minute sparks in the distance, as rockets, not launched by the defenders, homed and exploded.

There was a pause. Then many voices were audible, shouting at the same time, with scarcely any words clear . . . Several minutes passed like that. Then there was almost silence.

"So — has it happened?" Nelsen growled into his phone.

"It has," came the mocking answer. "Be cavalier, Nelsen. Salute the new top outlaw . . . Don't faint — I knew I'd make it . . . And don't try anything you might regret . . . I'm coming in with a couple of my Jolly Lads. You'd better not welsh on your promises. Because the others are armed and waiting . . ."

The guys with Tiflin looked more tired than tough. Out from under their fierce, truculent bravado showed the fiercer hunger for common things and comforts. Nelsen knew. The record was in his own memory.

"You'll get your bubbs right away," he told them. "Then send the others in, a pair at a time. After that, go and get lost. Make your own place — town — whatever you want to call it . . . Leland, Crobert, Sharpe — fit these guys out, will you . . . ?"

All this happened under the sardonic gaze of Glen Tiflin, and before the puzzled eyes of Joe Kuzak and Two-and-Two Baines. A dozen others were hovering near.

Nelsen lowered his voice and called, "Nance?"

She answered at once. "I'm all right, Frank. A few people to patch. Some beyond that. I'm in the hospital with Doc Forbes . . ."

"You guys can find something useful to do," Nelsen snapped at the gathering crowd.

"Well, Frankie," Tiflin taunted. "Aren't you going to invite me into your fancy new quarters? Joe and Two-and-Two also look as though they could stand a drink."

On the sundeck, Tiflin spoke again. "I suppose you've got it figured, Nelsen?"

Nelsen answered him in clipped fashion. "Thanks. But let's not dawdle too much. I've got a lot of wreckage to put back together . . . Maybe I've still got it figured wrong, Tiflin. But lately I began to think the other way. You were always around when trouble was cooking — like part of it, *or like a good cop*. The first might still be right."

Tiflin sneered genially. "Some cops can't carry badges. And they don't always stop trouble, but they try . . . Anyhow, what side do you think I was on, after Fessler kicked me around for months . . . ? Let Igor go. He's got law and order in his soul. I kind of like having him around . . . But keep your mouths buttoned, will you? I'm talking to you, Mr. Baines, and you, Mr. Kuzak, as well as to you, Nelsen. And I'm take my bubb along, the same as the other ninety or so guys who are left from Parnay's crowd. I've got to look good with them . . . Cheers, you slobs. See you around . . ."

Afterwards, Joe growled, "Hell — what do you know! Him . . . ! Special Police. Undercover. U.N., U.S., or what?"

"Shut up," Nelsen growled.

Though he had sensed it coming and had met it calmly, the Tiflin switch was something that Frank Nelsen had trouble getting over. It confused him. It made him want to laugh.

Another thing that began to bother him even more was the realization that the violence, represented by Fessler, Fanshaw, Parnay, and thousands of others like them back through history, was bound to crop up again. It was part of the complicated paradox of human nature. And it was hard to visualize a time when there wouldn't be followers — frustrated slobs who wanted to get out and kick over the universe. Nelsen had felt such urges cropping up within himself. So this wasn't the end of trouble — especially not out here in raw space, that was still far too big for man-made order.

So it wasn't just the two, opposed space navies patrolling, more quietly now, between Ceres and Pallas. That condition could pass.

The way people always chose — or were born to — different sides was another matter. Or was it just the natural competition of life in whatever form? More disturbing, perhaps, was the mere fact of trying to live here, so close to natural forces that could kill in an instant.

For example, Nelsen often saw two children and a dog racing around inside one of the rotating bubbs — having fun as if just in a back yard. If the stellene were ripped, the happy picture would change to horror . . . How long would it take to get adjusted to — and accept — such a chance? Thoughts like that began to disturb Nelsen. Out here, in all this enormous freedom, the shift from peaceful routine to tragedy could be quicker than ever before.

But is wasn't thinking about such grim matters that actually threw Frank Nelsen — that got him truly mixed up. In Parnay's attack, ten men and two women had been killed. There were also twenty-seven injured. Such facts he could accept — they didn't disturb him too much, either. Yet there was a curious sort of straw that broke the camel's back, one might have said.

The incident took place quite a while after the assault. Out on an inspection tour in his Archer, he happened to glance through the transparent wall of the sundeck of a prefab he was passing . . .

In a moment he was inside, grinning happily. Miss Rosalie Parks was lecturing him: " . . . You needn't be surprised that I am here, Franklin. 'O, tempora O, mores!' Cicero once said. 'O, the times! O, the customs!' But we needn't be so pessimistic. I am in perfect health — and ten years below retirement age. Young people, I suspect, will still be taught Latin if they choose . . . Or there will be something else . . . Of course I had heard of your project . . . It was quite easy for you not to notice my arrival. But I came with the latest group, straight from Earth . . ."

Nelsen was very pleased that Miss Parks was here. He told her so. He stayed for cakes and coffee. He told her that it was quite right for her to keep up with the times. He believed this, himself . . .

Afterwards, though, in his own quarters, he began to laugh. Her presence was so incongruous, so fantastic . . .

His laughter became wild. Then it changed to great rasping hiccups. Too much that was unbelievable by old standards had happened around him. This was delayed reaction to space. He had heard of such a thing. But he had hardly thought that it could apply to him, anymore . . . ! Well, he knew what to do . . . Tranquilizer tablets were practically forgotten things to him. But he gulped one now. In a few minutes, he seemed okay, again . . .

Yet he couldn't help thinking back to the Bunch, the Planet

Strappers. To the wild fulfillment they had sought . . . So — most of them had made it. They had become men — the hard way. Except, of course, Eileen — the distaff side . . . They had planned, callowly, to meet and compare adventures in ten years. And this was still less than seven . . .

How long had it been since he had even beamed old Paul, in Jarviston . . . ? Now that most of the Syrtis Fever had left him, it seemed futile even to consider such a thing. It involved memories buried in enormous time, distance, change, and unexpectedness.

Glen Tiflin — the sour, space-wild punk who had become a cop. Had Tiflin even saved his — Frank Nelsen's — life, once, long ago, persuading a Jolly Lad leader to cast him adrift for a joke, rather than to kill him and Ramos outright . . . ?

Charlie Reynolds — the Bunch-member whom everybody had thought most likely to succeed. Well, Charlie was dead from a simple thing, and buried on Venus. He was unknown — except to his acquaintances.

Jig Hollins, the guy who had played it safe, was just as dead.

Eileen Sands was a celebrity in Serene, in Pallastown and the whole Belt.

Mex Ramos — of the flapping squirrel tails on an old motor scooter — now belonged to the history of exploration, though he no longer had real hands or feet, and, very likely, was now dead, somewhere out toward interstellar space.

David Lester, the timid one, had become successful in his own way, and was the father of one of the first children to be born in the Belt.

Two-and-Two Baines had won enough self-confidence to make cracks about the future. Gimp Hines, once the saddest case in the Whole Bunch, had been, for a long time, perhaps the best adjusted to the Big Vacuum.

Art Kuzak, one-time hunkie football player, was a power among the asteroids. His brother, Joe, had scarcely changed, personally.

About himself, Nelsen got the most lost. What had he become, after his wrong guesses and his great luck, and the fact that he had managed to see more than most? Generally, he figured that he was still the same free-wheeling vagabond by intention, but too serious to quite make it work out. Sometimes he actually gave people orders. It came to him as a surprise that he must be almost as rich as old J. John Reynolds, who was still drawing wealth from a comparatively small loan — futilely at his age, unless he had really aimed at the ideal of bettering the future.

Nelsen's busy mind couldn't stop. He thought of three other-world cultures he had glimpsed. Two had destroyed each other. The third and strangest was still to be reckoned with . . .

There, he came to Mitch Storey, the colored guy with the romantic name. Of all the Planet Strappers, his history was the most fabulous. Maybe, now, with a way of living in open space started, and with the planets ultimately to serve only as sources of materials, Mitch's star people would be left in relative peace for centuries.

Frank Nelsen began to chuckle again. As if something, everything, was funny. Which, perhaps, it was in a way. Because the whole view, personal and otherwise, seemed too huge and unpredictable for his wits to grasp. It was as if neither he, nor any other person, belonged where he was at all. He checked his thoughts in time. Otherwise, he would have commenced hiccupping.

That was the way it went for a considerable succession of arbitrary twenty-four hour day-periods. As long as he kept his attention on the tasks in hand, he was okay — he felt fine. Still, the project was proceeding almost automatically, just now. The first cluster of prefabs had grown until it had been split into halves, which moved a million miles apart, circling the sun. And he knew that there were other clusters, built by other outfits, growing and dividing into widely separated portions of the same great ring-like zone.

Maybe the old problems were beat. Safety? If deployment was the answer to that, it was certainly there — to a degree, at least. Room enough? Check. It was certainly available. Freedom of mind and action? There wasn't much question that that would work out, too. Home, comfort, and a kind of life not too unfamiliar? In the light of detached logic and observation, that was going fine, too. In the main, people were adjusting very quickly and eagerly. Perhaps *too* quickly.

That was where Nelsen always got scared, as if he had become a nervous old man. The Big Vacuum had a grandeur. It could seem gentle. Could children, women and men — everybody sometimes forgot — learn to live with it without losing their respect for it, until suddenly it killed them?

That was the worst point, if he let himself think. And how could he always avoid that? From there his thoughts would branch out into his multiple uncertainties, confusions and puzzlements. Then those strangling hiccups would come. And who could be taking devil-killers all the time?

He hadn't avoided Nance Codiss. He talked with her every day, lunched with her, even held her hand. Otherwise, a restraint had come over him. Because something was all wrong with him, and was getting worse. Just one urge was clear, now, inside him. She knew, of course, that he was loused up; but she didn't say anything. Finally he told her.

"You were right, Nance. I was fumbling my way, too. Space fatigue, the medic told me just a little while ago. He agrees with me that I should go back to Earth. I've got to go — to take a look at everything from the small end, again. Of course I've always had the longing. And now I can go. It has been a year since the worst of the Syrtis Fever."

"I've had the fever. And sometimes the longing, Frank," she said after she had studied him for a moment. "I think I'd like to go."

"Only if you want to, Nance. It's me that's flunking out, pal." He chuckled apologetically, almost lightly. "My part has to be a one-person deal. I don't know whether I'll ever come back. And you seem to fit, out here."

She looked at him coolly for almost a minute. "All right, Frank," she said quietly. "Follow your nose. It's just liable to be right on the beam — for you. I might follow mine. I don't know."

"Joe and Two-and-Two are around — if you need anything, Nance," he said. "I'll tell them. Gimp, I hear, is on the way. Not much point in my waiting for him, though . . ."

Somehow he loved Nance Codiss as much or more than ever. But how could he tell her that and make sense? Not much made sense to him anymore. It seemed that he had to get away from everybody that he had ever seen in space.

Fifty hours before his departure with a returning bubb caravan that had brought more Earth-emigrants, Nelsen acquired a traveling companion who had arrived from Pallastown with a small caravan bringing machinery. The passenger-hostess brought him to Nelsen's prefab. He was a grave little guy, five years old. He was solemn, polite, frightened, tall for his age — funny how corn and kids grew at almost zero-gravity.

The boy handed Nelsen a letter. "From my father and mother, sir," he said.

Nelsen read the typed missive.

"Dear Frank: The rumor has come that you are going home. You have our very best wishes, as always. Our son, Davy, is being sent to his paternal grandmother, now living in Minneapolis. He will go to school there. He is capable of making the trip without any special attention. But — a small imposition. If you can manage it, please look in on him once in a while, on the way. We would appreciate this favor. Thank you, take care of yourself, and we shall hope to see you somewhere within the next few months. Your sincere friends, David and Helen Lester."

A lot of nerve, Nelsen thought first. But he tried to grin engagingly at the kid and almost succeeded.

"We're in luck, Dave," he said. "I'm going to Minneapolis, too. I'm afraid of a lot of things. What are you afraid of?"

The small fry's jutting lip trembled. "Earth," he said. "A great big planet. Hoppers tell me I won't even be able to stand up or breathe."

Nelsen very nearly laughed and went into hiccups, again. Fantastic. Another viewpoint. Seeing through the other end of the telescope. But how else would it be for a youngster born in the Belt, while being sent — in the old colonial pattern — to the place that his parents regarded as home?

"Those jokers," Nelsen scoffed. "They're pulling your leg! It just isn't so, Davy. Anyhow, during the trip, the big bubb will be spun fast enough, so that we will get used to the greater Earth-gravity. Let me tell you something. I guess it's space and the Belt that *I'm* afraid of. I never quite got over it. Silly, huh?"

But as Nelsen watched the kid brighten, he remembered that he, himself, had been scared of Earth, too. Scared to return, to show weakness, to lack pride . . . Well, to hell with that. He had accomplished enough, now, maybe, to cancel such objections. Now it seemed that he had to get to Earth before it vanished because of something he had helped start. Silly, of course . . .

He and Davy traveled fast and almost in luxury. Within two weeks they were in orbit around the bulk of the Old World. Then, in the powerful tender with its nuclear retard rockets, there was the Blast In — the reverse of that costly agony that had once meant hard won and enormous freedom, when he was poor in money and rich in mighty yearning. But now Nelsen yielded in all to the mother clutch of the gravity. The whole process had been gentled and improved. There were special anti-knock seats. There was sound- and vibration-insulation. Even Davy's slight fear was more than half thrill.

At the new Minneapolis port, Nelsen delivered David Lester, Junior into the care of his grandmother, who seemed much more human than Nelsen once had thought long ago. Then he excused himself quickly.

Seeking the shelter of anonymity, he bought a rucksack for his few clothes, and boarded a bus which dropped him at Jarviston, Minnesota, at two a.m. He thrust his hands into his pockets, partly like a lonesome tramp, partly like some carefree immortal, and partly like a mixed-up wraith who didn't quite know who or what he was, or where he belonged.

In his wallet he had about five hundred dollars. How much more he might have commanded, he couldn't even guess. Wups, fella, he told himself. That's too weird, too indigestible — don't start hiccupping again. How old are you — twenty-five, or twenty-five thousand years? Wups — careful . . .

The full Moon was past zenith, looking much as it always had. The blue-tinted air domes of colossal industrial development, were mostly too small at this distance to be seen without a glass. Good . . .

With wondering absorption he sniffed the mingling of ripe field and road smells, borne on the warm breeze of the late-August night. Some few cars evidently still ran on gasoline. For a moment he watched neon signs blink. In the desertion he walked past Lehman's Drug Store and Otto Kramer's bar, and crossed over to pause for a nameless moment in front of Paul Hendricks' Hobby Center, which was all dark, and seemed little changed. He took to a side street, and won back the rustle of trees and the click of his heels in the silence.

A few more buildings — that was about all that was visibly different in Jarviston, Minnesota.

A young cop eyed him as he returned to the main drag and paused near a street lamp. He had a flash of panic, thinking that the cop was somebody, grown up, now, who would recognize him. But at least it was no one that he remembered.

The cop grinned. "Get settled in a hotel, buddy," he said. "Or else move on, out of town."

Nelsen grinned back, and ambled out to the highway, where intermittent clumps of traffic whispered.

There he paused, and looked up at the sky, again. The electric beacon of a weather observation satellite blinked on and off, moving slowly. Venus had long since set, with hard-to-see Mercury preceding it. Jupiter glowed in the south. Mars looked as remote and changeless as it must have looked in the Stone Age. The asteroids were never even visible here without a telescope.

The people that he knew, and the events that he had experienced Out There, were like myths, now. *How could he ever put Here and There together, and unite the mismatched halves of himself and his experience?* He had been born on Earth, the single home of his kind from the beginning. How could he ever even have been Out There?

He didn't try to hitch a ride. He walked fourteen miles to the next town, bought a small tent, provisions and a special, miniaturized radio. Then he slipped into the woods, along Hickman's Lake, where he used to go.

There he camped, through September, and deep into October. He fished, he swam again. He dropped stones into the water, and watched the circles form, with a kind of puzzled groping in his memory. He retreated from the staggering magnificence of his recent past and clutched at old simplicities.

On those rare occasions when he shaved, he saw the confused sickness in his face, reflected by his mirror. Sometimes, for a moment, he felt hot, and then cold, as if his blood still held a tiny trace of Syrtis Fever. If there *was* such a thing? No — don't start to laugh, he warned himself. Relax. Let the phantoms fade away. Somewhere, that multiple bigness of Nothing, of life and death, of success and unfairness and surprise, must have reality — but not here . . .

Occasionally he listened to news on the radio. But mostly he shut it off — out. Until boredom at last began to overtake him — because he had been used to so much more than what was here. Until — specifically — one morning, when the news came too quickly, and with too much impact. It was a recording, scratchy, and full of unthinkable distance.

" . . . Frank, Gimp, Two-and-Two, Paul, Mr. Reynolds, Otto, Les, Joe, Art, everybody — especially you, Eileen — remember what you promised, when I get back, Eileen . . . ! Here I am, on Pluto — edge of the star desert! Clear sailing — all the way. All I see, yet, is twilight, rocks, mountains, snow which must be frozen atmosphere — and one big star, Sol. But I'll get the data, and be back . . ."

Nelsen listened to the end, with panic in his face — as if such adventures and such living were too gigantic and too rich . . . He hiccupped once. Then he held himself very still and concentrated. He had known that voice Out There and Here, too. Now, as he heard it again — Here, but from Out There — it became like a joining force to bring them both together within himself. Though how could it be . . . ?

"Ramos," he said aloud. "Made it . . . Another good guy, accomplishing what he wanted . . . Hey . . . ! Hey, that's swell . . . Like things should happen."

He didn't hiccup anymore, or laugh. By being very careful, he just grinned, instead. He arose to his feet, slowly.

"What am I doing here — wasting time?" he seemed to ask the woods.

Without picking up his camping gear at all, he headed for the road, thumbed a ride to Jarviston, where he arrived before eight o'clock. Somebody had started ringing the city hall bell. Celebration?

Hendricks' was the most logical place for Nelsen to go, but he passed it by, following a hunch to his old street. *She* had almost said that she might come home, too. He touched the buzzer.

Not looking too completely dishevelled himself, he stood there, as a girl — briskly early in dress and impulse, so as not to waste the bright morning — opened the door.

"Yeah, Nance — me," he croaked apologetically. "Ramos has reached Pluto!"

"I know, *Frankie*!" she burst out.

But his words rushed on. "I've been goofing off — by Hickman's Lake. Over now. Emotional indigestion, I guess — from living too big, before I could take it. I figured you *might* be here. If you weren't, I'd come . . . Because I know where I belong. Nance — I hope you're not angry. Maybe we're pulling together, at last?"

"Angry — when I was the first fumbler? How could that be, Frank? Oh, I knew where you were — folks found out. I told them to leave you alone, because I understood some of what you were digging through. Because it was a little the same — for me . . . So, you see, I didn't just tag after you." She laughed a little. "That wouldn't be proud, would it? Even though Joe and Two-and-Two said I had to go bring you back . . ."

His arms went tight around her, right there on the old porch. "Nance — love you," he whispered. "And we've got to be tough. Everybody's got to be tough — to match what we've come to. Even little kids. But it was always like that — on any kind of frontier, wasn't it? A few will get killed, but more will live — many more . . ."

Like that, Frank Nelsen shook the last of the cobwebs out of his brain — and got back to his greater destiny.

"I'll buy all of that philosophy," Nance chuckled gently. "But you still look as though you needed some breakfast, Frank."

He grinned. "Later. Let's go to see Paul, first. A big day for him — because of Ramos. Paul is getting feeble, I suppose?" Nelsen's face had sobered.

"Not so you could notice it much, Frank," Nance answered. "There's a new therapy — another side of What's Coming, I guess . . ."

They walked the few blocks. The owner of the Hobby Center was now a long-time member of KRNH Enterprises. He had the means to expand and modernize the place beyond recognition. But clearly he had realized that some things should not change.

In the display window, however, there gleamed a brand-new Archer Nine, beautiful as a garden or a town floating, unsupported, under the stars — beautiful as the Future, which was born of the Past.

A Bunch of fellas — the current crop of aficionados — were inside the store, making lots of noise over the news. Was that Chip Potter, grown tall? Was that his same old dog, Blaster? Frank Nelsen could see Paul Hendricks' white-fringed bald-spot.

"Go ahead — open the door. Or are you still scared?" Nance challenged lightly.

"No — just anticipating," Nelsen gruffed. "And seeing if I can remember what's Out There ... Serene, bubb, Belt, Pallas ..." He spoke the words like comic incantations, yet with a dash of reverence.

"Superbia?" Nance teased.

"That is somebody's impertinent joke!" he growled in feigned solemnity. "Anyhow, it would be too bad if something *that* important couldn't take a little ribbing. Shucks — we've hardly *started* to work, yet!"

He drew Nance back a pace, out of sight of those in the store, and kissed her long and rather savagely.

"With all its super-complications, life still seems pretty nice," he commented.

The door squeaked, just as it used to, as Nelsen pushed it open. The old overhead bell jangled.

Pale, watery eyes lifted and lighted with another fulfillment.

"Well, Frank! Long time no see ... !"

THE END